Caught Inside
(A Boys on the Brink Novel)

by
Jamie Deacon

Beaten Track
www.beatentrackpublishing.com

Caught Inside

Published 2016 by Beaten Track Publishing
Copyright © 2016 Jamie Deacon

ISBN: 978 1 78645 035 7

Cover Design: Natasha Snow
www.natashasnow.com

Beaten Track Publishing,
Burscough. Lancashire.
www.beatentrackpublishing.com

To everyone who knows how it feels to be young and falling wildly, irresistibly, heartbreakingly in love for the first time in your life, this one's for you.

Acknowledgements

I owe a huge thank you to Ian Madden from BoardShop.co.uk for helping me negotiate the mysterious world of surfboards, and also to Jere' Fishback for sharing his firsthand knowledge of surfing. Without your advice, I would have been utterly clueless!

Next, I'd like to extend my heartfelt thanks to my wonderful Beata readers: Sherri, Laura, David, Heather, Molly, Rory, Nadia, Cyn, and Jules. You told me what I needed to hear and helped shape this into the story it is today.

I'm indebted to Debbie McGowan at Beaten Track for her thoughtful editing and for giving me this chance to share my novel with the world, as well as to Natasha Snow for creating such a stunning cover.

My final shout out goes to my family. Thank you from the bottom of my heart for believing in me, not to mention all the good-natured teasing that keeps me grounded and prevents me from taking myself too seriously!

Prologue

I have to get away.

Half running, half stumbling, I emerge from the trees and onto the beach. At once, the storm re-launches its assault. Clouds, thick and black, race each other across the sky, taking the last of the daylight with them. A fierce wind drives me backwards, hurling rain and clumps of wet sand into my face. Drops the size of bullets pelt my cheeks, the bare skin of my arms. It doesn't matter. Anything to escape the depths of his betrayal.

The sea rises ahead of me, filling my vision. A huge steel-grey vortex, indistinguishable from the swirling clouds above, it batters itself in a frenzy against the shore. The sheer force of it, the angry ferocity, unleashes a tendril of fear in my heart. This is madness, far more advanced than anything I've ever attempted. I'll never make it.

Don't stop. Don't think.

I drop my surfboard to the sand and strip to my boxers. My clothes are too wet to offer any protection from the chill, and they'll only drag me down. My mind flashes to the wetsuit I left back at the cottage. No time to worry about that now. Frigid pellets ping off my back and shoulders. I'm shivering but scarcely feel the cold. I take a final look at the wall of water; imagine riding it as though on the back of a blue whale. For a moment, my nerve fails.

I grit my teeth and stoop to retrieve my board. Any hesitation and my common sense will butt in. I can't let that happen, not when this is the one thing that has the power to help me forget. With a final deep breath, I gather my courage and hurl myself into the waves.

Chapter One

"Where are you?"

Zara's words, shrill with indignation, drill holes in my aching skull. I wince, edging the phone away from my ear. "Huh?"

"Luke, you should've been here half an hour ago. We're supposed to be going on holiday today, or did that slip your mind?"

Shit. Reality slaps me across the face. I shoot up in bed, but a giant hand grasps my room, tipping it on its side. My stomach rolls, and I collapse onto the pillows with a groan. An untouched mug of tea reproaches me from the bedside cabinet. I have a vague memory of Mum shaking me awake before she went to work, but I'd taken it for a dream.

"Luke?"

"Sorry." Christ, am I slurring? "I'll, uh, be right there."

A pause, then Zara's voice, heavy with menace. "Please tell me you're not still in bed."

"No." Too defensive. I palm my throbbing brow and try to sound casual. "Got held up, but I'm on my way." And I hang up before she can start shrieking again.

I sit up, more carefully this time. My gut protests, and I take a deep breath to steady it. Satisfied I'm not about to throw up, I swing my legs out of bed. My feet land on a pile of folded T-shirts, and I squint through the curtained dimness of my room. The limited floor space is heaped with the clean clothes Mum insisted on ironing for me, clothes I should have packed last night. I stifle a moan. Behind me, my bed beckons, cosy and inviting. Resisting the temptation to burrow back under the duvet, I lurch to my feet.

This isn't how I'd expected to spend the summer before my final year of sixth form. Normally, I'd be joining Dean's family on their annual holiday, staying in a caravan in Brittany, or an apartment on the Costa del Sol. Money was just too tight this year, though, his parents told us, what with takings at the shop being down. Instead, I imagined passing the days in a miasma of barbecues, sleeping in till noon and sunbathing at Zara's. That was until a month ago.

***

It was one of those sultry June evenings, the end of term so close you could almost taste the freedom on the air. We were sprawled on the grass in Zara's back garden, our feet dangling in the pool, when she leaned into me. Her golden-brown hair tickled my arm. "I have a surprise for you."

I flashed a crooked smile. "Should I be worried?"

"You'll like it, I promise."

"Go on then."

"You don't get to find out just like that." Zara drew her legs from the water, straddling my lap, her lips a whisper from mine. "You have to earn it."

I tilted my head. "If you wanted me to kiss you, you only had to ask."

"Luke, do you want your surprise or not?"

She pressed against me, her body curvy and soft through the thin material of her dress. I kissed her, lying

4

back on the grass and pulling her down on top of me. Zara moaned against my mouth, her lips parting for my tongue. She tasted of lip gloss and lemonade, and her hair smelled like coconut. I ran my hands over her back, giving in to the feel of her, until she reached for the zip on my shorts.

"Whoa." I captured her wrists. "Your parents."

Usually this wouldn't have been an issue. John and Celia Scott-Palmer, partners in a prestigious law firm, are scarcely ever home. That night, however, they were hosting a dinner party and could have walked in at any moment.

Zara's eyes danced. "Scared?"

"Hey, you're the one who'll be stuck making polite conversation with them over dinner. It's no wax off my board."

Not strictly true. I had the sneaking suspicion the Scott-Palmers' tolerance towards a boy from East Brookminster tramping over their threshold would evaporate if they caught me having it off with their precious only daughter on the manicured lawn.

Zara sat up, laughing, and pushed her hair away from her face to look down at me. "So, want your surprise?"

"The suspense is killing me."

"You can mock. Just wait till you hear how we're going down to my family's cottage in Cornwall for the summer."

"We?"

"Yes, Luke, we, as in the two of us. You and me."

"With your parents?" I raised an eyebrow. The Scott-Palmers had been nothing but friendly to me when our paths crossed, which wasn't often, and as far as I knew, they hadn't tried to dissuade Zara from seeing me. Still, inviting me on holiday with them would be beyond the call of duty.

"God, no, that wouldn't be any fun. Anyway, they're flying out to our villa in Saint-Tropez, remember?"

How could I have forgotten? Between the holiday cottage in the West Country and a villa in the South of France, I was certainly learning about life on the other side of town.

"So it would just be us?" I wound a blade of grass around my finger. Zara was great fun, we always had a laugh, but the two of us alone in Cornwall for weeks... I wasn't sure how I felt about that.

"And Theo will be there. My cousin. I told you about him."

"The one at Oxford, right?"

"And my favourite person in the world. Apart from you, obviously." Zara grinned. "So, what do you say?"

I stared up at a sky streaked with golden fire. Some of my mates, fellow players on the school rugby team, had tossed around the idea of a lads' weekend if we could get the money together, but I didn't have any specific plans.

"Just think," Zara nuzzled my ear, "we'll be able to do whatever we want."

"Yeah?"

"No parents to walk in on us at inconvenient moments."

"Uh huh?"

"Plus," her tone was one of a chess master about to make the definitive move, "the cottage is right by the sea and has its own private beach."

That clinched it, just as Zara knew it would.

I didn't set out to land a girl from the west of town with its million-pound houses and security gates. If it's one thing I've discovered, however, it's that nothing stops

Zara Scott-Palmer when she wants something. And that night around Easter, when our respective groups of friends ran into each other at the cinema, she decided she wanted me.

Not that I'm complaining. Zara's precisely my type—pretty and outgoing and easy to be with. Besides, it does have its advantages. If we're not watching DVDs on the giant flat-screen that takes up an entire wall of her basement, we're hanging out in the landscaped grounds, which are straight out of the pages of the magazines Mum's always poring over, even though the closest we've ever had to a garden is a potted plant.

And now this, a rural retreat in Cornwall with its very own beach and all the surfing room I could ask for.

Surfing is my passion. My obsession, Dean calls it. From those earliest lessons, when I felt the board untamed and alive beneath my feet, the one thing between me and the powerful swell of the ocean, I fell in love for the first and only time in my life. Now, I head down to the coast whenever schoolwork and my Saturday job allow, but it's never enough to satisfy the constant craving. Cornwall is a hot spot for water worshippers around the world, and any surfer would give their life's blood to have the waves all to themselves. How could I resist a lure like that?

"Well?" Zara's face glowed with triumph.

I'd need to run it past Mum, and also check with Dean's parents who own The Inkwell, the bookshop where I work, but...

"OK," I said, "let's do it."

With a squeal, Zara smothered me in a hug and covered my face in kisses. I laughed, throwing my arms up in self-defence. She cuddled against me, bubbling over with excitement, chattering non-stop about the amazing summer we were going to have. I barely heard her. In my imagination, I was already soaring over foam-flecked water, wind and spray in my face, exhilaration humming through my veins.

"Luke?"

I blinked, and Zara swam back into focus. Her eyes, which a moment ago had been bright with anticipation, were cobalt slits of suspicion.

"What's wrong?" she asked. "Is this about Theo?"

I hesitated. What had she been saying while I was away with the waves? Something about a breakup?

"It is, isn't it?" All at once she looked as fierce as a lioness protecting her cubs. "You have a problem with him being gay."

"What? No!" My brain scrabbled to catch up. Distantly, I'd caught the phrase 'his boyfriend' but paid it no attention.

"Really? I need to know, Luke, because if you can't handle it, you'd better tell me now, and we'll forget the whole thing."

It was unclear whether she meant Cornwall or our relationship full stop. Either way, I had no wish to find out.

I put a hand on her back. "Zara, it's cool, I promise."

My smile, the one my mates refer to as my come-and-get-it smile, warped slightly at the corners. Zara relaxed, obviously having no idea she'd touched on a raw subject. Why would she? It isn't as if I've ever told anyone. It's something I've scarcely even acknowledged to myself, keeping the truth hidden under a jumble of half-forgotten memories in the deepest, most secret recess of my mind.

***

Now, vision blurring with tiredness, I stagger across the tiny hallway to the bathroom. Sweat sticks my T-shirt and boxers to my body. I'm desperate for a shower, but there's no time. In the act of splashing cold water on my face, I catch a glimpse of my reflection in the mirror above the sink, eyelids red and puffy against my pallor. Zara wouldn't say I have take-me-to-bed eyes if she could see me now. Hide-before-someone-mistakes-you-for-a-zombie eyes, more like. I grimace and grab my toothbrush to rid my mouth of its taste of stale beer.

Still feeling like death, I fumble my way to the kitchen. I flip on the light, cringing at the glare, and raid the medicine cupboard for breakfast. The windowless room is stuffy, the air thick with the aroma of mince and herbs from last night's lasagne. My gut twists, and I force down a couple of painkillers with an Alka-Seltzer.

The previous evening, Mum left work early to cook me my favourite dinner and see me off. As I devoured my second plateful, she watched me from across the rickety table that takes up an entire corner of our living room. "Excited?"

I'd nodded, my mouth full of pasta, and she'd smiled at me. As always, the years rolled off her when she smiled. The lines of weariness, etched there by too many hours working at Pardo's, grew fainter. Her face softened into the familiar expression of tenderness and pride, mingled with an ever-present sadness—sadness for my dad, the one I've only seen in photographs. Whenever she looks at me—at the broad shoulders, the unruly tangle of brown hair, the eyes, sleepy and dark—she sees the boy she fell in love with.

"You'll have a great time. It's such an amazing opportunity." Mum didn't add what I knew she was thinking: that it was the kind of opportunity she could never give me, regardless of how many extra shifts she put in at the supermarket.

I grinned across at her, hoping to convey without words how little it mattered that we couldn't afford the same luxuries as other people. "Can't wait to get out on my board. It'll be incredible to have the waves to myself."

Mum's smile dimmed a fraction. She's never been one of those overprotective parents and generally lets me do my own thing, provided I tell her where I am. All the same, the prospect of my first surfing trip without adult supervision worried her.

"Luke," she said, "I know how sensible you are. Just text me regularly to let me know you're safe, OK? And never, ever go out on your board without someone being close by. Promise me."

"I promise." I met her gaze without flinching. It wasn't much to ask, and I had every intention of keeping my word.

Back in my room, I pull on the first clothes that come to hand. Everything else, I hurl into my rucksack, moving as fast as I can without heaving. No time to worry about folding or checking to make sure I have everything. I'll just have to hope for the best. Ten minutes after Zara's irate phone call, which is pretty impressive if you ask me, I sling my backpack over one shoulder and hoist my board in its padded bag onto the other.

Closing the front door behind me is like crossing into another realm. Our poky hallway with its crimson rug and plant in matching pot gives way to a dingy stairwell, plaster flaking like dandruff from the walls. It isn't much. Yet, the flat on the fifth floor of Paradise House—

whoever built it must've had a sick sense of humour—is the only home I've ever known.

In a reflex learnt from years of experience, I hold my breath against the stench of urine and pot. The descent down the concrete stairs with my bags, negotiating the occasional dog end and empty beer bottle, proves as awkward as I anticipated. With considerable relief, I push open the entry door with its peeling paint and emerge onto the street. Sunlight stabs at my eyes, half blinding me. I suck in a lungful of stifling air, but the combined stink of petrol fumes and overflowing rubbish bins does nothing to settle my stomach.

Fighting an urge to retreat to the peace and solitude of my room, I walk through the east of town. Even with the summer sky almost blotted out by the buildings on either side, the heat bears down on me. A burnt-out car that wasn't there last night greets me on the corner of my street. The sounds of a man and woman arguing spills from a downstairs window, competing with a blast of drum and bass.

The Brickwell Estate—a sprawl of council houses and high-rise flats, graffitied walls and litter-strewn gutters—is the section of Brookminster its good citizens would rather pretend doesn't exist. Not Zara, though. She would willingly have collected me at my door. After the first time she ventured into my neighbourhood, however, when a group of kids battered her with insults and threatened to scratch up the brand new midnight-black Mini Cooper her parents bought her for her seventeenth birthday, I persuaded her to steer clear. She took some convincing; she was all for a rematch.

When I arrive at Pardo's, our agreed meeting spot, Zara is pacing the supermarket car park, hands on hips.

The moment she sees me, she jumps into her car and revs the engine. "Just chuck your stuff in the back and get in."

"Good morning to you, too." Despite Zara's impatience boring into me, I stow my board bag in the boot with extra care. Zara has folded down the rear seats for me, but it's still a snug fit, especially alongside her two large suitcases. I toss my rucksack into the back and squeeze myself into the passenger side. My bulk, so at home on the rugby pitch, feels big and awkward in the confined space of Zara's Mini. My surfboard digs into my scalp, and I shift forward until my knees are rammed up against the dash.

"About time." Zara puts the car in gear before I even have the door shut, and roars out of the car park. "So, what happened?"

My gut churns, and I hastily buzz down the window. In all the rush, I've forgotten to invent a plausible excuse. I rack my brain, but it doesn't appear to be working.

Zara turns onto the main road, heading towards the motorway. She shoots me a withering glare. "You look like crap."

I glance down at myself. In my befuddled state, I'd thrown on my oldest denim cut-offs, the ones unravelling at the bottoms, and a Metallica T-shirt so faded the writing is barely legible. Mum didn't iron them, knowing I wouldn't be taking them with me. They're so wrinkled they might have been slept in. "Uh, yeah. Iron packed up."

Zara snorts. She scrunches her nose in distaste, eyes narrowing. "So that's it. You went out on the piss."

"Course I didn't." I scowl down at my seat belt. The stupid thing refuses to cooperate.

I hadn't meant to get drunk last night. I'd fully intended to spend the evening packing, before getting an early night in preparation for the following day. Then Dean called to ask if I wanted to come over.

"Can't, mate, sorry." My gaze had darted between the stacks of clothes and my empty rucksack. "I need to pack."

"You don't have to come for long. Mum and Dad are out at some work thing, and there are some beers in the fridge. We can give you a proper send-off."

I wavered. Even with the window flung wide, my room was like the inside of a kiln. An ice-cold beer sounded like the best thing in the world. "All right, but only for a bit. I really do need to pack."

Several hours later, we'd progressed to Jack Daniel's and Cokes. I was still sprawled on Dean's bedroom floor, and the knowledge that there was something else I should be doing, somewhere else I ought to be, was muted by a fuzz of alcohol.

Zara's voice reclaims my attention. "You're hungover, Luke, I can tell. How could you? You know I wanted to leave early. Now we'll get stuck in all the traffic."

"Keep it down, will you? My head's killing me."

"And my heart's bleeding. Perhaps you should've thought about that before you went and got rat-arsed. And you almost made me miss the exit."

Zara yanks on the steering wheel and the car swerves. My stomach heaves, almost vomiting its contents all over the plush leather seat. I turn my face to the window and take several deep breaths.

"And if you dare throw up in my car, Luke Savage, I swear I'll dump you by the side of the road and you can walk home."

"You do that." Afraid to open my mouth, I grind the words out through clenched teeth.

Zara ignores me. Extracting a CD from the glove compartment, she slips it into the player. A wall of disco music slams into me. My head throbs, surely about to explode.

"What the...?" Eyes screwed up against the pain, I reach for the controls, reducing the music to a background thrum.

Immediately, Zara cranks up the volume again. Every drumbeat is a nail gun firing into my temples.

"Zara, I'm serious. Either you turn this racket off, or I'll—"

"Fine!" She jabs her finger on the power button. Blessed silence descends. "Just sit still and shut up. I've had as much of you as I can take."

She stares straight ahead, her face set. I'm too relieved to heed the guilt tugging at my conscience. I'll make it up to her later. When I feel less like crawling onto the back seat to die. I rest my head against the window, the breeze a soothing hand on my brow, and close my eyes.

***

Warmth caresses my cheek. I sit up, blinking against the brilliant sunshine, and stretch experimentally. My headache has receded to a faint pulsing, and my stomach remains steady.

Zara glances over at me. "Feeling better?"

"Much." Beyond the window, hills rise and fall like a pod of humpback whales against the sky, cattle dozing in the fields at their feet. "Where are we?"

"Devon. You've been asleep for hours."

"Seriously?"

"Yup. Didn't even stir when I stopped for petrol, which reminds me. I bought you something." Zara indicates a carrier bag at my feet.

I bend to scoop it up. Inside is a bottle of water and a sandwich in a cardboard carton. It's more than I deserve. I unscrew the cap and gulp half the water in one go. It's lukewarm and tastes of plastic, but it's a balm to my parched throat. Thirst quenched, I attack the sandwich. Egg and bacon. My favourite.

"Zara," I say around a mouthful, "you're the best."

"You're welcome." She rests a hand on my thigh and gives it a gentle squeeze. "Sorry I was such a bitch."

"You weren't." The corner of my mouth quirks in response to her raised eyebrow. "Well, maybe a bit, but it was my fault. I shouldn't have drunk so much."

"So you *were* out on the piss last night. I knew it." She slaps my leg, but her eyes are amused.

We fall quiet, the earlier tension evaporated. I finish my sandwich, content to sit back and gaze at the view. Gradually, as we cross the border into Cornwall, the roads become narrower, the signs of civilisation fewer and farther between. Towns give way to fishing villages surrounded by woodland and rolling fields. And then I get my first glimpse of the sea. The swell is visible even from this distance, rippling in the afternoon sun. My heart leaps in recognition.

"How long's Theo been down here?" I ask a while later.

"A couple of months, since he finished uni for the summer."

I try to imagine burying myself in the countryside for weeks on end, with only the waves and the occasional cow for company. The concept is too alien. Even in the holidays, when Mum's working and I have the flat to myself, there's a constant banging and creaking from the residents above and below me, the roar of traffic from the street outside. How might it feel to be really, truly alone?

Zara slows the car to manoeuvre a tight bend. "I think he just wanted to get away for a while. He's been like that since the breakup, shutting himself away, refusing to talk about it. Don't bring it up in front of him, will you?"

"What do you think I'm going to say? 'Nice to meet you, Theo. By the way, sorry about your boyfriend.'"

"I'm serious, Luke. It really messed him up. He hasn't even talked to me about it. Not yet."

"Zara, I get it. It's fine."

All the same, with the countryside closing around us, the doubts set in. Perhaps Zara's made a mistake bringing me. If Theo's as cut up as she says, he might not be in the mood for company, especially that of some guy he's never met.

A quarter of an hour later, Zara swings through a gate set in the hedge and onto a gravel driveway. "We're here."

I'm allowed only a fleeting glimpse of the cottage before she veers into the garage, its entrance standing open in readiness. She parks beside the only other car, a silver Golf, its scratched body a marked contrast to the Mini's gleaming paintwork.

Zara kills the engine. Silence descends, a silence more profound than any I've ever known. It presses in on my eardrums, a physical force. But for the fact that I can hear myself breathing, I would've sworn I've gone deaf.

"Well, come on." Zara reaches for the door handle, her eyes alight. "Come and meet Theo."

Chapter Two

Zara opens the car door and jumps out. I follow more warily, not sure I should be here, that I want to be. Desperate as I am to get out on the water, I can't shake the sense that I'm intruding.

We leave the garage and crunch our way over the gravel driveway. At my first proper look at the place, I turn to Zara, eyebrows raised. "Cottage?"

I'd conjured up an image of something quaint, all thatched roof and walls shrouded in honeysuckle. The double-fronted house before us is nothing like that. It may not be on the same scale as the Brookminster house, but there's nothing rustic about the elegant façade, white stone inlaid with floor-to-ceiling windows. I should have known better. The place has a private beach, for Christ's sake.

Zara waves a dismissive hand. "That's what Dad christened it after our first summer here, and the name kind of stuck."

She runs ahead and bounds up the front steps, keys jangling. By the time I join her, she has the door unlocked and is calling out. I'm hit with an impression of space and light, at odds with my expectation of low ceilings and dark beams. Then a young man, barefoot and wearing a baggy T-shirt and shorts in marginally better condition than mine, appears in the doorway at the end of the hall.

"Ah, a camp invasion." He comes to meet us, running a hand through his hair. He doesn't look especially screwed up, just tousled and a bit distracted.

"Theo!" Zara rushes him, almost sending them both crashing to the parquet.

"Whoa." He laughs and hugs her back. "Good to see you, too."

I hang back, excluded from the reunion, feeling more like an interloper than ever. The family resemblance between the cousins is strong. They have the same golden-brown hair, the same soft curve to their mouth, but it goes deeper than that. There's a poise about them, an effortless grace to their movements I could never imitate. It's what comes of being born into money, I suppose.

"Theo, this is Luke," Zara says, releasing him.

"I surmised as much." His eyes, hazel and amused, find mine. "Hey."

"Hey." I offer an embarrassed smile. All at once, I'm aware of my rumpled clothes and the fact that I haven't showered since the previous morning.

"I'll help you with your stuff," Theo says. "If I know Zara, she's brought her entire wardrobe."

"For your information, I had to leave half my stuff behind to make room for Luke's precious surfboard."

"The sacrifices we make in the name of love." Theo evades Zara's swipe, laughing, and ducks past me on the threshold. On our way to the car, he glances at my frayed shorts and Metallica T-shirt. "Wouldn't have had you down as a surfer."

I shrug. "What can I say? I'm one of a kind. Anyway, why else do people come to Cornwall?"

"For the fudge, obviously." Zara moves ahead of us to unlock the boot. "You haven't lived unless you've tried authentic Cornish fudge."

"Guilty as charged, I'm afraid." I shoulder my rucksack and lift out my board bag, while Theo grabs the larger of Zara's suitcases.

"My uncle thought it would be fun if we all learned to surf a few years back," Theo says. "He bought a couple of boards for us to mess around on, but I never really took to it."

It shouldn't surprise me, not having seen how the Scott-Palmers live, but the concept of being able to splash out on boards purely for the hell of it blows my mind. I grin at him. "It's a doddle once you get the hang of it. All you need is practice. And a good teacher."

"Tell you what." Theo's eyes light up. "I'll buy you some fudge in exchange for a few lessons."

"Deal, but on one condition. It has to be maple and walnut."

Zara rolls her eyes, lips twitching, and leads the way inside. Theo tells me I can leave my board in the hall. I cast the white paintwork a doubtful look, but the others have already started up the stairs, so I prop my board bag against the wall and follow.

It's as if the Scott-Palmers have captured as much of the ocean as possible and brought it indoors. Carvings of shells and seahorses decorate the banisters, and the walls are hung with polished brass, intricate replicas of anchors and tillers. In the sunlight pouring through the windows on either side of the front door, the oak staircase gleams a warm russet. I expect to feel uncomfortable, the way I always do in the house on Clarenden Avenue with its leather sofas and glass coffee tables. Instead, the cottage seems to welcome me.

19

"I've saved you the master." Theo opens a door to the left of the landing and grins at Zara. "Thought you'd appreciate it more than me."

Zara's gaze settles on the king-size bed before meeting mine. Her eyes glitter with mischief. And something else.

I dump my rucksack in a corner and look around. This room with its en suite and walk-in wardrobe that's bigger than my bedroom at home belongs in an up-market hotel. Again, the sea is everywhere—in the curtains and bedspread striped blue and pale grey; the piles of fluffy turquoise towels in the bathroom; the painting over the bed of a harbour at dawn.

Unable to resist, I step through the open glass doors onto a balcony. Below me, a swimming pool shimmers in the afternoon haze, smooth lawn sloping to meet a wooded area. And beyond it, a glimmer of blue-grey between the trees, lies the sea.

"The beach is along there." At my shoulder, Theo points out a path winding away through the woods. "We'll show you later."

He sets Zara's suitcase on the bed, and leaves us to settle in. Without bothering to unpack, Zara changes into a bikini and hurries back downstairs, while I shoot off a quick text to Mum to let her know I've arrived safely. I'm about to replace my mobile in my bag when it rings. Dean's name flashes on the screen. I'm amazed my relic of a phone even has a signal out here.

"Hey," Dean says when I pick up. "You made it then?"

"Only just. Thought Zara was gonna leave me behind when I overslept this morning."

"Yeah, right. That girl's crazy about you. Christ knows why."

"Because I'm irresistible, obviously."

Dean snorts. I can picture him sprawled on his rumpled bed, Xbox controller beside him, the walls plastered with posters of Alter Bridge and Manchester United. Over the years, since that first morning of primary school when Mrs. Smith kept us in at playtime for making willies out of Play-Doh, I must have spent as many hours in that room as I have in my own.

"So, what's it like?" he asks. "Did Zara's cousin get out the pink hair and rainbow flags to welcome you?"

This is so far from reality I have to grin. "It's amazing. I can actually see the sea from my window. Can't wait to get out on my board."

"Man, what's wrong with you? You're getting to spend some proper alone time with your gorgeous girlfriend, and all you can talk about is surfing. You're obsessed."

I shake my head, even though he can't see me. Dean never took to surfing the way I had, didn't have the patience. Unless you've experienced it, felt the sensation of weightlessness as you're swept along on the crest of a wave, your mind wiped clean of everything but the present, you can't possibly understand the buzz that drives the surfer to do it again and again.

"I swear," Dean says, "I'd give up playing Xbox for a year just for one night with Yasmin."

"That's because you're in love and sexually frustrated. Dangerous combination."

Yasmin's parents are Iraqi and strictly Catholic. While they've welcomed Dean into the family in the three years he and Yasmin have been together, they're incredibly protective of their youngest daughter. Dean's forever bemoaning the fact that he's only allowed in Yasmin's room with the door propped wide open, and can't even watch a film in their living room without Mrs. Hassani checking up on them every ten minutes.

"Smug bastard," Dean says. "One day you'll fall for someone so hard you won't know what hit you, and I'm just going to sit back and gloat."

I hang up, laughing, and head into the en suite for a well overdue shower. Zara and Theo will have plenty of catching up to do, so I take my time, luxuriating under the hot water. The spray pounds the stiffness from my muscles, and washes thirty hours' worth of sweat and grime from my body. The misgivings that had formed on the drive swirl down the plughole on a tide of soap suds. If Theo is as cut up as Zara claimed, he's hiding it well, and couldn't have made me feel more at home.

Half an hour later, dressed in fresh shorts and my favourite Pantera T-shirt, I set out to explore the cottage. An open door on my way along the landing reveals an unmade bed, the duvet spilling onto the floor, mounds of clothes and books everywhere. It isn't unlike my room back home. Obviously some things don't change, whether you're brought up in a run-down flat in the city or a grand country estate.

Downstairs, I peer into a dining room to one side of the hallway and a lounge to the other. Both are high ceilinged with full-length windows and decorated in ocean hues. Everything oozes extravagance—I wouldn't expect anything else—but it's bright and inviting, a house to be lived in, not merely admired.

I push open the door at the end of the hallway, the one Theo emerged through earlier, to find a kitchen/living area stretching the width of the cottage. One section of the room is given over to polished wood worktops and stainless steel appliances, while a sofa and armchairs huddle around the large fireplace to my right. Judging by the numerous books, damp towels and empty glasses crammed onto the dresser and strewn over the scrubbed pine table, this is where Theo has been spending much of his time.

Curious, I pick up the book lying face down on the arm of the sofa. *The Lord of the Rings*. Theo's name, Theodore Benedict Scott-Palmer, is written in a childish scrawl on the inside cover. The pages, as dog-eared as my own copy, mark him out as a true Tolkien fan.

I replace the book where I found it, and the sounds of splashing and laughter tug me through the sliding glass doors onto a terrace overlooking the pool. It has two tiers, the top level shaded beneath a stone awning, with steps leading down to a sunny patio.

The cousins don't notice me; they're too busy fooling around in the water. For a moment, I simply stand there, breathing the smell of grass and sea and freshness. I hold it in my lungs, the way you're supposed to when smoking a joint, then let it out in a long sigh.

"Luke." Zara catches sight of me and waves. "Coming in?"

I shake my head. "Think I'll sit this one out."

"Help yourself to a drink or anything else you want," Theo calls, before Zara tackles him, and he disappears beneath the surface.

I fetch a can of Coke from the fridge and descend the terrace steps, settling at a table in the late afternoon warmth. With the first mouthful soothing my parched throat, I absorb my surroundings. Despite the pool and tennis courts, there's an untamed quality to the overflowing flowerbeds and too-long grass, as though the woods have snuck some of their wildness into the grounds.

I sit there, half watching Zara and Theo fool around, thinking about nothing very much. A sensation entirely disconnected from the fizz bubbles up inside me. Freedom. The summer extends before me, mine to do with whatever I like. It's intoxicating.

"Feeling better?" Theo asks when he and Zara join me. "Zara said you had a heavy night."

I glance at her. "Did you also tell him how you threatened to abandon me on the side of the motorway?"

Theo laughs.

"He deserved it," Zara says, "turning up an hour late, reeking of booze. What would you have done?"

Theo meets my gaze with a faint smile. "Bought him a bottle of water and told him to sleep it off, maybe?"

"Which, I think you'll find, is what I did," Zara points out.

"Actually, you told me to sit there and shut up."

"Same difference." Zara slips her hand into mine, interlacing our fingers. "Anyway, I'm glad I didn't leave you behind."

"Me too." My eyes stray to the wood. The waves are screened behind the trees, but I know they're there, waiting for me. All that potential, lying unused and unappreciated for years. What a waste. I turn to Theo. "So, if you don't surf, what do you do down here?"

He shrugs. "Swim. Read a lot. Sketch, when I'm in the mood."

"Sketch, huh?" I nudge Zara's knee with mine. "He any good?"

Her smile brims with pride. "Fantastic. You should see the one he did of his Lab Cocoa."

"Give over." Theo blushes. "I'm OK," he tells me, "but nowhere near good enough to do it professionally. Keeps me out of trouble, though."

"What about telly? I didn't see one anywhere."

"That would be because there isn't one," Theo says. "Aunt Celia and Uncle John have always said they come here to escape all that."

"And to have 'quality family time'," Zara adds. "We have to play board games and talk about our feelings. Imagine."

It sounds kind of nice, actually. Between Mum's hours at the supermarket, and the demands of my social life and rugby practice, we barely have any quality time, simply to talk or do things as a family. On the other hand, the realisation that Theo's been out here all these weeks without even a TV for company makes his solitude seem even worse.

"You here for the summer?" I ask him. "Or are you going home to see your parents?"

The awkward pause alerts me to the fact that I've put my foot in it. Theo shoots Zara an exasperated look, and she grimaces in apology. Clearly something else I wasn't supposed to mention.

Theo gets to his feet. "Who wants another drink?"

As soon as he's out of earshot, I round on Zara. "Thanks for the heads up."

"God, I'm sorry. There's been so much going on with the breakup and everything, I forgot to warn you. Just don't bring up Theo's family, OK?"

"Yeah, think I got that."

Before either of us can say anything else, Theo returns with more drinks. We stick to general topics after that, and the brief tension dissolves. When Zara and Theo discuss people and places I'm unfamiliar with, I lean back in my chair, happy to let the conversation eddy around me. Through half-closed eyes, I gaze into the aquamarine water of the pool, more relaxed than I can remember feeling in my life.

When the trees fringing the woods cast long shadows over the grass, Zara goes upstairs to shower and Theo gets up to light the barbecue. I join him, hands in the pockets of my shorts, observing as he arranges the charcoal. "Sure you can handle that thing?"

He glances up at me, eyebrows raised.

"I mean, surely you have servants to do this stuff at your mansion." When Theo looks taken aback, I touch him on the shoulder. "Hey, I'm kidding. Want a hand, though?"

His expression relaxes. "Don't tell me. When you're not perfecting your surfing prowess, you're pursuing world domination as King of the Barbecue."

"Watch and learn. Got any newspaper?"

Theo disappears inside, returning a moment later with a folded copy of *The Times*. "My uncle has a whole stash of them. He likes to do the crossword."

I remove a few sheets, balling them up in my fist. Then I show Theo how to place them around the barbecue and cover them with charcoal, the way I've helped Dean's dad to do so often.

Theo looks impressed. "Maybe I can't handle this thing so well, after all."

With the barbecue lit, we sit on the terrace to wait for the coals to heat up. Theo opens a couple of beers and passes me one. "Zara's talked a lot about you."

"Now why does that make me nervous?"

"No need. She's crazy about you, but you must already know that."

I look down at my bottle, twisting it between my hands. I hadn't known. Not really. I feel guilty without understanding why. Theo's studying me, head tilted, expecting an answer.

"Zara's great." It's the most honest response I can muster.

"Yes," Theo smiles at me, "she is."

***

After feasting on burgers and hotdogs, the three of us wind our way along the path that coils through the trees. Zara takes my hand, her smile a promise, Theo a few paces behind us. Though the evening's still golden, the wood engulfs us in twilight. The quiet steals my breath. The only sounds are our footsteps scuffing on the dirt track, the rustle of leaves overhead, and the waves, their constant swoosh wrenching at me as irresistibly as the moon pulls the tide.

With an abruptness that catches me off guard, the path opens out, and I'm brought up short. The beauty of it traps the air in my chest. The setting sun, a fiery crescent on the horizon, strikes sparks off the water and the smooth expanse of sand. I have the sense that I've stepped into an enchanted world, like waking to find everything beyond my bedroom window blanketed in snow, its crisp whiteness unmarred by footprints or tyre tracks.

And the waves. Swift and powerful, they throw themselves at the shore, their crests tipped with foam like the head on a pint. Frothy tendrils reach out across the stretch of sand that separates us, before once more retreating. I can almost imagine they're beckoning to me, daring me to join them.

With a whoop of joy, Zara releases my hand and races to meet the water, kicking off her flip-flops as she runs. I follow more slowly, halting a wave's span from the breaking surf, and take it all in.

"What do you think?" Theo speaks beside me, making me jump.

"It's…" I search my brain for the right word, one that won't make me sound like the soppy romantic poets we're force-fed in English Lit. None of the adjectives that spring to mind come close to doing the view justice.

He smiles. "Looking forward to testing out your board on those waves?"

"For Pete's sake, Theo," Zara looks over at us, knee-deep in the water, "don't get him started on that again. He's talked about nothing else for weeks. I'm in serious danger of developing a complex."

"Heaven forbid." Theo bumps my shoulder. "Take no notice of Miss Prima Donna here. It's good for her to learn she isn't the centre of the universe."

"I should at least be the centre of Luke's universe, and whose friend are you, anyway? If I'd known you two were going to gang up on me, I would've stayed home."

I catch Theo's eye, grinning, and he winks at me.

***

"Told you you'd like him, didn't I?" Zara says much later, as we're getting ready for bed. Her expression is impossible to make out in the silvery moonlight, but there's no mistaking her smug tone.

"So you did." I drop my clothes to the floor and crawl into bed. The mattress is marshmallow soft, the sheets cool against my skin. Despite having slept through most of the journey, I stifle a yawn.

"Well, Theo definitely likes you," Zara says. I can hear the rustle of clothes as she rummages in her suitcase.

"You think?"

"Luke, he was totally flirting with you."

I smother a laugh in the duvet. "He was not."

"Was, too. Good job you have me here to defend your honour."

"Lucky me."

Zara throws her T-shirt at my head, and I roll over, hiding my grin in the pillow. By the time she climbs into bed beside me, I've drifted into that relaxed state on the brink of sleep.

"All right?" Zara drapes an arm over me and nestles into my back.

"Uh huh."

"Hey, no falling asleep on me." Her fingers trace a path down my chest to my stomach. "I've been looking forward to getting you to myself all day."

She presses against me, hand inching towards the waistband of my boxers. About to slip into oblivion, I curl in on myself, burrowing deeper into the mattress.

"Luke?"

"Hmmm?"

"Oh, never mind." Zara exhales, planting a kiss on my shoulder, and turns onto her other side.

Chapter Three

The cry of seagulls and the soft hum of voices worm their way into my consciousness. I stretch and open my eyes. Sunshine floods the room, drenching my pillow. It's a miracle it hadn't roused me sooner. I lie there for a while, savouring my drowsy contentment, until the smell of bacon calls to my stomach, which rumbles in appreciation. I throw off the covers and cross to the window, flinging it wide.

Zara and Theo are seated on the sunny patio; the remains of breakfast litter the table between them. Unnoticed, I lean out over the sill and inhale lungfuls of salty air. A stiff breeze ruffles my hair, a relief after the intense heat of yesterday.

My focus shifts to the trees. Blown by an offshore wind, their branches salute me, and the patches of water visible between the trunks ripple like silk. Perfect surfing conditions. My blood thrums. In less than an hour, I'll be out on my board. The sea, every one of those sweeping, unstoppable waves, will be mine and mine alone.

"Hey!" Theo grins up at me, drawing my attention back to the patio. "Get yourself down here. Bacon sandwiches."

I give him the thumbs up, and retreat to pull on last night's clothes. In a matter of minutes, I emerge onto the patio and flop into the chair beside Zara's.

"Morning, Sleeping Beauty." She kisses me, a soft peck on the mouth. "We were just taking bets on whether you'd be up before lunchtime."

I reach for a sandwich, and accept the mug of coffee Theo passes me. "Must've been all that sea air."

"Well, it wasn't because you were worn out after a night of passion, that's for sure."

"Zara."

"What? It's true. Can you believe him, Theo? The first time we get to share a bed and he falls asleep on me."

"Tell the world, why don't you?" I make a big show of stirring sugar into my coffee.

"You know," Theo's mouth twitches, "I think you're embarrassing him."

I glare at him, though I'm suppressing a smile. He raises an eyebrow, but thankfully changes the subject.

***

After breakfast, we head down to the beach, armed with towels and books, Theo lugging a cool box packed with a hastily prepared lunch. Even hampered by the awkward weight of my board, I stride ahead through the woods, shorty wetsuit hugging my skin, impatient to be out on the water.

"For heaven's sake, Luke, the sea isn't going anywhere." Zara pants from the effort of keeping up with me.

I take no notice, and a moment later, step from the shade of the trees. Late morning sunlight sparkles off the surface of the water, turning it a dazzling blue-grey. The breeze, stronger here on the seafront, messes with my hair and whips sand into my face. Zara and Theo join me, and we walk along the beach until the ground to our left begins to slope upwards, the trees thinning and giving way to rocky boulders.

Theo points to the distant cliff top, etched dark and rugged against the sky. "There's a path that takes you all the way up. We'll show you sometime. It's a bit of a trek, but the view's incredible."

We set up camp in the shelter of the cliff wall. While Zara and Theo spread out their towels, I deposit my board bag and unzip it. As I slide my prize possession onto the sand, a low whistle makes me look up.

"Wow." Theo runs an admiring gaze over my board. "Decent bit of kit you have there."

The grin I flash him is one of pride, as if the compliment were directed at me. I stroke a hand over the board's newly waxed surface. With its diamond tail and step-down tail rail, The Firewire Spitfire has the thrust of a much thinner board, but without compromising on speed or flotation. In short, it's six feet of utter perfection.

"Luke, would you do my back for me?" Zara, stripped down to her bikini, holds out a bottle of sun cream.

Theo reads my hesitation and takes it from her. "Here, I'll do it. Go on, Luke, I can see you're dying to be off."

"You sure?" I cast Zara a doubtful look. "Do you mind?"

She waves me off. "Go on. I'm sure I'll get over it eventually."

I don't wait for her to change her mind. After securing the leash that connects my ankle to my board, I hoist the Spitfire over my head and race for the shore. The first slap of surf against my shins sends goose bumps prickling up my legs and sets my pulse buzzing like nothing else can. I wade out until the water is waist high, then stretch out on my board to paddle. The sea is like a living creature underneath me, its back rising and falling as it moves. I duck through an oncoming wave, and for an instant my vision becomes shimmering and opaque. Salt stings my eyes, filling my senses with the smell of the ocean.

Once I feel the swell rolling in from behind me, I stop and guide my board around. Already the beach is a long way off. I can just make out Theo, who has walked to the water's edge to watch me. In that case, I'd better give him something worth watching.

"The hardest lesson to master as a surfer," Dean's dad told me seven summers ago, "is learning to catch the wave. Stand too early and you lose your footing. Move too late and you risk missing it altogether."

In fact, once I found my balance, I picked it up quicker than he expected. I was a natural, or so he was fond of claiming. Certainly, from those earliest days on a board, I felt in tune with the sea, able to read the pull of the current, the eddy and flow of water beneath me.

"It's like learning a new language," I once tried to explain to Dean, "completely indecipherable at first, but once you understand it, everything makes sense."

And now, seven years after losing my surfing virginity, here I am with the best surfboard I've ever ridden, the only one I've actually owned, and with what may as well be the entire Atlantic to myself. I crouch, every muscle tensed, awaiting the perfect moment. My timing is spot on. Just as the wave begins to break beneath me, I explode to my feet. And then I'm flying, moving with the Spitfire as though it's an extension of my body, spray lashing my face, the wind whipping the hair back from my forehead.

Nothing else comes close to this feeling. Nothing. Only out on a board do I experience such a rush of pure exhilaration or feel so at peace. For those few seconds, it's as though the world stands still. The present wipes my mind clean of everything, every thought, every emotion. Nothing matters save for the wave and the sensation of being wholly at one with nature.

By the time I rejoin the others, they've unloaded the cool box and started on lunch. I remove the fins and pack my board away in its bag, my stomach protesting at the smell of crusty bread.

"Sorry," Zara says through a mouthful of baguette, "we meant to wait for you, but we were starving, and it looked like you were going to be out there all day."

"No worries." I zip up my board bag and unroll my towel. The breeze is cool against my wet skin, so I wrap it around my shoulders and settle beside Zara.

Theo reaches across her to hand me a Coke. "How was it?"

"Amazing." I snap open the can, downing half the contents in one go. It bubbles down my throat, sweet and refreshing.

"You're seriously good," Theo says. "You were in your element out there."

I bite into a baguette. "I've had a lot of practice. You have to be a bit obsessive to be a surfer."

"Isn't it the same with any hobby? One you're really passionate about, anyway."

"Maybe. I dunno. Surfing's just one of those things where there's no middle ground. You either get it or you don't, and if you don't, we surfers sound like a load of pseudo-hippie water worshippers. Or so my mate Dean tells me." I flash Theo a sheepish grin. "Sure you want to take lessons from a crazy wave junky?"

Theo laughs. "So long as you don't mind when I make a total idiot of myself."

"Trust me, making an idiot of yourself is sort of compulsory when you're starting out." I turn to Zara. "How about you? Want to give it a try?"

She wipes a dribble of peach juice from her chin. "Honestly, my balance is atrocious, can hardly even ride a bike. Much safer for everyone if I stay on dry land."

"Chicken." I stretch out my legs, toes digging into the powdery sand. My workout with the waves has left my muscles gratifyingly sore, and my appetite, always considerable, multiplies several times over after a session on my board. I demolish the remainder of the picnic—baguettes, followed by peaches and fresh strawberries and chocolate cake. Somehow, it all tastes so much better eaten with the sea air on my face.

When the sun ducks for cover behind a bank of clouds, we pull on our clothes, collect our stuff, and wander back to the cottage.

"Think I'll go for a walk," Theo says in the kitchen. "Feel a bit lazy. How about you two?"

"Actually," Zara catches my eye, "we have other plans. Luke has some making up to do."

"God." I throw up an arm to shield my eyes, a display of embarrassment that isn't entirely put on.

Theo chuckles. "I'll leave you to it then. Have fun."

"We will." Zara takes my hand, and with a significant look at Theo, leads me from the room.

I let myself be tugged up the stairs. "Do you have to be quite so obvious?"

"I didn't realise you were such a prude, Luke Savage."

She draws me into our room and closes the door behind us, pushing me up against it. Her mouth finds mine, warm and demanding and sweet with the aftertaste of chocolate and peaches. My self-consciousness, which I can't entirely explain, fades into the background. I press her closer, my hands in her tangled hair, my tongue

36

stroking hers until she moans and I fumble with the button on her shorts.

"Uh uh." Zara breaks the kiss, flushed and breathless. "You'll have to wait. I need a shower."

I groan. My mouth goes to her neck, nibbling the sensitive spot below her ear. She gasps, but disentangles herself from me with a visible effort.

"Shower first." Her smile is teasing, confident, and I know this is her way of paying me back for last night. With a parting kiss, she disappears into the en suite.

I drag in a breath, suspended between amusement and frustration. I'm tempted to follow Zara into the shower, but that would be playing right into her hands. Instead, I grab my towel and head along the landing to the main bathroom.

The shower is still running in the en suite when I get back, so I dry myself off and crawl into bed. My tired muscles sink into the mattress. I stretch, and gaze through the window towards the wood. The treetops sway in the breeze, their branches spelling out their secret language against the sky. I watch them, the movement almost hypnotic, and let my thoughts drift.

***

When I open my eyes, the room is quiet. I sit up, dazed and disorientated. Where did Zara go? Orange tongues of sunlight lick at the window frame, throwing long shadows over the floor. A cool breeze raises goose bumps on my arms and carries with it the scent of charcoal.

Hell. I toss back the covers and stumble out of bed. Brain muggy with sleep, I pull on jeans and a sweatshirt against the evening chill, and head downstairs to face the ribbing I suspect is coming my way.

"Look who it is." Zara's voice accosts me the moment I step onto the terrace. "Managed to tear ourselves out of bed, did we?"

She and Theo are gathered around a table on the patio, close to the smoking barbecue. I amble over to join them, my smile rueful. "I'm sorry. Really. Didn't realise I was so worn out."

"I can't believe you fell asleep on me...again." Zara seizes my hand, yanking me into the chair beside hers. "Once I can just about forgive, but twice?"

"I know, I know. I'm a pathetic excuse for a boyfriend. I'll make it up to you, I promise." I appeal to Theo.

He meets my gaze, his eyes amused. "Give the guy a break, Zara. He's had a heavy morning."

"You can mock," Zara says. "Maybe you should try coming second to a lump of fibreglass, see how you like it."

"He wouldn't mind. Unlike you, he actually appreciates my board. Right, Theo?"

"Well, it is a very attractive lump of fibreglass."

"I give up." Zara scrapes back her chair. "You two do something useful and get the sausages on. I'm going to make a salad."

Theo watches her go with a roll of his eyes. "Sounds like we have our orders."

As we had the night before, we take our places on either side of the barbecue, Theo in charge of the sausages, while I watch over the chicken legs. I sweep my gaze over the coals, the heat evenly distributed. "Nicely done."

Theo smiles. "I picked up some tips from an expert."

"You're a fast learner. Reckon you'll be as quick to master surfing?"

"I seriously doubt it." He laughs and turns a sausage with his tongs.

Zara re-emerges a while later, with a bowl of salad and a French stick. Theo opens bottles of beer for him and me, and pours Zara a vodka and Coke. Then we sit on the patio to eat, the heat from the barbecue taking the edge off the chill.

"How come the sausages are always burnt?" Zara grimaces through her mouthful of hotdog.

"Nothing to do with me," I say. "That was Theo's domain."

Theo sighs. "Some people just don't understand the difference between burnt and authentically charred."

Zara snorts, and I lean close to her ear, my tone confidential. "Go easy on him. I'm still training him up."

"Watch it, surfer boy." Theo stabs his fork in my direction, but his laughter is obvious behind the threat.

We sit out on the patio long after we've eaten. Overhead, the sky darkens to a dusky blue, and stars flicker into life. The conversation flows easily, the collection of beer bottles growing on the table between us. Mostly we stick to general topics, but sometimes Zara and Theo talk among themselves. I don't mind. With my body tingling from a morning's surfing and alcohol singing through my veins, there's nowhere else I'd rather be than right here, right now.

"So, where's Giles?" Zara asks Theo. "He doesn't normally pass up the chance to tag along down here."

"He's with Meredith, visiting her family for a few days."

"They're still together then, Giles and Meredith? And it's been how long?"

"Don't know. About three months, maybe?"

"Wow, that must be a record for Giles."

Theo grins. "I think it is."

Zara shakes her head. "They're just so unsuited."

"From the outside, perhaps, but it seems to work. I'm starting to think Meredith might be just what Giles needs."

"What Giles needs is a girl to tell him where to get off."

I smile, only half listening, part of me straining to catch the rush of the waves, just audible beneath their voices. Moonlight brushes the treetops and illuminates the path with splashes of silver. Even though it's too far to see from here, I imagine the sea, glistening and mysterious in the darkness.

Zara touches my leg, making me jump. She runs her hand up and down my thigh. "What're you thinking? And it had better not have anything to do with that blasted board. I need all your energy for later."

"It doesn't." I push myself to my feet, beer bottle in hand, and include Theo in my grin. "Come on, I have an idea."

***

Under the night sky, the water gleams like onyx. The waves, calmer than they'd been earlier, caress the shoreline in a shower of glitter. For once, my thoughts don't stray instantly to my board. I'm content simply to absorb it all. I've never seen anything so incredible as this expanse of sea and sky and stars.

We sprawl on a blanket, Zara sandwiched between Theo and me, the well-stocked cool box on the sand beside us.

"Luke, this is amazing." Zara leans into me and takes a gulp from her Smirnoff Ice. Her words slur around the edges. "Can't believe we've never done this."

"Never?"

"You forget, we've only ever come here with our parents. Well, Theo's been here without them, haven't you, Theo?"

"Once." His response is flat.

I look over at him, but he's staring off towards the horizon. Even if I'd been able to see his face, his expression would have been hard to read in the dark.

Zara claps a hand over her mouth. "Oops, I'm not supposed to mention that, am I? Sorry, Theo. Anyway, we've had barbecues on the beach before, big parties where my parents invite everyone we've got to know in the summers we've been coming here. This, though." She gestures with the hand holding her bottle, encompassing our surroundings, the quiet stillness. "This is special."

"Yeah, it is." I smile and put an arm around her.

She nuzzles into me, the warmth of her body seeping through our sweatshirts, her breath tickling my neck. "Have you ever thought about having sex on the beach? Want to try it?"

"Not right now." My laugh is half awkward, half amused. I glance Theo's way, but he's intent on drawing something in the sand with a finger.

Zara pouts. "You're no fun."

Downing the rest of her drink, she discards her bottle on the blanket and pushes herself to her feet. She stumbles to the water's edge, where she waits, body tensed. When the next wave rolls in, she turns and runs, hysterical with giggles, barely staying ahead of the surf.

I watch her strange game of chicken while I finish my beer. Instead of grabbing another, I lie back on the blanket, arms pillowing my head, and stare up at the stars. My entire body feels fluid, weightless. The sky sways above me, as though I'm stretched out on the deck of a ship.

"OK?" Theo's voice is closer than I'm expecting, and I glance sideways. He's lying beside me, studying the sky.

I smile and return my gaze to the stars. "I never knew they were so bright."

"That's because you're a city boy. I was fascinated with the stars when I was younger. In the summer, I used to persuade my sister Clemmy to camp outside with me so I could watch them before I went to sleep."

Sadness lurks beneath the surface of his words. I wonder if it has anything to do with his reluctance to talk about his family.

"So," I say to distract him, "you know all the constellations, right?"

"Of course. Let's see." Theo points to a large grouping of stars to our left. "Over there, we have the Great One-Armed Baboon, and that small cluster just below it, that's the Squashed Toad."

"Yeah," I grin, my eyes scanning the sky, "and that one has to be the Leering Skull."

"No way. That's the Chocolate Chip Cookie. Everyone knows that."

We fall into a contest, competing to find patterns in the pinpricks of light, arguing over whether one is an Easter egg or a rugby ball, a tennis racket or a banjo.

"All right," Theo says, "I'll give you that last one, but that's a rocket, no doubt about it. Look, you can see the fire trailing behind it."

I bump his shoulder with mine. "Nah, you need your eyes tested. That's definitely a surfboard. Those are the fins."

"I don't know. They're a bit wonky."

"And you're a bit pissed."

Theo laughs, just as Zara lets out a shriek. I push myself up on my elbows in time to see her topple backwards into the water. She sits there, fully dressed, giggling to herself as the waves lap around her.

"Time to head back, do you think?" Theo asks, sitting up beside me.

Together, we scramble to our feet and hurry over to Zara. She's struggling unsuccessfully to get up, which only makes her giggle harder.

"Come on," Theo's voice vibrates with mirth, "let's get you out of there. On the count of three." He grasps one of Zara's hands, while I take the other. "One…two…three!"

We pull. Zara grips my fingers, allowing us to haul her up. She's just found her balance, when her flip-flop catches on something and she goes down. I try to steady myself, but I'm already falling. The next thing I know, we're tumbling in a drunken heap in the water, our limbs entangled, all three of us helpless with laughter.

Chapter Four

"OK, ready to impress?" I pull my T-shirt off over my head and turn to Theo, squinting against the late morning sun. Beyond him, the sea stretches out like a sleeping monster, tranquil and vast. The barest breeze ruffles the surface of the water and takes the edge off the heat. Terrible surfing conditions, but ideal for teaching Theo the basics.

He grimaces. "Think I'm still hungover."

"Not making excuses already, I hope." Sprawled on the blanket in her bikini, Zara pushes herself up on her elbows to watch us, eyes shielded behind dark glasses.

"Why?" Theo asks. "You up for showing us what you're made of?"

"Hardly. I'll leave it to you to make a fool of yourself."

"Hey, have some faith," I say. "He's learning from a master, don't forget."

Theo shakes his head with a smile. "Still, somehow I don't think I'll be impressing anyone. Not after that display of surfing prowess yesterday."

"Trust me, you'll be an expert in no time."

Theo looks sceptical, but crosses to dump his T-shirt on the blanket and retrieve the longboard we unearthed in the shed. His stomach muscles, tanned the same pale gold as the rest of him, ripple as he straightens and lopes to join me. My cheeks warm. I glance away, gesturing for him to lay the board on the sand.

To begin with, I show Theo the correct way to stand, left foot centred in front, right foot at an angle towards the back. Then I lie flat on the board and demonstrate propelling myself to my feet in a single fluid motion. The first time Theo tries it, I laugh.

"What?" He shoots me a quizzical glance. "Did I do it wrong?"

"No, that was fine. It's just…you're goofy footed. You put your right foot forward instead of your left."

"Oh, is that bad?"

"Never did me any harm. Seriously, that was great for a first try. Have another go."

I make him practise a dozen more times. Once I'm satisfied he has it down, I clap him on the back. "Knew you'd be a natural. Ready to try it on the water?"

"As I'll ever be." With a thumbs-up to Zara, who returns the gesture from behind her magazine, Theo hefts the board and we plunge into the waves.

Being a strong swimmer, he masters the art of paddling with ease, and his upper body strength helps him keep the board stable.

"You're doing brilliantly," I tell him. "But now for the tricky part."

I get him to turn and head a little inland. With the water lapping around my chest, I hold the board as steady as I can on the swell while Theo attempts the same manoeuvre we practised on the beach. He powers to his feet, struggling to find his equilibrium, before toppling away from me into the water.

He emerges, grin rueful, and pushes the sopping hair out of his eyes. "That went well."

"Hey, you almost had it there. No one does it first time."

"Not even you?"

"Not even me. Give it another go."

This time, he manages to stay upright for a few seconds before losing his balance, almost collapsing on top of me. I reach out to catch him, and for a split second the leanness of his chest grazes mine. Something hot, embarrassment spiked with a reaction I can't define, jolts through me.

"Sorry." Theo hooks an arm over the board and pulls himself upright, his smile sheepish.

I let out a long breath. "S'all right. You did really well then. You're picking it up much quicker than I did."

"Right, and you were how old? Twelve?"

"Ten."

Theo laughs. "Wow, I'm officially a faster learner than a ten-year-old. So who taught you? Your Dad?"

"My dad's dead." Grateful for the reprieve, I rest my forearms on the board and stare into the distance. A faint haze shimmers on the horizon, the sea blending into the paler blue of the sky.

"Gosh, I'm sorry. What happened?"

"Motorbike accident. He died before I was born, so I never knew him."

"I'm really sorry." Theo's silent for a few moments. Then he says, "My mum, too, four years ago. Breast cancer."

"Shit." I hadn't known. Something else Zara conveniently forgot to tell me. And there I was the other night, asking about his parents. I look sideways at him. "You must miss her."

Theo nods. He leans on the board beside me, his expression faraway. "Dad and I get on all right, but Clemmy's his favourite. I was always closer to Mum. She understood me better than Dad ever has."

47

"That must've been tough." I try to imagine losing my own mum, the one person in the world who has been there for me my entire life. It's unthinkable.

"It was. Still is, but I have a lot of good memories." Theo's gaze shifts to me. "Must be hard for you, too, never to have known your dad."

I drop my eyes to my hands where they rest on the board. No one has ever said anything like that to me. People are always nice when I tell them about Dad, but their sympathy is somehow detached. They assume it's easier on me because I never had a relationship with him, didn't have to suffer through the loss. It isn't easier, just different. I might not have grieved for my dad the way I would if I'd been alive, but often I think the pain would have been worth it to have a single memory to hold on to.

And Theo gets it.

I swallow against the lump in my throat. "Sometimes. Harder for Mum, though. She's had to bring me up on her own."

"What about her parents? Your grandparents."

"They've never wanted anything to do with me. Mum comes from this respectable middle-class family. They never approved of my dad, thought he was a bad influence. After Dad was killed and Mum discovered she was pregnant, her parents gave her an ultimatum—get rid of the baby or be cut off from the family."

"They disowned her, after she'd just lost your dad?"

I shrug. I try not to think about it too much; it makes me too mad.

"So," Theo can't mask his shock, "what about your dad's family?"

"Wasters, apparently. Mum wouldn't have let them anywhere near me even if they were interested, which they weren't. They're probably in prison by now, or dead of an overdose."

Theo opens his mouth, but seems at a loss. Horror and empathy battle each other across his face.

For reasons I can't explain, I have the urge to reassure him. "It hasn't been all bad. I've had Dean and his family. Brian, that's Dean's dad, was the one who taught me to surf. He and Sue have always treated me like a second son."

It's true. To begin with, I think they felt sorry for me for being without a dad and because Mum worked such long hours. As I got older, they invited me on day trips with them, and away on holiday. In short, they've been the family I never had.

We're quiet for a while. I rest my chin on my folded arms, letting the waves push and tug at my body. I'm not generally so open about myself, and never with people I barely know. Yet, Theo puts me at ease in a way that makes talking to him feel like the most natural thing in the world.

I rouse myself and turn to him. "Break over. Ready to have another go?"

Again and again I get Theo up on the board, and each time he stays on for longer. Finally, he grins down at me, face alight with triumph. "Think I've got it."

"You sure about that?" I smirk, tilting the board, and he crashes into the water.

The lesson deteriorates after that. We take it in turns to stand on the board, the other waiting to tip us off when we least expect it.

Resurfacing for what must have been the tenth time, Theo blinks the water from his vision. "Looks like we're being summoned."

I follow the direction of his gaze. Zara has wandered to the water's edge and is gesturing for our attention. "Well, we've probably done enough for one day. We can carry on tomorrow, if you like. We'll get you riding some actual waves."

"You think so? Thanks for this, Luke. It's been great."

"You're welcome. Just don't forget you owe me some fudge."

"I haven't forgotten."

We smile at each other. A shyness that wasn't there a moment ago trembles between us. Then it's gone, and we splash our way back to shore.

As soon as we're within shouting distance, Zara throws us each a towel. "Nice of you to remember my existence. You've been out there for hours."

"We have?" I'd completely lost track of time.

Zara rolls her eyes. "Yes, and I'm starving. You're taking me out to lunch to make up for ignoring me all morning."

"Yes, Ma'am." Theo salutes, and catches my eye with a complicit grin.

***

Theo drives us into a local fishing village for lunch. We sit at a table that overlooks the bustling harbour, eating golden fries and cod in crispy batter. I feed mine to the seagulls, having left my appetite out on the water.

Zara does most of the talking. Oblivious to the fact that Theo and I are quieter than usual, she amuses herself, inventing increasingly sleazy stories about our fellow diners.

"You see her?" She points a chip in the direction of a mousy young woman who is nodding earnestly as she listens to the stern-looking couple seated across from her. Her parents, I assume. "She pretends to be the good little daughter, while all the time conducting a secret life as a dominatrix."

"Um, Zara, I know I'm not exactly an expert," Theo says, "but come on."

"Appearances can be deceptive. She might not look like much, but dress her up in leather and put a whip in her hand, and she's a slave driver in the bedroom."

"Luke?" Theo appeals to me, eyebrows raised.

"Just tie me down," I drawl, and he chokes on his Sprite.

"And that guy over there," Zara indicates a sneering, bald man perspiring a table with his sour-faced wife and two taciturn children, "he plays the part of the dutiful husband and father, but he's actually pining for his gay lover."

"How'd you work that one out?" Theo asks.

"Easy. He keeps eyeing you up whenever he thinks no one's watching."

Theo shudders. "Don't. You're making me feel contaminated."

***

Back at the cottage, Theo and I take shelter from the heat on the under-cover terrace, but Zara insists she needs to do some more work on her tan.

"You'll get sunstroke," Theo warns.

Zara pokes her tongue out at him, and spreads a blanket over the grass by the pool.

Stretched out on a lounger, I open my copy of *A Game of Thrones*. Somehow, though, I'm not in the mood. A drowsy contentment drags at my body, so that I have no desire to do anything other than lie here and drift.

I find myself watching Theo. He's hunched over the table, pencil making a faint scratching sound against his sketchpad. "What're you drawing?"

"Oh," his arm shifts to block the page from view, "nothing really. Just doodles." He glances at the book propped on my chest. "You enjoying that?"

I grin. "Haven't started it yet."

Theo laughs, returning his attention to his doodles, and I pick up my book with renewed determination. I start over from the beginning, but hanging on to my concentration is like trying to hold back the tide. I end up staring at the opening line, smiling without caring why, letting my thoughts wander.

**

When I open my eyes, I'm alone on the terrace. I roll off the lounger, stretching, and pad inside in search of the others.

Theo's just entering the kitchen from the hall, his hair damp from the shower. He smiles at me. "Lightweight."

"Hey, this teaching lark is hard work. Zara upstairs?"

"Yeah. Washing her hair, I think."

In fact, I find her retching over the toilet bowl in the en suite. I hover in the doorway, at a loss as to what to do, until she straightens, supporting herself against the sink.

"You OK?" Stupid question, since she clearly isn't.

She grimaces. "Sunstroke. Theo was right."

"Anything I can do?"

"You could get me a drink of water, and there are some paracetamol in my case, inside pocket."

"Be right back." I make a hasty exit. Doling out painkillers—I can handle that.

"She does this every year without fail." Theo sighs, passing me a glass to fill from the tap. "She never learns."

When I return to our room, the curtains have been drawn against the evening light and Zara's huddled in bed, shivering as though she has a fever. I unearth the painkillers, watching her gulp them down with the water. "Will you be OK? Anything else you want?"

"No, I just need to sleep it off." She collapses onto the pillows and gives me a weak smile. "Thanks, Luke."

"You're welcome." I smooth her hair away from her hot forehead, overcome with a surge of affection, and leave her to rest while I shower.

In the short time it takes to rid my body of its coating of sweat, sand and salt, Zara has fallen asleep. Careful not to disturb her, I pull on jeans and a clean T-shirt and close the door behind me.

In the kitchen, Theo's crouched on the floor inspecting the contents of the fridge. I lean against the table and peer over his shoulder. "She's asleep."

"That's good. She'll feel better after some rest." He glances up at me. "So, looks like it's just us for dinner. How're you at wielding sharp knives?"

I hold up my fingers. "All present and correct. I can't vouch for the state of my co-chefs, though."

"I'll risk it." Theo gets to his feet, a bottle of beer in each hand. He flips the top off one and passes it to me. "You're on salad duty."

I take a swig of my beer. "No problem. Just stay out of slicing range and you'll be fine."

"Thanks for the warning." Theo lowers his bottle to study my T-shirt. "Is that some kind of political statement?"

"Lamb of God? You have to be kidding me. You're talking about one of the best metal bands of all time."

"News to me. You'll have to play me some of their stuff."

"Somehow I doubt it'll be your thing."

"No? What's my thing?"

"I dunno." I pretend to consider him. "Mozart, something poncy like that."

Theo laughs. Seizing a knife from the wooden block behind him, he thrusts it at me. "Get chopping, surfer boy, and stop making assumptions."

While I slice tomatoes, Theo sets about making a dressing—actually making one from scratch, which impresses the hell out of me. It's easy, companionable, as if we've known each other far longer than forty-eight hours.

"So," I say, as Theo sets a pan of oil on to heat, "if you don't like Mozart, what music do you like?"

He grins. "I never said I didn't like Mozart, just that you shouldn't make assumptions. I prefer Handel, though. How do you want your steak?"

"Bloody."

"Good to know you're not a complete philistine. Zara always makes me burn hers to a crisp."

We take our food onto the terrace to eat, washing it down with a steady flow of beer. After we've demolished a tub of Rocky Road ice cream, Theo heads indoors and reappears with a bottle of Bourbon and two glasses. I lose all sense of time passing. Only the sky, darkening as the sun slips below the treetops and a velvety night closes around us, bears witness to how long we sit there.

And we talk. We talk about anything and everything and nothing at all. We debate England's performance in the Six Nations, the arguments for legalising cannabis, and whether Sam or Aragorn is the true hero of *The Lord of the Rings*. Once we start, we can't stop. We throw subjects back and forth, exchanging smiles of comradeship when our views coincide, challenging one another when they don't. And all the while I'm conscious of being on the edge of something, something new, unknown.

Theo reaches for the bottle to refill our glasses. "Any idea what you want to do? After school, I mean."

"Not really." The whisky trails a fiery path down my throat to my stomach. When I lean back in my chair, the stars twinkle down at me, fuzzy around the edges. "I've been wondering about sports journalism. How about you?"

"That's easy. For as long as I can remember, I've wanted to run my own gallery, discover the next Hockney or Constable. Wouldn't that be a legacy to leave behind?"

"Yeah, I suppose it would." I smile at him. Art means about as much to me as Chinese, but his passion touches me.

"Of course," he adds, "I've always known it would never happen."

"Why not, if that's what you want?"

"Because I'm expected to take over running our estate, as well as the family business. My dad breeds and trains racehorses, owns one of the top yards in the country, and it'll be mine one day."

I mull this over. Many people, most even, would envy Theo his life, his wealth and privilege, but I doubt any of them would stop to consider the sense of duty and responsibility that goes along with it. Despite everything, I feel lucky.

"Mind you," Theo's tone is thoughtful, "that may not be the case anymore."

"How come?"

He stares into the contents of his glass. "You asked me the other night whether I'd be going home over the holidays. Well, I'd like to. The problem is, my dad doesn't want to see me, not now he knows about me being gay."

"Shit." There doesn't seem to be anything else to say to that.

"Yeah." Theo glances at me, then away again. "I told him last summer, a couple of weeks before I left for Oxford. Now I wish I'd done it earlier, when Mum was alive. Maybe it would have been easier on Dad. It just never felt like the right moment. It isn't exactly something you bring up over dinner, is it? Or maybe it is. Maybe that's what I should've done, got it out of the way years ago, put an end to their hopes for me before they took root. I don't know." He pushes the hair out of his eyes. "Anyway, I finally plucked up the courage. I had to. Dad kept going on about all the great opportunities for meeting 'nice young ladies' and I couldn't take any more. I couldn't face the idea of going away under false pretences. So I sat him down after lunch one day and told him."

"And he took it badly?"

"That's one way of putting it. At first, he tried to brazen it out. 'It's just a phase,' he said. 'You'll grow out of it.' Then, when I explained this is how I am, how I always will be, he shut down. He said he'd speak to me once I came to my senses and decided to be a real man." Theo winces. "I've called home a few times, just to check he's OK, but after establishing I haven't abandoned 'this gay nonsense' he hangs up."

"He'll come round," I say. "In time."

"I hope so." The look he flashes me is part gratitude, part sadness. "I'm just not sure he'll ever forgive me."

"What do you mean, forgive you? You haven't done anything wrong here."

"To Dad, I have. Rowanleigh has been in the Scott-Palmer family for generations. It's vital to him that the line continues, and now I've told him this isn't going to happen. At least, not in the way he wants."

"There's still your sister, right?"

"Yeah, there's still Clemmy, and if Dad can't learn to accept me, she'll have to take over. She's more than capable, better with the horses. Still, there's no getting away from the fact that, regardless of whether she marries or not, the family name will die out. That's a massive blow for my dad. As far as he's concerned, I've failed him as a son."

I set down my empty glass and rest an elbow on the table, propping my chin on my hand. I suppose I can see why Theo's Dad might be gutted, but that doesn't give him the right to basically disown him. Theo's already lost his Mum; now it must feel like he's lost his dad, too. "So, you haven't been home since you told him?"

"Nope. I spent Christmas with my aunt and uncle, Zara's parents, and over Easter I stayed at the flat in Oxford. It's easier that way, for both of us."

I hesitate, wanting to ask, unsure whether it's off limits. "So, your dad never met... He didn't know about..." I realise I don't know the guy's name.

"Francis?" Theo averts his gaze. "No, he didn't."

Immediately, I wish I'd kept my mouth shut. Theo sort of hunches in on himself, his body language the equivalent of a 'no trespassing' sign.

"Look," I fiddle with my glass, "I'm sorry. None of my business."

At once, Theo turns back to me. "No, Luke, I'm sorry. You must think I'm pathetic, the poor little rich boy, complaining because his bed of roses turned out to have a few thorns in it."

"No." I meet his eyes. "No, I don't think that."

"Thanks, that means a lot." Theo rests his elbows on the table, studying me. "Things can't have been easy for you, though, not having your dad around."

I shrug, conscious of Theo's forearm mere inches from mine. "I haven't had it bad. Mum's the one working fourteen-hour shifts to feed me and keep a roof over our heads."

"And there's never been anyone else? No stepfather?"

"Honestly, I don't think Mum's ever got over losing my dad, although she claims she's just too busy to meet anyone. She works so hard to make sure I have everything I need, but I know she feels it isn't enough."

"You don't see it like that, though," Theo says, "I can tell."

I shake my head. "Mum's never been able to buy me the latest iPhone or whatever, but she's always there. Even when she comes in after being on her feet all day, she's never too tired to listen to what I have to say. That means more than whether my clothes come from Pardo's or Jack Wills."

"Your mum sounds great."

"She is. I'm lucky to have her, I guess."

"And I bet she'd say the same about you."

I contemplate my empty glass. It isn't that I think Mum regrets having me; I know she doesn't. All the same, if she'd done what her parents wanted and got rid of me, her life would have been very different. She might have gone to university, had a career, been free of the daily grind of stock-takes and money worries.

"Trust me," Theo says. His eyes, when I glance up at him, are warm and full of something I don't dare put a name to. I meet his gaze. For an instant, it's as if I'm riding the crest of a wave, suspended in that halfway state, where time simultaneously stands still and stretches into eternity. The darkness closes in around us, settling like a fleecy blanket over our shoulders.

Theo looks away first. He pushes back his chair and gets to his feet. "Think I'll go up. OK?"

"OK." My voice sounds strange, scratchy, as though I'm coming down with a cold.

Theo scuffs the ground with his toe. "You staying out here?"

"Think I will, yeah."

Still he stalls. "Night, then."

"Night."

Finally, Theo turns and makes for the glass doors, stumbling a little up the step. I watch him go. It's only once he's disappeared inside and I let out a long sigh that I realise I'd been holding my breath.

Chapter Five

Brilliant blue shimmers above me, the sun shining full on my face. I blink, disorientated. Where am I? How did I get here? Slowly, as I lie there, fragments of the previous evening come back to me—sitting with Theo into the early hours, the whisky and confidences, me stretching out on a lounger, gazing up at the stars until I fell asleep.

I yawn, languid with contentment. There's just something about waking up in the open air, something liberating. The murmur of voices drifts through the open glass doors, along with the smell of coffee. I run a furry tongue over my teeth. My mouth's as dry as a rusty beer barrel, and doesn't taste much better. I work the kinks from my shoulders and stand. My sweatshirt sticks to me in the mid-morning heat. No, not mine. Theo's. I'd found it draped over the back of a chair and pulled it on against the night chill. Somehow, I don't think he'll mind.

I run a hand through my dishevelled hair and make for the kitchen. About to step inside, I'm brought up short on the threshold, my greeting dying in my throat. Theo is seated at the table, hands wrapped around his mug, but there's no sign of Zara. A rangy young man lounges in the chair across from him, his arm slung over the shoulders of a dark-haired girl.

Back to the door, Theo doesn't notice me, but the young man does. He breaks off mid-sentence. "Theo, did you know there's a tramp in your back garden?"

His drawling, upper-class voice sets my teeth on edge. I lean against the doorframe, deliberately casual, and stare him down. This guy is handsome in that sickening way—blond, with a straight nose and strong jaw—that makes me want to punch his perfect teeth in.

Theo glances over at me. His eyes meet mine for an instant, but then he turns away. "It's all right, Giles. That's Luke, Zara's latest."

I frown at the back of Theo's head. No smile. Not even a greeting. If I didn't know better, I'd swear there was a coolness to his tone, but that makes no sense. I fish a clean mug from the dishwasher and saunter over to the table, reaching past Theo for the coffee pot. "Not going to introduce me?"

He shrugs without looking at me. "Giles and Meredith, friends of mine from Oxford."

This time, there's no mistaking the dismissal. Whatever connection had been forming between us is gone now. Our time out on the water, everything we'd shared about our lives, our dreams... It's as though it never happened.

"Hi." It's an effort, but I give Giles and Meredith the benefit of my smile. Giles completely blanks me, which earns him a sharp look from Meredith.

"Hi." Her answering smile is more a grimace of apology. She's pretty in a head-girlish sort of way, her hair pulled back in a long plait, plain white T-shirt worn over navy shorts. She regards me, her grey eyes thoughtful, as though I'm an abstract painting she's trying to puzzle out.

In the awkward silence that follows, I spoon sugar into my coffee and perch on the edge of the table. Theo's gaze remains fixed on his mug, although he shifts away from me, like I'm a virus he's afraid of catching.

Just to make him feel uncomfortable, I prop my foot on the edge of his chair. "Borrowed your sweatshirt last night. Hope that's OK."

"It's fine." He edges away still farther. If he isn't careful, he'll end up on the floor. "Just dump it in the machine when you've finished with it."

His meaning is clear. He has no desire to wear it after it's been contaminated. I swallow a mouthful of coffee; it tastes bitter on my tongue.

Zara enters the kitchen then, shattering the tension. She's tousled and has on only a baggy pink T-shirt. When she spots Giles, her smile vanishes. "What's he doing here?"

"Hey." Theo's expression softens with concern. My fingers tighten around my mug. "Feeling better?"

"I was," she shoots Giles a dark look, "until I saw who the bad fairy spirited in during the night."

Giles raises an eyebrow, toying with the end of Meredith's plait. "What a warm welcome. You could at least pretend to be pleased to see me."

"What would be the point? You'd know I was faking it."

"Something you've never had to do, I'm sure." He smirks in my direction. "Roughing it a bit these days, aren't you, Zara?"

She ignores him. Moving behind Theo's chair, she puts her arms around my neck and kisses me full on the mouth. It's a lingering kiss, even though I must taste rank, and I hug her, overcome with affection.

Giles makes a revolted sound. Zara draws away, opening her mouth to retort, but I lay a hand on her back. I know Giles's type, arrogant pricks who think they're superior to everyone else, and they're not worth it.

Zara nestles into me. "So, where'd you get to last night?"

"Ended up being a bit of a late one. I didn't want to disturb you."

"What a gentleman." She kisses me again, quick and sweet. With a smile, she accepts the mug Theo hands her and pulls out a chair, helping herself from the toast rack.

I touch her shoulder. "Gonna jump in the shower. Have a feeling I need one."

She nods, focused on prying the lid from a jar of peanut butter. Downing the remainder of my coffee, I slide off the table and make my escape. Out in the hallway, I take the stairs three at a time. Theo's sweatshirt is starting to irritate my skin, as though it's infested with lice. I need to get rid of it.

When I barge into Theo's room, the scent hits me, alcohol mingling with something unmistakably masculine. Despite myself, I pause, looking around. His personality leaps out at me from every corner. The curtains half pulled, teetering towers of books that a single careless nudge would surely send spilling across the rug, the jumble of odds and ends—broken pencils, loose change, weirdly shaped pebbles—on the chest of drawers...it's all testament to his distracted geekiness. In a violent motion, I yank the sweatshirt off over my head and fling it to the floor.

In the shower, the water pounding my body, a hard anger unravels in the pit of my stomach. It doesn't take a genius to work out what's behind Theo's sudden change of attitude. He had no problem hanging out with me yesterday, but now his posh friends have turned up, I'm not good enough. Had his friendliness been nothing more than an act? Give the guy an Oscar. He certainly had me fooled. Or maybe it was genuine, and he doesn't want to be seen to associate with me in front of Giles. So he's either a liar or a disgusting hypocrite. I can't decide which is worse.

More to the point, why do I give a shit? So Theo and I aren't going to spend the summer hanging out. There'll be no more meandering conversations late into the night, no more teaching Theo to surf. I'm sure I'll survive.

At least the weather is on my side. As I tug on a T-shirt and shorts over my shorty wetsuit, the view from the bedroom window shows the trees tossing in a stiff breeze. Though it's mostly out of sight beyond the wood, I imagine the sea rising and falling in a ceaseless rhythm. My body aches to be at one with the waves, to put all this shit behind me, if only for a few hours. Flip-flops in hand, I head downstairs.

The others have progressed to the shade of the upper terrace. Meredith has a stack of brochures on the table before her and is sifting through them. "Tintagel has to be worth a visit, the birthplace of King Arthur and all that. Oh, and I'd love to visit the Charles Kingsley Museum in Clovelly. I've read *The Water Babies* too many times to count."

I slip behind the group and make straight for my board, where it's propped up against the cottage wall.

"Sounds fascinating," Zara says. "You'll have to buy me a postcard. Luke," she beseeches me, "help me out here. Theo's being an idiot."

"Really?" I try to sound as though this isn't old news.

"He's banned, yes, banned me from going anywhere today, even the beach. Can you believe that? He says I have to stay in the shade. All day."

"Zara, don't be difficult." Theo rubs his forehead. He looks tired. "You got sunstroke because I let you stay out too long. Now I'm telling you to take it easy, just for today."

"Theo, in case you've forgotten, I'm not five years old."

"And in case you've forgotten, your parents are trusting me to look out for you. If anything happens, it's my responsibility."

"Luke," Zara appeals, "tell him."

I wrestle with myself. Siding with Zara, purely for the satisfaction of annoying Theo, is tempting. I sense him watching me, wondering if I'm really that petty. Without glancing at him, I say, "No, he's right. You probably should take it easy."

"I hope this doesn't apply to the rest of us, Theo," Giles says. "I didn't drive all the way down here to play nanny to your baby cousin."

"As I remember it, no one asked you to come at all," Zara snaps.

I leave them to it. Board bag slung over my shoulders, I slide my feet into my flip-flops and descend the terrace steps, starting along the path to the woods.

"Luke?" Theo's voice stops me. When I turn back, his eyes find mine. "Where're you going?"

Resentment squeezes my chest—like it's any of his business—but I keep my tone light. "Just down to the beach for a bit."

"On your own? You think that's a good idea?"

"Yeah. I think it's an excellent idea. Unless you want to come, pick up where we left off."

Theo's expression flickers, and I know he recognises the challenge behind the words. He averts his gaze. "Another time, maybe."

I shrug and continue along the path. I walk fast, as fast as I can with the awkward weight of my board, and soon the cool dimness of the woods embraces me. Just let me get out on the water where I won't have to think, won't have to feel.

"Luke!" Running footsteps pound behind me. "Hold up."

My instincts urge me to ignore him, to feign deafness in the hope that he'll take the hint, but what would be the point? It isn't as if I can outrun him. Not with my board. He'll catch up to me sooner or later, whether I like it or not. Blood sizzling, I lean my board bag against the nearest tree and wait for Theo to join me.

"What do you want?" Away from the others, I drop any pretence at civility.

"I..." He falters, but only for an instant. "You can't go out alone. It's too dangerous."

I'm reminded of my promise to Mum, my promise never to go out on the water without someone close by. Guilt gnaws at my gut, which only pisses me off more. I glare at Theo. "Thanks for the health and safety lecture," I tell him, and move to reclaim my board.

He's too quick for me. A couple of strides and he's blocking my path. "You know I can't let you do this."

"And you know there's nothing you can do to stop me."

Theo appraises me, perhaps trying to gauge the level of my stupidity. He glances in the direction of the cottage, expression conflicted. At last, he sighs. "Go ahead."

"You what?"

"Go ahead. You're right. I can't stop you."

My eyes narrow. "And what're you going to do?"

"Do I have a choice?" He hurls the words at me. "I'm going to stand there and make sure you don't drown."

I regard him, the stubborn set to his jaw, his mouth uncharacteristically hard. He doesn't want to do this, but he will. He will because it's the right thing to do, and because he doesn't want my death on his conscience. And I'm supposed to lose myself in the waves when the person I'm trying to escape is watching my every move. "Forget it."

"Sorry?" Theo rakes a hand through his hair, frowning.

"I said forget it." The fight gusts out of me. More drained than angry, I heft my board and trudge back the way I came.

***

It's settled. Theo, Giles and Meredith will go to Tintagel to visit the ruins of King Arthur's birthplace, while Zara and I stay behind. Zara grumbles, but her protests are half-hearted. I have the feeling she's as glad to see the back of Giles as I am.

I'm perched on the edge of a lounger, keeping out of the way, when Theo approaches, car keys dangling from one hand. He speaks to me in a low voice. "Watch out for Zara, won't you? See she stays out of the sun?"

I don't dignify this with a response. Does he think he's the only one around here who cares about Zara?

Theo must see something in my expression because he holds up his hands. "No, I'm sorry. I know you will. Forget it."

"Already forgotten." It's unclear, even to me, whether I'm referring to his comment or everything that's happened over the past two days. It doesn't matter. Giles calls to Theo to get a move on, and he leaves to join his friends.

The moment the purr of the engine has faded, the tension drains out of me. I hunch forward, elbows on my knees, and rest my throbbing head in my hands.

The springs sag as Zara sits beside me. "Was he foul to you before I came down?"

It takes me a second to realise she isn't talking about Theo. I flick her a wry smile. "Nothing I couldn't handle."

"Believe it or not, Giles isn't always such a dickhead."

"I'll take your word for it."

Zara grins. "As you may have noticed, he isn't my favourite person either, but Theo thinks a lot of him, so he can't be all bad."

No, they're just as bad as each other. Theo's worse, in fact. At least I know where I stand with Giles. No elaborate charade for him. No attempt to conceal his utter contempt for me.

"Why did he and Meredith have to come?" Petulance creeps into Zara's tone, a side effect of being the only child of rich parents. "They get to spend all term with Theo. This was supposed to be my time."

I nod, trying to appear sympathetic. Actually, I'm glad Giles showed up when he did. If he hadn't, Theo might never have revealed his true colours. He might have kept up the farce all summer, gone on day after day acting out a friendship that was nothing more than a sham. And like the idiot I am, I would've swallowed it whole.

"Still," Zara's tone brightens, "Theo told me they're only staying a few days. We'll just have to put up with them until then."

At which point, I'll have to leave. Once Giles and Meredith have gone and the three of us are alone again, what choice will I have? The situation will be impossible.

And Theo must know that. He must know I won't want to stay, that there's no going back now everything's out in the open.

"Luke?" Zara rests a hand on my back. "You all right?"

I focus on her with an effort. Despite the heat, a leaden coldness weighs on my insides. "Yeah, I'm fine."

She smiles and kisses me, her hands sliding under my T-shirt. I kiss her back, but my mind is all over the place.

Zara draws away. "Someone's distracted this morning."

"Sorry." I put my arm around her, and she leans into me.

"That's OK. Come on, let's go down to the beach. I can sunbathe while you take your board out."

"Appreciate the offer, but a couple of hours surfing aren't worth what Theo would do to me if he found out."

"I won't tell him if you don't. Not scared of big bad Theo, are you?"

"'Fraid so. Think I'll go for a swim, cool off a bit. Can I trust you to stay in the shade like a good girl?"

"Go on." Zara collapses against the lounger cushions. "I'll just lie here and endure the torture of eyeing up your body."

"Don't knock it. There are some who'd pay good money for that." I push myself to my feet, pulling my T-shirt over my head, and make for the pool.

The water, when I plunge in, sends shock waves along my nerve endings. I launch myself into a series of lengths, pushing my body hard, arms slicing the surface as though intent on beating it to a pulp. After a while—I lose track of how much time passes—the anger recedes to a dull emptiness.

I return to the terrace on rubbery legs, my muscles on fire. Zara has laid lunch out on the table: cheese and crackers, watermelon and grapes. I don't have much of an appetite, despite missing breakfast, but I force some down to please her.

She hands me a beer, and I'm reminded sharply of last night, of Theo doing the same. I swallow the memory and take a swig. "So, do Theo and Giles go back a long way?"

"Almost five years." Zara pops a chunk of melon into her mouth and licks the juice from her fingers. "Since their first term at Eton."

I have a mental image of Theo in a top hat and waistcoat, looking like a schoolboy in a Frank Richards novel. Yet another reminder, if I needed one, of the gulf between our two worlds.

"Before that," Zara says, "it was just the two of us, Theo and me. After Giles came on the scene, though, Theo didn't need me so much. I was left to tag along, when they let me."

At least that explains her less than ecstatic reaction to Giles showing up this morning.

Zara grimaces. "Even worse—God, this is really embarrassing—I had this major crush on Giles."

"Wow! Now that *is* embarrassing."

"I know, I know. Makes me cringe when I think about it, and obviously I'm way over him. Jealous?"

I raise an eyebrow. "Should I be?"

"No way. You're much hotter than Giles. Speaking of which," Zara's eyes sparkle, "we should make the most of having the place to ourselves."

I down the rest of my beer. "Have anything specific in mind?"

In answer, she removes the bottle from my grasp and straddles me. My arms go around her and she presses close, soft and inviting, her mouth seeking mine. This time, I kiss her with an intensity that catches us both off guard. There's no thought, no second guessing myself. My mind simply steps aside and lets my body take charge, trampling my doubts into the ground.

My hands roam over Zara's back, and I push my tongue into her mouth, hungry, devouring, until she moans and thrusts against me. When I stand up, she winds her legs around my waist, fingers tangled in my hair. I stumble across the terrace, hampered by Zara's weight and my own impatience. My mouth moves to her neck, sucking on the delicate skin, as I reach beneath her top to unhook her bra. She gasps, tugging up the hem of my T-shirt, raking her nails down my spine. Then we're collapsing onto the nearest lounger, a confusion of hands and lips and burning need that blocks out everything but the present.

Afterwards, Zara dozes with her head nestled against my shoulder, one arm draped over my stomach. I can't sleep. I lie there, gaze on the gilded treetops, and wonder at the hollowness inside me.

***

When the others arrive back towards early evening, we're sitting fully clothed on the terrace, me with another beer, Zara on her second vodka and Coke.

"How were the ruins?" she asks as they join us.

"It was a long climb," Meredith says, "but so worth it. The view was amazing."

"Pity you couldn't come, Zara," Giles adds. "We would've had such a laugh watching you struggle up there. I know how much you love heights."

Zara only rolls her eyes, her earlier animosity evaporated. It's amazing what sex and a long nap can do.

"Take no notice." Theo lays an arm across the back of her chair. "As I recall, he was the one who almost had a heart attack. You have a good day?"

"Mmm hmmm." Zara smiles at me, hooking her leg over mine in a way that can't be misinterpreted.

"I'm glad." Expression neutral, Theo drops a paper bag into her lap. "Something to make up for missing the trip."

Zara snatches it up to peer inside. "Ooh, chocolate fudge. Thanks, Theo." She breaks off a square and pops it in her mouth. "Mmmm."

"It's from Granny Wobbly's, this little shop in Tintagel," Meredith says. "The owners make all their fudge by hand."

Zara chews slowly, savouring it, and holds the bag out to me in invitation. I shake my head. I expect her to mention our deal, Theo's and mine, reminding him that he owes me payment for the surfing lesson, but she doesn't. Most likely she's forgotten about it, just as Theo has. I stare over the lawn towards the woods, and tell myself I'm relieved he didn't feel obliged to honour our bargain. I would have choked on it, anyway.

Meredith retreats indoors to unpack the food shopping they'd picked up on their way home, while Theo and Giles get the barbecue going. As the smell of charcoal fills the air, I watch the two of them out of the corner of my eye, my fingers entwined with Zara's. Giles says something and Theo shakes his head, punching him on the shoulder. They laugh, easy, relaxed. Even if Zara hadn't told me, their years of friendship would have been obvious.

That was us two nights ago, Theo and me. We'd fooled around like that, me teasing him about burning the sausages, as the beginnings of a connection sparked between us. A connection that had never existed.

"Just going to grab another beer," I tell Zara.

She nods, squeezing my hand, and I wander into the kitchen. Meredith has a book resting against the toaster, a glass of wine at her elbow, reading while she chops spring onions. A saucepan of new potatoes bubbles on the hob beside her.

I skirt around her to open the fridge. "Hey."

"Hey." She spares me a glance, keeping one eye on her book.

I grab a beer and nudge the fridge shut with my thigh. On my way back past her, I pause to read the title printed at the top of the page. *The Private Lives of the Impressionists*. "Some light holiday reading?"

"Yes," Meredith darts me an amused look, "actually."

"If you say so." I laugh, and rummage in the drawer next to her for the bottle opener.

Attention on her chopping, she says, "Sorry about earlier, Giles being so difficult."

I raise an eyebrow. 'Difficult' was certainly one word for it, although 'pompous arsehole' would be nearer the mark.

The corner of Meredith's mouth twitches. "OK, he was downright rude, but he isn't normally like that."

"Don't worry about it. Must've been a shock to his system, being forced under the same roof as someone like me."

"That isn't it, you know."

I don't answer, but my silence must convey my scepticism, because Meredith lays down her knife and fixes me with a direct gaze. "Not everyone at Oxford has been to Eton or Roedean."

I look at her, uncomprehending, and she sighs. "Luke, you clearly have me down as some upper-class girl. Not true. My dad teaches art at a secondary school and my mum works at the Tate."

She has me. Seeing her in the kitchen with Theo and Giles that morning, I'd presumed she was from their world. The idea that she might be closer to mine had never entered my head.

"So you see," Meredith says, "Giles is no snob."

I prop myself against the worktop, and take a swig of my beer. Though I can't doubt her words, they don't tally with Giles's hostility. For whatever reason, he took against me on sight, and Theo, like the faithful lapdog, is following his lead. "Clearly I'm just obnoxious, then."

"Oh," Meredith's grin transforms her earnest face, "I think you're all right."

She isn't flirting. There's a straightforwardness about her, a candour that appeals to me, and I can't help grinning back.

"How's it going in here?"

We turn to see Giles standing in the doorway. At the sight of me leaning beside his girlfriend, his smile vanishes. He shoots me a suspicious glare, which I rebuff with cool defiance. So Giles has a jealous streak. Interesting.

He crosses the kitchen, sliding a possessive arm around Meredith's waist. "Need a hand?"

"No, everything's under control." If she noticed the look that passed between us, she gives no sign. "Steaks ready?"

"About another five minutes. Theo can handle it." Giles nuzzles her neck, a display of familiarity I'm guessing is for my benefit.

I leave them to it, escaping with my beer onto the patio.

***

"How's Clemmy?" Giles asks Theo a while later. "I'd hoped you might have managed to tempt her down here."

We're gathered on the patio, eating lamb steaks and potato salad washed down with a steady supply of alcohol, dusk smudging the sky the deep mauve of a day-old bruise.

"And drag her away from her precious horses? Hardly." Theo smiles, though there's sadness behind it. "I'd really like to see her, but she won't leave the estate for long, and…well."

He doesn't finish the sentence. Doesn't need to. I'm assailed by the memory of last night, Theo pouring out his troubles with his dad to me, and I have to swallow hard to shift the mouthful of steak that has lodged itself in my throat.

Giles takes charge of the conversation, purposely sticking to topics that exclude me, pouncing on every opportunity to drive home the fact that I'm an outsider. A wasted effort on his part. I lean back in my chair and let the conversation wash over me. Any world inhabited by Giles isn't one I want to belong to.

Giles, it transpires, is Giles Jardine of the renowned banking dynasty. His dad, he takes obvious pleasure in boasting, has just agreed a gigantic sum with *The Financial Times* for an exclusive interview, something about balancing family commitments with running a multinational company. No one shows much interest in the announcement, so I assume it was made for my benefit, another detail to emphasise how little I fit in. Like I give a shit.

Perhaps sensing my immunity to him, Giles turns an insincere smile on me. "And how about you, Luke. What do your parents do?"

Theo winces. He grimaces at me, the first time he's so much as acknowledged my existence since returning from Tintagel. I look away, pretending not to see.

Zara glares. "God, you're such an insensitive prick, Giles. Luke's dad is dead."

"Oh, sorry." His tone is offhand, as though apologising for bumping my shoulder in the street. "So, what does your mum do?"

I regard him over my fork. He really does believe he's better than me, that his money and privileged background makes him somehow superior. "She's a stockbroker. In the city."

"Yeah, right." Giles snorts. "And I'm a lap dancer."

I shrug. As if Mum's job has anything to do with him. Besides, she is a stockbroker of sorts. As manager of Pardo's, buying and selling is her domain, and she does work in the city, just not the city my comment implied.

Giles glowers at me, while Zara smothers a grin in her wineglass. I turn away, dismissing him, and find myself looking straight at Theo. He catches my eye, and for the briefest instant I swear he's about to wink. Hope, warm and uninvited, flares to life in my chest. Then he averts his gaze, and the moment passes.

Chapter Six

Whatever Giles's problem with me, he can't seem to find a single insult to fling at my board. As the five of us make our way along the wooded path to the beach the following morning, I glance over my shoulder to catch him studying my board bag with its Firewire logo. When he sees me eyeing him, his expression hardens into a sneer. "So, who did you have to rob to get your hands on that?"

I ignore him and step from the trees into the dazzling sunshine. It's another perfect day, just enough of a breeze to take the edge off the heat without blowing grit into our eyes. We wander a short way along the beach and get settled in, the others extracting books and sunglasses, while I unzip my bag to slide my board onto the sand.

"Sure you're a match for that?" Giles stands above me, the malice in his expression failing to mask his admiration.

"You wait and see." Zara pulls her T-shirt off over her head to reveal the bikini top underneath. "Luke's a marvel."

"Yes, well, I wouldn't expect you to say anything else." Giles calls across to Theo, who's unfolding one of the blankets. "Hey, is Zara's man any good with this flash board of his?"

"He is, actually. Surprisingly good." Theo answers without warmth; he's simply stating a fact.

I focus on slotting the fins into place. "Of course, Giles, if you think you can show me a thing or two about how it's done, be my guest."

I'd live off raw jelly fish for a year before letting him lay so much as a toe on my board, but I suspect it won't come to that. Sure enough, Giles merely snorts in disgust and turns to help Meredith with the second blanket.

Zara waves a bottle of sun cream under my nose. "Will you do the honours? Not that Theo wasn't an adequate stand-in, but he doesn't have your touch."

An image pops into my mind—Theo's hands, slender and capable. An artist's hands. Where did that come from? I blink, clearing my vision, and take the bottle from Zara. "Sure."

She smiles at me and joins Theo on the blanket, rolling onto her front. I kneel beside her, careful to keep my distance from Theo, and squirt a blob of sun cream into my palm. Zara gasps at the coldness, shivering with obvious pleasure as I smooth it over her back and shoulders.

More than once, I'm certain I sense Theo's gaze on me, but when I sneak a peep at him, he's busy with his puzzle book. Giles, on the other hand, makes no attempt to hide his scrutiny. Whenever I look his way, I find him watching me with a calculated shrewdness that grates on my nerves.

"You're done." I recap the bottle and brush a loose strand of hair off Zara's neck. "Gonna take my board out for a bit, OK?"

"Mmm hmmm." She stretches, the picture of languor. "Go and show Giles what you're made of."

The need to escape is so overwhelming I have to resist the impulse to run. With studied nonchalance, I scramble up and collect my Spitfire. I'm aware of Giles following my every move, a prickle of discomfort along my spine. I pretend not to notice. Wading into the surf, I lay down my board and paddle out to sea.

The beach is far behind me when I realise my mistake. I swear under my breath, cursing my stupidity. In my haste, I hadn't paid enough attention to the water, hadn't taken the time to read the signs. A set of oncoming waves barrels towards me. They'll be on me long before I have time to push my way through to the calmer water beyond. I'm trapped, caught inside, the bane of every surfer's life.

"The most elemental rule of surfing," Dean's dad told me that first summer, "is to stay calm. There will be times when things don't go your way and you get into difficulty, but the key is not to panic."

I assess the nearest wave as it hurtles closer. It isn't especially large, nothing I haven't handled before. I paddle faster, speeding straight for the oncoming breaker. Just as it reaches me, I push down on the rails with both hands, fill my lungs with air, and dive beneath the water. The surf rolls over me, a torrent of energy that buffets me from all directions, and I grip my board to hold it steady. As soon as I judge it to be safe, I point the nose of my Spitfire towards the surface and burst once more into the sunlight. I blink the salt from my vision, reorientating myself. There, that wasn't too bad. Another couple of those and I'll be through.

I paddle for the next wave, gathering speed. When I emerge, something has adhered itself to my face. Something wet and slimy. I put up a hand to push it away and grimace. Seaweed. I work to disentangle the tendrils from my hair. Intent on what I'm doing, I don't notice the wave until it's right there, rising above me.

Adrenaline surges through my veins. There's no time to duck through it, no time to do anything other than clutch my board and suck in a quick breath. Then it's on me, an unstoppable wall of water throwing me backwards. I don't fight it; resisting will merely tire me out. I let the surf have its fun with me, pulling me under, tossing me about as though I'm nothing but a lump of driftwood. With cruel suddenness, it spits me gasping and spluttering into the shallows, where I'm greeted by applause and wolf whistles.

"Go Luke," Giles calls. "You should try out for the belly-boarding Olympics. Amazing."

Jaw clenched, I detach myself from my board and stagger to my feet. This wasn't my first pummelling, not by a long stretch. Getting knocked about a bit is par for the course when surfing, and normally I'd emerge grinning and exhilarated, ready to do it all over again. Not today. Today my whole body aches, inside and out. I'm tempted to give up, collapse beside Zara and sleep, but the prospect of a morning spent enduring Theo's silent treatment and Giles's snide comments doesn't appeal.

So, I allow myself a moment to collect myself and assess the conditions, before heading out once more. With an immense sense of relief, I paddle outside. My territory. And finally I'm up, carving the surface of the wave, wind driving the smell of salt into my face.

Only…it doesn't feel right. Though my technique is faultless, the Spitfire perfectly poised beneath my feet, I'm aware of going through the motions. For the first time ever, an invisible barrier separates me from the ocean, severing our connection. Thoughts crowd in on my peace—the need to put on a display for Giles, and memories of the last occasion I'd come out on a board. With Theo. Christ, what am I doing here? If I'm not even enjoying the surfing, where's the point in any of it?

When I eventually haul my board to shore, a sleepy
lethargy has descended over the group. The girls are lying
on their stomachs, Meredith absorbed in a book, Zara
dozing with her iPod headphones trailing from her ears.
Her bikini top is undone, permitting the sun full access to
her back, a fact which hasn't escaped Giles. Though he
has a book propped against his knees, his eyes are on Zara,
on the spot beneath her folded arm where the side of her
breast is visible.

I glare at him as I pass. Bastard. He has no right
gawping at Zara, not without her knowledge, and
especially not in front of his own girlfriend. Meredith
seems absorbed, her eyes darting across the page, but the
tautness in her shoulders gives her away.

I dump my board on the sand beside Theo, near where
I've left my change of clothes, and shake out my towel.
Engrossed in his crossword, Theo doesn't look up as I dry
myself off. Either he's oblivious to Giles checking his
cousin out, or else he doesn't care.

Annoyance flares in my gut and I toss him my towel.
"Here, hold this up for me."

"Huh?" He blinks, body stiffening. He glances from me
to his puzzle book, wariness in every line of his features.
Still, he can't exactly refuse. Jaw tense, he sets his book
aside and scrambles to his feet.

I step a few paces along the beach to draw him out of
earshot of the others. Theo follows, looking everywhere
but at me, and raises the towel to shield my lower half
from view.

I begin peeling off my wetsuit, my voice low. "I'd watch
out for your friend, if I were you."

83

"What?" Theo's head snaps towards me before he catches himself. Twisting, he stares past the girls at Giles. "Ah."

I reach for my dry shorts. "I swear, Theo, if he doesn't put his eyes back in, I'll do it for him."

"It's all right, I get it." Theo rakes his fingers through his hair. I have the feeling he wants nothing more than to sink into the sand and vanish. "I'll talk to him."

"I have a better idea." I shrug into my T-shirt, leaving Theo holding the towel, and advance on the others. When I reach Meredith, I kneel and touch her shoulder. "Come on, we're going for a walk."

"Oh?" She lowers her book, eyebrows raised. "Is that a command or a request?"

I flash my lazy smile. "I can beg if you like. See, I'm already on my knees."

Giles yanks his attention from Zara, his glare a loaded gun against my temple. I school my expression into one of bland innocence.

Meredith lays down her book and rises gracefully, the shadow of a smile toying with her lips. Giles opens his mouth, but voices no objection. What can he say? Forbid Meredith to go? Insist on coming with us? Either way, he'll end up sounding like a jealous idiot, and we both know it. He can only glower after us, wishing me a thousand painful deaths with his eyes.

We walk without speaking for a while, the waves rushing in to fill the silence. The sand slides soft and warm against my feet, stretching ahead of us in an expanse of white-gold. I've always wondered how it might feel to have a beach to myself, no over-excited kids charging in and out of the water, no harassed parents trying to keep track of them. The reality is more stunning than I ever imagined. I should be happy.

"It won't work, you know," Meredith says at length, "what you're doing."

I cock my head, half submerged in my thoughts.

She elaborates. "You can't tie Giles down. No one can. He goes out with a girl for a while, a couple of months if she's lucky, then moves on to someone new."

"And you're OK with that?"

"It's just the way he is. I've always known it. No point pretending otherwise."

I kick out at a loose pebble, which skitters away over the sand. "I don't get what you see in him."

Meredith glances at me. "I'm sorry he's given you such a hard time. I don't know what's got into him. He's not normally like this."

"Strangely enough, Zara said the same thing."

"Because it's true. You think Theo and I would put up with him otherwise? Giles is a good friend—generous, funny, fiercely loyal if anyone dares hurt either of us."

But what if he's the one doing the hurting? I bite my tongue on the retort. The softness in Meredith's expression wards off my cynicism. "You love him, don't you?"

She shifts her gaze to the horizon. "I have almost from the moment I met him."

"And how did you? Meet, I mean."

"I sat next to him and Theo in the lecture hall on our first day at Oxford. They pulled me into their conversation, asked me to go for a coffee with them afterwards. It went from there. Of course, I never dreamed Giles and I would get together. I'm not his type. At least, I didn't think I was."

I remember Zara saying something similar on our first full day here, and Theo defending the relationship. "Why, what's his type?"

Meredith shrugs. "Party girls, mostly—confident, sexy, stunningly pretty—you know the sort."

Put like that, Giles goes for the same kind of girls as I do. What a thought. I banish it to a dusty corner of my mind and nudge Meredith's shoulder with mine. "So when did Giles see sense and ask you out?"

"Actually, I'm not sure he did." She sounds amused. "It happened so gradually. We were used to it being just the two of us a few evenings a week when Theo was out with Francis, but things really changed after the breakup. You know about that, I suppose."

"Yeah, Zara told me."

"Well, with Theo barricaded in his room, Giles and I were on our own all the time. We were used to spending most of our free time together, but it was different without Theo. When we weren't trying to get him to come out with us, or simply to eat something, we went to dinner and to the cinema. Afterwards, we'd stay up talking for hours, and one night, when Giles walked me back to my room, he kissed me. That was about three months ago."

We've reached a point where the sand gives way to rocks, jagged and slippery and inlaid with shallow pools. By unspoken agreement, we turn and wander back to the others. We arrive as they finish packing up. As soon as he sees us, Giles is at Meredith's side, wrapping a proprietary arm around her.

"You were gone a long time." His tone is casual, but he shoots me a look that's cold with dislike. "We're going to grab some lunch."

He leads Meredith along the beach to catch up with Theo, leaving me to gather my board bag and follow with Zara.

"Nice walk?" she asks.

"Yeah, it was OK."

Zara adjusts the strap of her beach bag. "I would've come with you. If you'd told me you wanted to go for a walk."

"You were asleep. I didn't want to disturb you." Mostly true, and better than filling her in on the real reason.

Zara nods, but she's chewing on her bottom lip, the way she does when she's troubled.

***

My phone rings as we're getting ready to go out for dinner. Damp from the shower, a towel wrapped around my waist, I snatch it off the bedside cabinet.

"Hey," Dean says, "how's the jet setter?"

"I'm in Cornwall, not California." I perch on the edge of the bed, a grin spreading across my face. He'll never know how glad I am to hear his voice.

"Some people are so picky. How's it going?"

"Good. Great."

"Yeah, sounds it. Don't tell me. Trouble in paradise?"

I glance towards the en suite, the trickle of running water audible through the closed door. "Something like that."

"Man, what're you like?" Dean's tone hovers between exasperation and amusement. "A few weeks of sun, surfing and sex, and without having to fork out a penny. Any normal guy would give his balls for a chance like that."

"I know. It's just not how I thought it would be."

"With Zara?"

"Yeah. No. Kind of."

Dean expels a long breath, something he does when he's thinking. "Look, if it isn't working out, you can always come home."

"I suppose." I twist the edge of the towel around my finger. "I just don't want to let Zara down."

"Luke, you're on holiday. You're meant to be having a good time. If you're not, say goodbye to the life of Riley and get your arse back here. Jack's having a party this Friday. You should be there."

A tide of homesickness knocks me off balance. I'm reminded of that morning, lying prone on my board, wave after wave crashing over me. Brookminster, my mates, the familiarity of my room all feel a thousand leagues away, another world entirely, one where life is simple, predictable.

The shower falls silent, and I hear Zara moving about in the bathroom. "I have to go."

"No worries, but keep me posted, OK?"

"OK."

When Zara enters the bedroom draped in a towel and wafting coconut-scented steam, I haven't moved. She eyes me seated on the bed. "Not getting ready?"

I stare down at the phone in my hands. "Dean called."

"How is he? Not trying to lure you away from us, I hope."

"Course he was. I'm a popular guy."

"And I've stolen you for the whole summer." Zara sits beside me, sliding an arm around my waist. "So long as you weren't tempted."

I try to smile, but my mouth won't cooperate.

Her eyes widen. "You were, weren't you?"

I bite down on the denial that leaps to my tongue. I'm fed up. Fed up of pretending everything's hunky-dory. Fed up of Giles and his smart-arsed remarks. Fed up of avoiding Theo's gaze. I look away. "Would it matter if I were?"

"It would matter to me. I wouldn't have invited you if I didn't want you to come." She leans forward, trying to see my face. "Aren't you having a good time?"

"It isn't that. It's been great. You've been great."

"What then?"

I fiddle with my phone. "I dunno. I don't really fit in here."

"Oh, for heaven's sake." Zara springs off the bed to stand in front of me, nearly dislodging her towel. She hoists it up and folds her arms across her chest. "This is about Giles, isn't it? You're letting him get to you."

I shake my head. No way I'm letting Giles take the credit for driving me out, especially as it wouldn't be true. "Zara, don't you think you'd have a better time without me?"

"No," her expression grows fierce, "I don't. Who would I talk to if you weren't here? You've seen how Theo and Giles are when they're together, and Meredith and I don't have much in common. Don't dare even think of leaving for my sake, Luke Savage, promise me."

I scrub a palm over my brow. "OK." If I do leave, it won't be for Zara's sake. That much I can promise.

She obviously doesn't believe me. We dress in tense silence, Zara casting me anxious looks, shoulders rigid as though preparing to tackle me if I decide to run for it. I keep my head down and attempt to ignore the dull ache behind my eyes.

"Luke?"

I glance up, in the act of buttoning my jeans. "Yeah?"

"Do you think Meredith's pretty?"

I stare at her, thrown by the change of subject.

"Not that it matters," she adds. "I was just curious."

I shrug, reaching for my T-shirt. "She's nice-looking, yeah. Why?"

"No reason." Zara bends to put on her sandals and her hair swings forward, hiding her face.

***

The evening is the earthly embodiment of hell.

Theo offers to drive so that the rest of us can drink, and Giles, after shooting me a warning glare, joins the girls in the back. Left with no option, I climb into the passenger seat. While the others talk amongst themselves, Theo and I spend the entire journey in stony silence, his gaze glued to the road ahead, me staring fixedly out of the window.

Via Italia lives up to its name, being small enough to give an impression of exclusivity, and busy enough to serve as an advert for its food. The proprietor, an exuberant man with salt-and-pepper hair who has clearly feasted on too much of the restaurant's cuisine, greets Zara and Theo like old friends, and shows us personally to a table by the window.

"We've eaten here at least once every summer since we've been coming to Cornwall," Zara explains, sliding onto the padded bench beside me. "Best carbonara you'll ever have."

She takes my hand and squeezes it, her smile coaxing. All through the meal, she does her best to act normal, parrying Giles's teasing with barbs of her own, debating with Theo whether Clemmy's love affair with horses might ever wane sufficiently for her to find herself a boyfriend. "Or a girlfriend, as the case may be."

Yet, even as I force down my pepperoni pizza, I'm aware of Zara's frequent glances in my direction, the way she keeps biting her lip. I know that look. She's biding her time, waiting to get me alone so she can present me with all the hard-and-fast reasons why leaving would be nothing short of insanity.

I'm determined not to give her the chance. As soon as we get back to the cottage, I plead a headache, which by this point has escalated to a full-frontal drum solo beating against the inside of my skull, and slip upstairs.

I haven't been in bed long when the door inches open. "Luke? You awake?"

I stay motionless under the covers, eyes closed, my breathing deep and even, and after a moment's pause, Zara's footfalls pad away along the landing.

I don't sleep. Hours after Zara has slipped into bed beside me and quiet descended over the house, I lie scowling into the darkness, thoughts grappling for dominance in my tired brain. Am I really done here? Am I really going to walk out on Zara when she's so desperate for me to stay? She'll be upset, furious even. It's possible she'll never forgive me. Maybe that's for the best. At least then I won't have to see her again, won't have to see any of them again.

With the pale mist of dawn creeping between the curtains, I reach a decision. Groggy with exhaustion, I slip out of bed, pull on shorts and a T-shirt, and steal downstairs. In the hall, I leaf through the Yellow Pages lying on the telephone table beside the front door and dial National Rail Enquiries. The journey to the station involves two buses, but from Exeter St. David's I can catch a train to Paddington, and from there, change for Brookminster. All I need is a ride into Bude.

I wander into the kitchen, the cottage eerily silent. The others won't be up for ages yet. I'll grab my board and head down to the beach for a while. Theo's face, stubborn and disapproving, flashes across my vision. I blink the image away. If this is going to be my final day in Cornwall, I may as well make the most of it. Besides, if I'm lucky, I can be there and back without anyone realising I'm gone.

I'm stepping out onto the terrace, the morning breeze cool on my face, when I see him. He's huddled on the grass by the pool, arms wrapped around his drawn-up knees. A weight presses in on my diaphragm, cutting off my air supply. *This is what you wanted*, I remind myself, *the chance to get him alone*. So much easier than asking in front of an audience.

I suck in a painful breath. With deliberate slowness, I stroll over to him. Theo darts me a wary glance as I approach, but doesn't speak. Neither of us does. I stand there, studying him with my hands thrust in my pockets, determined I won't be the first to crack.

"Listen," Theo shifts beneath my scrutiny, "if you want to use the pool—"

"I don't." I'd intended to sound offhand, but my tone comes out flat and cold. "I have a favour to ask."

"Of…" Theo catches himself. "What can I do for you?"

"Don't look so worried. It's nothing taxing, I promise. I need a lift into Bude, have a bus to catch."

"A bus?"

"Yeah, a bus. You know, that mode of transport for common people. I need to get to St. David's. There's a train leaving for London at midday and I'd like to be on it."

"Oh." He winds a blade of grass around his finger. "Does Zara know?"

"Not yet."

"Well, I'm sure she'd take you. Why don't you ask her?"

Truth is, I don't know. Maybe I want to have a plan before confronting Zara, who will certainly try and talk me out of it. Maybe I want to make Theo squirm, a tiny act of revenge for his hypocrisy. Or maybe, and I hate myself for it, I just want a reaction. Out loud, all I say is, "Because I'm asking you."

"Luke." Theo drags a hand through his hair. He looks more uncomfortable than I've seen him. Perhaps he'd convinced himself I wouldn't confront him, that I'd let him get away with it.

"Luke," he tries again, "Don't feel you have to go."

I laugh. It's an unpleasant bark, bitter, unfamiliar. "Right, and why wouldn't I want to stay? Everyone's making me so welcome."

He has the decency to wince. "Look, about Giles. I'm sorry he's been a bit… He's not normally—"

"No." I cut him off. "If one more person tells me how Giles is actually a great guy who just happens to be masquerading as a total arsehole, I swear I'll—"

"OK, OK." Theo extends his palms in a placating gesture. "At least let me talk to him, get him to lay off."

I lose it. He can lie to himself all he wants, but he can't pretend with me. Not anymore. The anger and hurt of the past two days spews out of me in a toxic rush. "I don't give a fuck about Giles, all right? This has nothing to do with him, and you know it."

Theo meets my glare, seeming at a loss, before averting his eyes.

"See?" I spit. "You can't even bring yourself to look at me. What's wrong, Theo? Scared the sight of me will turn you to stone?"

"Luke, you know that isn't—"

"No, that's right. You didn't always have a problem with me, did you? I was good enough to hang out with a few days ago. Then your posh friends turn up, and suddenly you're too ashamed to have anything to do with me."

"Luke—"

"Go on, deny it. Look me in the face and tell me it isn't true." I drop to the grass, seizing Theo by the shoulders. "But you can't, can you? You can't because you know I'm right. You're nothing but a—"

He kisses me, and the words get jammed in my throat. Shock judders along my nerves, a hundred volts of white-hot electricity. My brain freezes; I can't process what's happening. But I can feel it. Christ, I can feel it.

There's nothing gentle or Theo-like about the kiss. His mouth crushes mine, fierce and rough and full of a desperate urgency. And I'm melting. My blood is turning to custard in my veins, so sweet and hot it'll surely burn me up from the inside out. I collapse onto the grass, pulling him on top of me, and the lean hardness of his body presses me into the ground. This is nothing like being with a girl, nothing anything I've ever experienced.

Theo's tongue probes my mouth and I open up to him, my own tongue wrapping around his. In a distant alcove of my mind, I can hear myself, hear the groans being torn from my throat, but I don't care. I bite down on Theo's lip and he gasps. His hands come up to trap my face, while mine are everywhere—tangling in his floppy hair, sliding over his back, fisting in the waistband of his shorts to haul him closer.

Theo wrenches himself from my grasp. He rolls away from me and sits up, burying his face in his hands. "Oh, God. God, I'm sorry."

"Don't be." My voice is hoarse, shaky. I struggle up, my head spinning as though I've stepped off a fast ride. "Theo, it's fine."

"No." The words are muffled behind his hands. "No, it isn't."

He raises his head to look at me. His eyes are huge, his expression stricken. I reach out to touch his arm, but he flinches, propelling himself to his feet. He backs away from me, step by cautious step, a hunter fearful of provoking a mountain lion.

"Theo?"

He shakes his head. "I'm sorry. We... I shouldn't have. I'm sorry."

And with that, he's gone, vanishing into the cottage. A puddle of confusion on the grass, I'm left to stare after him, my world in pieces around me.

Chapter Seven

I can't stop shaking.

Before I realise what I'm doing, I'm up and running. Fuelled by panic, I run faster than I ever have on the rugby field, sprinting across the lawn and into the safety of the trees. I need to get away. When I hit the beach, I keep going. I scarcely know where I'm headed, don't much care. Everything is too bright; blades of sunshine bounce off the sand, the surface of the water, stabbing at my eyes until I'm half blinded. My breath comes in ragged gasps. I can't breathe. It's as though my lungs have shrunk, making it impossible to draw in enough air. Still, I keep going. Mustn't stop. Mustn't think. It'll all be fine so long as I don't think.

My foot connects with something, a rock partially submerged in the sand. I go down hard, falling to my knees. The impact jars along my thighs. I don't get up again. What's the point? There's no running from what just happened. Christ, what did just happen? I bury my face in my hands, eyes screwed shut, willing the reality away.

Immediately I'm back by the pool, Theo's body thrusting me into the grass, his tongue in my mouth. And I'd wanted him. Fuck, I'd wanted him more than I can remember wanting anyone in my life.

"Are you really surprised?" A voice, soft but insistent, whispers in my ear. "You honestly never saw this coming?"

My mind presents an image of Max, muscular legs caked with mud and sweat, eyes bright and triumphant. I groan against my palms, fingers digging into my eyelids. Steel ropes have my chest in a strangle hold. I drag in a breath, try to calm down, because what does it matter? What does any of it matter?

The connection I shared with Theo from my first evening here, all the complicit smiles and soul-baring, the fact that my attraction to him goes beyond anything I've ever experienced...it's all irrelevant. Despite that kiss, Theo wants nothing to do with me. His coldness over the past couple of days has told me that loud and clear. The question is: where does that leave me?

***

By the time I've composed myself and trudged back to the cottage, the others are finishing breakfast on the patio.

"There you are." Zara's face brightens, and she pulls out a chair for me.

I collapse into it, careful not to look at Theo. For his part, he keeps his head down, staring into his mug.

"Where were you?" Zara asks. "We were starting to worry."

"Walking." My voice comes out croaky, as though I've swallowed a beach load of sand. I clear my throat. "Woke up early, thought I'd get some air."

For the briefest instant, Theo's eyes skim mine. Something flickers behind his indifference. Relief? Was he worried I might throw myself into the waves like some jilted bride? More likely he was afraid I'd bring up what happened between us in front of his friends. "Hey, enjoyed the snog, Theo. Fancy doing it again sometime?" I suppress a grim smile. That would shake things up a bit, that's for sure.

"Want some coffee?" Meredith proffers the pot. "And Theo made bacon sandwiches."

My stomach stages its objection at the mere mention of food. "Coffee would be great. Thanks."

I accept the mug Meredith pushes across to me with the ghost of a smile, grateful she'd done the pouring. I wouldn't trust a pot of hot coffee in my hands right now.

"Before you graced us with your presence, Luke," Giles drawls, "we were discussing what we should do today."

He glowers at me, his expression even more sour than usual. I get the feeling he would have liked nothing better than for me to disappear, for my bloated corpse to be discovered washed up several miles along the coast.

"It was hardly a discussion," Zara says. "You and Meredith decided we're going to Clovelly. End of conversation. What's so special about it, anyway? It's only a village where some author just so happened to live a zillion years ago."

"Not quite that many," Meredith rolls her eyes, "and you must have heard of Charles Kingsley. Didn't you ever read *The Water Babies*?"

"No hot vampires and not enough sex. Are we really going to waste a whole day paying homage or whatever to some long-dead author?"

"I'd like to," Meredith says. "That book was such a big part of my childhood. Still, if you'd rather not—"

"We're going." Giles puts his arm around her. "It's already decided. Of course," he throws Zara a dirty look, "no one's forcing you to come. You can always stay behind."

"Maybe we will. Luke?" She lays a hand on my thigh.

I flinch; can't help it. My every nerve is charged, sensitised, so that the merest touch sends electricity crackling through me. Confusion shadows Zara's face.

"Sorry," I say, meaning it. "I was miles away."

Her smile is forgiving. "As usual. So, what do you think? Shall we take advantage of having the place to ourselves?"

She trails her fingers up my thigh. I resist the impulse to jerk away, but it's an effort. I glance at Theo, who's examining the dregs of his coffee with the concentration of a fortune-teller reading the tea leaves. "No, let's go. Might be interesting."

"If you say so," Zara hides her disappointment well, "but you're the one who'll have to give my parents the tragic news when I die of boredom."

Theo shakes his head as if to clear it, then gets up and begins stacking the plates. "Shall we get ready, then?"

His tone is light, measured. It's as if the kiss never happened. Maybe, as far as he's concerned, it didn't.

The others head indoors, leaving me alone with the tangled mess of my thoughts. Coffee mug cradled between my hands, my gaze drifts to the pool, to the spot where Theo flipped my world on its head. I sit there, enveloped in a curious kind of numbness, until a movement behind me catches my attention.

"You know," Giles drops into Zara's vacated chair, "for a moment there, when we woke up and couldn't find you, I thought you'd done a runner."

I shrug, turning away. "Sorry to disappoint."

Giles snorts. He rests his elbows on the table, cupping his chin in his hands. I can feel his eyes on me. "This thing with Zara, you do realise it won't last."

I swallow a mouthful of lukewarm coffee, barely listening.

"She's toying with you," Giles says. "You're a novelty, the unsuitable boyfriend she can flaunt in front of her parents. It's her way of rebelling."

On any other day, his idea of a heart-to-heart would have been quite entertaining. Now, the words collide and meld into one another, a meaningless buzz in my ears.

Giles persists, undeterred. "You must see there's no future in the relationship. Zara's out of your league, and sooner or later she's going to wise up."

I stare into my mug, swirling the remains of my coffee, watching it slosh about like a storm-tossed sea.

"Ignore me all you want," Giles says. "It doesn't change the facts. Stay with Zara, and you're going to get hurt. If I were you, I'd end it now and get it over with."

Christ, he's worse than a fucking bulldozer. I round on him. "And if I were you, I'd shut up before I get the wrong idea."

His eyes narrow. "Meaning?"

"Meaning, if you don't watch out, I'm going to think you only care so much because you want Zara for yourself."

Giles rocks back in his chair, expression hardening. When he speaks, it's clear he's making an effort to keep his tone even. "Why don't you leave? You'd be doing everyone a favour, including yourself. You don't fit in here. You should go home."

"Back to my own friends, you mean?" The irony of Giles echoing my words of yesterday isn't lost on me.

"Exactly." His smile is conciliatory. "You know it makes sense. I'm sure you'd have a much better time."

I consider him; smug complacency oozes like treacle from his every pore. In a sudden movement, I get to my feet. "And why don't you fuck off?"

Shock passes over Giles's face. With a surge of vindictive triumph, I leave him sitting there and head inside.

***

Giles gets his revenge on the drive to Clovelly. He insists we go in his car, a gleaming red Audi A3 Cabriolet, even though it's much more of a squeeze than in Theo's Golf. His way of flaunting just how little I belong in their world. He rolls the top down, so that the slipstream blows the scent of leather and money into my face. Like I needed another reason to despise him. I fix my gaze on the window, pretending to be unaware of Theo crammed into the back seat on Zara's other side.

Clovelly has no vehicle access—it must be one of the few settlements in the developed world that doesn't—so we leave the Audi in the car park at the top of the village and walk. A cobbled slope, so steep it has steps carved into it at intervals, descends between rows of Hansel-and-Gretel cottages. The front doors open directly onto the footpath and barely reach my shoulder. I guess people were much shorter back then. On another day, I might have appreciated the quirkiness of this place. Not today. Today I feel weird, disconnected, like my body's here, but my spirit has buggered off somewhere else entirely.

Theo walks ahead with Giles and Meredith, keeping his distance from me with a diligence that verges on obsessive. I try not to look at him, but every now and then I catch myself staring at his tanned thighs, the down of short hairs on the back of his neck. I remember the soft prickle of those hairs against my palm as he kissed me. Heat floods my belly. Christ, that kiss. Theo can play Mr. Indifferent all he likes, but that kiss gave him away.

"OK?" Zara loops her arm through mine. Her eyes are anxious, protective, and I know she's picked up on my tension.

"OK." Unable to look at her, I concentrate on absorbing our surroundings. What would it be like to live in one of these cottages, to have a never-ending trickle of tourists tramping past your window every summer?

We locate the Charles Kingsley museum in the heart of the village. Zara shows no interest in going inside, so we arrange to meet the others at the harbour and continue the descent. Neither of us says much. Zara takes my hand, interlacing our fingers, and I have to resist the impulse to pull away.

By the time we reach the foot of the slope, the midday heat has plastered my T-shirt to my skin. A welcoming breeze blows in off the sea, cooling the sweat on my brow. We perch on the harbour wall and look out along the quay, at the boats bobbing gently in the swell.

"Sure you're OK?" Zara asks. "You're very quiet."

"I'm always quiet." I try to smile at her.

Zara scans my face, forehead creased. "You're not still thinking of leaving?"

I avert my eyes, staring at the scuffed toes of my trainers. Honestly, I haven't given it a thought. Not since the kiss.

"Luke?"

"No." I rub the bridge of my nose. "I'm staying for now." I have to, at least till I've had it out with Theo. He can't kiss me like that, can't throw my life into chaos, without some kind of explanation. He owes me that much.

The others join us a while later, Meredith buoyed up with enthusiasm. "You two should've come in. It was really interesting."

"Whatever." Zara hops down from the wall. "Can we eat? I'm starving."

We order sandwiches and a cream tea at the Red Lion, a hotel overlooking the quay. The tables are crowded with tourists, parents coaxing their kids with ice creams before dragging them back up the slope. I pick at a scone, forcing it down with several cups of tea. It churns unpleasantly in my stomach.

"I read about this place in the guidebook." Meredith spreads strawberry jam on a scone. "It used to be three cider houses, apparently, where the fisherman would meet up to boast about their catches."

"And their mistresses," Zara says.

"That, too. And of course Salvation Yeo from Charles Kingsley's book *Westward Ho!* was born here."

Zara snorts, almost spitting out her mouthful of tea. "What sort of name is that? Bet his mates called him Sally for short."

***

After dinner that evening, when we're all languid with food and too much alcohol, Zara disappears inside. She re-emerges a minute or so later, waving a book at us. "Hey, Theo, do you remember the party we had at mine a couple of years back? Ollie's boyfriend, the one who worked at Bar Basco, mixed cocktails for everyone until half of them passed out on the floor."

"I'm hardly likely to forget, am I?" Theo grimaces. "Your parents trusted me to look after you while they were away. I thought they were going to kill me when they came back and found the house trashed."

"Don't exaggerate. It was only a bit of puke on the carpet." Zara drops into her chair besides mine and flips through the book she brought with her. "So, what shall we try? A Goodnight Kiss? Sex on the Beach?" She winks at me, pressing her thigh against mine.

"Get a room." Giles leans over to scan the page. "Look, here's one for Theo." He adopts a Texas twang. "A Piece of Ass."

Theo rolls his eyes and gets to his feet. "I'll see what we've got and surprise you."

Once he's gone inside, the others take turns leafing through the cocktail recipes, seeing who can spot the ones with the most obscene names—Liquid Viagra, Slippery Nipple, Cock Sucking Cowboy.

I'm jittery, on edge. My leg bounces as if to a beat only it can hear, and I keep darting glances towards the kitchen. This is it, my chance to get Theo on his own. I stand, heart pounding like a sledgehammer against my ribs. In my clumsiness, I knock my chair to the patio with a crash.

"Where're you off to?" Zara asks.

I bend to right the chair, heat burning like red-ant bites over my skin. I can hardly think straight. "I, uh, thought I'd see if Theo needs a hand."

"Adios, motherfucker," Giles says.

"Giles!" Zara and Meredith's shocked voices follow me up the terrace steps and into the cottage.

"What? It's a cocktail. Here, look if you don't believe me."

I slide the glass door shut, muffling the conversation.

Theo shoots me a look, then goes back to arranging glasses on a tray beside a jug of something dark. "It's OK. I was just about to bring these out."

I swallow against the dryness in my throat. "We need to talk."

No response.

Slowly, as though wading through deep sand, I cross the room until I'm standing right behind him. He grips the edge of the worktop.

"Theo?"

Still nothing. Only the convulsive tightening of his fingers shows he even heard me.

"Theo," my voice cracks, "don't do this."

Theo sucks in a breath. When he replies, his tone is even. "Do what?"

"This. Shutting me out."

"I'm—"

"And don't say you're not, because we both know that isn't true." I'm aware of my voice rising, and lower it with an effort. "Just...don't."

Theo exhales in a long sigh. He turns to me, his expression distant but not unkind. I wish he'd glare at me, shout, whatever. Anything to show he gives a damn.

"Luke, I'm sorry about this morning. It was a mistake. If you got the wrong impression—"

"The wrong impression? You kissed me. What impression was that supposed to give me?"

He casts a nervous glance at the window.

"What's wrong, Theo? Worried Giles might hear? I don't blame you. He'd probably make you bathe in disinfectant for a year if he knew you'd kissed scum like me." Theo starts to protest, but I shake my head. "You know what? Forget it. So sorry I embarrassed you."

I need to get out of here. Humiliation, hot and clammy, coils like tar through my veins. Still, what did I expect? Theo's made it perfectly clear how he sees me, that he thinks I'm beneath him. I grab for the nearest glass, intending to pour myself a liver full of whatever's in that jug, but my hand shakes so much it slips through my fingers. Glass collides with oak in a minor explosion, glittering fragments flying.

"Shit." I drop to my knees, begin picking up the larger pieces. I fumble, a jagged shard slicing my palm. "Shit."

"Luke?" Theo crouches beside me.

"I'm fine." I turn away from the phony concern in his eyes, fist clenched around the cut to hide it from view. Blood trickles through my fingers and onto my jeans. The pain is almost a relief.

"Let me see." Theo holds out his hand, but I jerk away.

"I said I'm fine."

He ignores me. With gentle firmness, he takes hold of my wrist, uncurling my fingers to examine the wound. My body stills. I scarcely breathe. Every nerve ending, every particle of my being is aware of him, the pressure of his fingers on my wrist, his warm palm supporting the back of my hand.

"What's going on?"

Zara's voice filters through to me from a long way off. In slow motion, I twist my head to find her framed against the evening sky.

As though it's the most natural thing in the world, Theo lays my hand in my lap and stands, motioning to her. "Whoa, blood alert."

"Oh." Zara pales. "We heard something break. Are you OK?" Her gaze seeks mine, expression concerned. She keeps her eyes on my face, averted from the blood.

I nod, not trusting myself to speak.

"He's fine," Theo says. He lifts the tray from the worktop and carries it over to Zara. "Here, get started on these while I patch Luke up."

He nudges the door to and reaches down to take my uninjured hand. I'm beyond resisting. I let him help me to my feet and steady me as my legs threaten to give way. He lowers me into a chair at the table and tears off a square of kitchen roll, which he wads up and presses against my cut, folding my fingers over it.

"Just hold that there. I'll clear up the glass."

"I should do that. It was my fault." My tongue feels too big in my mouth, and the words emerge indistinct.

Theo shakes his head, glancing at my hand with a faint smile, and turns to rummage in the cupboard under the sink.

I stay where I've been put, watching Theo sweep the broken glass into a dustpan. The quiet wraps itself around me. Voices waft in from the patio, muted and indecipherable, snatches of dialogue from another planet. A clock I've barely noticed before ticks from the wall behind me. If not for its hands counting off the seconds, I could have been fooled into believing time had halted, waiting. I picture myself perched on the edge of a cliff, unsure whether I'm about to step back from the precipice or fling myself forward into the unknown.

Glass dealt with, Theo returns to me with the first-aid box. He turns his chair so that he's sitting at right angles to me, his knee a whisper from mine. "Let me see."

This time, I don't even pretend to object. Theo takes my hand in his, peeling the kitchen roll aside to inspect the cut. "I think you'll live."

Will I? It seems to me I'll die if he lets go of my hand, and die if he doesn't.

He does let go, but only for a moment to rummage in the first-aid kit. Then he's back to cradling my hand in his, while he smoothes a plaster over the cut. It's the lightest of touches, a mere brush of fingers against my palm, but it sends all the blood to my groin. I bite my lip on a gasp. I'm trembling, or perhaps it's Theo. Impossible to tell.

He should have released me by now, but he hasn't. His thumb keeps rubbing my palm, although the plaster must be well and truly stuck. Has he any idea what he's doing to me? I look at him, and he returns my gaze, his expression softer than it's been since that night, the night of whisky and confidences.

"Theo?" It's all I can croak out, but it's enough. I've never begged in my life, never needed to. It's always been the other way around, girls chasing after me, doing the running. All I had to do was stand still and wait for them to catch up. It's only now that I realise the power they were giving me, the power I've just handed over to Theo.

He knows what I'm asking; it's obvious in the way his eyes flicker to my mouth. I moisten my lips with my tongue. Theo leans in, and I sway towards him. He's so close his breath mingles with mine.

In a sudden decisive movement, he drops my hand and gets up, stepping away from the table. "I'm sorry."

I don't know what I expected. I'm here with Zara, Theo's cousin. I was wrong to ask, just as he would've been wrong to give in. All the same, his rejection punches me in the gut. The air whooshes out of me. I can feel my face hardening, shutting down. I let him see my vulnerability—Christ, I practically threw myself at him—and he chucked it back at me like it meant nothing.

I push my chair back, heading for the door to the hall. When I speak, I'm amazed how composed I sound. "No problem. Sorry if I...how did you put it? Got the wrong impression."

"No." Theo puts out a hand, then lets it fall to his side. "Don't apologise. It was—"

"A mistake. Yeah, you said." Without looking at him, I escape from the kitchen and up the stairs before I can humiliate myself any further.

Chapter Eight

"No." Her tone is flat, final.

We confront each other across the kitchen table, Zara with her back to the dresser, me leaning against the sink. Beyond the sliding doors, the sky hangs heavy and grey, a light drizzle pinging off the glass. Even the weather is sad to see the end of something which began with such promise.

"No." Zara folds her arms over her chest, face set.

I drop my gaze, study the breakfast things littering the table. "I have to."

And I do. There's no way I can stay, not even for Zara. Not after last night.

"You don't have to do anything, Luke, and you know it. If you want to go, just come right out and say so. Don't pretend you're being forced into it."

"Fine, I want to. Happy now?"

Zara's face crumples. "It's Giles, isn't it? He's been getting at you. I swear I'll—"

"Zara, this has nothing to do with Giles, or you, or...anyone."

"Then why?"

I rub my aching forehead. Two sleepless nights in a row are taking their toll; my thoughts intermingle, sticking together like overcooked spaghetti. "OK, so you remember I spoke to Dean the other day? Well, he mentioned this party—"

"Whoa." Her eyes narrow. "You're leaving me in the lurch so you can go to some stupid party with your mates? Is that what you're telling me?"

I shrug. What else could I say? Sorry, Zara, but I've fallen for your cousin, only he's made it clear he isn't interested and now I can't bear to be near him? That would go down well.

"No!" Zara stamps her foot, voice rising. All at once, I'm faced with the pampered princess used to getting her own way. "You can't do this to me, Luke. I won't let you."

My head throbs. I take a deep breath, keeping my tone even with an effort. "Correct me if I have this wrong, but I wasn't aware I needed your permission to go home."

"And how are you going to get there? Because I'm bloody well not driving you."

"Like I expected you to. Luckily, though, there's that great invention called a train. You may have heard of them. They're what we commoners use when we don't have rich daddies to buy us a flash car."

Zara flushes. "Stop being such a prick, Luke. God, I don't know why you came in the first place, seeing as you obviously can't wait to get away from me."

"Yeah, well," I turn away, "that makes two of us, doesn't it?"

"What's going on?" Theo appears in the doorway, feet bare, hair damp from the shower. He glances between us, forehead creased. My gut twists. I swallow, staring down at the frayed bottoms of my jeans.

Zara rounds on him. "Luke says he's leaving. Seems he'd rather be with his mates than his girlfriend."

"Oh." The single word reveals nothing. I risk a peep at him, catch the brief flicker of emotion in his expression. Relief? Did he imagine I'd told Zara about the kiss out of some desire for revenge? Don't worry, Theo. Your shameful little secret will go with me to the grave.

"Oh?" Zara glowers at him. "My boyfriend's threatening to dessert me, and that's all you can say?"

"Be fair, Zara. What else can I say?"

"Say you'll talk to him, make him change his mind."

Theo sighs and runs a hand through his hair. "Look, this might sound harsh, but if Luke wants to go, maybe it's for the best."

It shouldn't hurt. I mean, after everything that's happened, it isn't as if I have any choice. Still, it does. It hurts like hell.

"How can you say that?" Zara demands. "How can having my heart broken possibly be for the best?"

"Zara, Luke's his own person. If this is what he wants, there's nothing we can do." Theo's eyes meet mine, just for an instant, and I get it. He can't return my feelings, so he's going to do the next best thing and help make my departure as easy as possible. And there I was thinking I couldn't feel any worse.

"Well, thanks a lot, Theo." Zara kicks out at the nearest table leg; cutlery rattles against china, and a knife clatters to the floor. "I would have thought you of all people would understand, but apparently you don't give a damn about me. In fact, why don't you go home as well? Why don't you all just go away and leave me alone?"

A slow handclap issues from the hallway. A moment later, Giles materialises at Theo's shoulder, smirking. "That was pretty impressive, Zara. Merrie and I could hear you all the way upstairs."

"Go fuck yourself, Giles," Zara says. "Luke's just announced that he's running out on us, and whatever he claims, I know it's your fault."

"Shame." Giles's smirk broadens. He's actually deluded enough to think he's responsible, that he holds that much power over me. "Need a lift to the station, Luke?"

Zara glares at him with such ferocity it's a wonder his eyebrows don't catch fire. "I swear, if you dare let Luke within a mile of the station, I'll smash up your precious car so badly it'll never drive again."

"OK, OK." Giles raises his palms in surrender. "Just trying to help. The offer's there, Luke, if you want it."

"Thanks." The word sticks in my throat. All the same, I'm grateful to him. Having Giles drive me will be far less awkward than going with Zara or Theo.

Zara opens her mouth to protest, but Theo shakes his head. "Leave it. You can't keep Luke here against his will."

Her eyes dart from face to face, begging one of us to come to her rescue. No one does. It must feel as though the whole world's against her. A tear slides silently down her cheek.

Theo lays a hand on her shoulder. "Look, Luke doesn't have to go today. Let him pack, get himself sorted, and Giles can drive him to the station in the morning. That'll give him time to change his mind. OK?" He addresses this last question to me.

I nod once. We both know I won't, can't, change my mind, but he's given Zara the only comfort he can—the chance to come to terms with the situation.

"Fine," Zara shrugs him off and wheels on me, "but I mean it, Luke, if you get on that train tomorrow, we're finished."

***

"So, who's playing?" Giles has unearthed a Monopoly board from somewhere, and is setting it up on the kitchen table amidst the remains of a late lunch.

Sprawled on the sofa, I pretend to be engrossed in *A Game of Thrones*. With the rain drumming against the windows and soft lamplight dispelling the gloom, it should be a cosy scene, would have been if not for the glares Zara keeps hurling my way, and Theo behaving like I don't exist.

When no one responds, Giles glances up from sorting the cards to beam at us; my imminent departure has put him in an excellent mood. "Come on, guys, it'll be fun. You'll play, won't you, Zara?"

"Monopoly's boring." She hunches down farther in her chair and flings me another dirty look, as if the dullness of the game is somehow my fault.

"You only say that because I always win," Giles says.

"Um, excuse me." Meredith rescues a pile of plates before they can slide off the table. "You're conveniently forgetting all those times I bankrupted you."

"Only because you insist on playing when I'm hungover. You'd never have beaten me otherwise."

"Patronising bastard. Well, you can't hide behind that excuse today. I'll be the top hat."

"And I'll be the racing car. Zara can be the iron."

"No I cannot. You're only giving me that because I'm a woman."

"For crying out loud. Fine, you be the racing car, I'll be the iron. I really don't care. Theo, you're the Scotty dog."

"Wruff," Theo says without enthusiasm from the armchair beside the fire. He abandons the charade of reading and pushes himself to his feet, walking past me to join the others as though I'm an extra cushion.

"Great." Giles sets the cards in two neat piles in the centre of the board. "I'll be the banker."

"I can think of another word for you," I say under my breath.

Giles arches an eyebrow in mock surprise. "Sorry, Luke, I forgot you were there. Did you want to play?"

"Piss off." My hands itch to punch the smug grin right off his face. If not for Meredith, maybe I would.

Head resting on the arm of the sofa, I watch them play for a while. Giles and Meredith's light-hearted bickering does a passable job of making everything seem normal. The longer I sit here, the more disconnected I feel. Even with Zara's foul mood and Theo being quieter than usual, there's a togetherness about the four of them, a sense that they're the only members of some exclusive club. I don't belong with them; perhaps I never could.

Unnoticed by anyone, I get up and slip from the room. Away from the light and warmth of the kitchen, the cottage is dingy, cold. I let out my breath, some of the tension leaving my shoulders. It's a relief to be alone. Back there, I was starting to feel like someone's embarrassing past, the one everyone knows about but does their best to pretend never happened.

I seek refuge in the sitting room. Without turning on the light, I flop into an armchair by the dead fire and curse the Scott-Palmers for not having a telly. A pang drags at my stomach. I wish I were at Dean's, sprawled on his bed playing Xbox. Blowing up a few enemy soldiers would have been therapeutic. Instead, all I can do is stare out of the window, watching the rain leave tear tracks on the glass, and cling to a single thought. By tomorrow evening, I'll be home.

Some time later—it could be hours or even days—the door edges open and Meredith pokes her head into the room. "There you are."

"Hey." I blink, disorientated. "Game finished?"

"Tea break." She holds up a mug and plate of sandwiches. "Could go on for a while yet."

"Not letting Giles win, I hope."

"What do you take me for? I've brought you these. You didn't eat much lunch. Thought you might be hungry."

"Not really. Appreciate the thought, though."

"At least drink this." Meredith sets the plate on the coffee table beside me and forces the steaming mug into my hands.

I clutch it like an abused dog pouncing on a scrap of kindness. The heat seeps into my numb fingers. I realise I'm shivering.

Meredith eyes me for a moment, then leaves the room without a word. Her light footsteps hurry up the stairs, and a moment later she's back, a hoody slung over one arm. She tosses it to me. "I got this out of your bag. Hope that's OK."

"You didn't have to," I say. "I'm fine."

Meredith raises an eyebrow. "Just put it on, Luke."

"Since when did you get so bossy?"

"Since always. Ask the boys. Now put that on before you freeze to death."

When I hesitate, she removes the mug from my grasp and stands over me, radiating disapproval, until I relent and pull on the sweatshirt.

She returns my mug, her expression sympathetic. "You don't have to punish yourself, you know."

I frown. Is that what I'm doing? Punishing myself for hurting Zara, for caring too much about Theo?

117

"This isn't your fault," Meredith says. "Sometimes things don't work out the way we want them to, that's all. Zara's tough. She'll get over it."

I manage a weak smile. Truth is, it isn't Zara I'm worried about. She's tough, like Meredith says. She'll probably have landed herself a new boyfriend before the summer's out. Me, though, that's another matter entirely.

Meredith perches on the armchair across from me. "I'll be sorry to see you go."

"Will you?"

"Of course. I like you."

My smile is real this time. "At least someone does."

She chews her lower lip, her gaze troubled. "I hope you leaving has nothing to do with Giles. I know he hasn't been exactly easy to get along with."

If only she knew. Should I mention our little chat of yesterday, Giles's none too subtle attempt to drive me out? Somehow, I don't think Meredith would be overly impressed. But Giles doesn't need my help in screwing up his relationship; he's more than capable of doing that himself.

"No," I tell her with total honesty, "this has nothing to do with Giles."

***

I must have dozed off after Meredith left, hardly surprising given my recent lack of sleep. When I open my eyes, the sky beyond the window is several shades darker, and the smell of garlic and tomatoes wafts from the kitchen. My stomach rumbles, protesting against my blatant neglect. Then it catches up with the rest of my body and my appetite vanishes.

It's tempting to stay where I am, to simply sit here all night and wait for this to be over. But I can't. I need to pack. When I uncurl myself from the armchair, pins and needles scrape like shards of broken glass up my legs. I wince, rolling the stiffness from my shoulders, and hobble upstairs.

It doesn't take long. In a burst of manic energy, I scoop everything up—the dirty underwear strewn over the floor, the flip-flops with their fine dusting of sand, the book I've barely opened—and throw them into my backpack. I cram it all in, all apart from my toothbrush and the clothes I have on. And my surfboard.

Energy spent, I sink onto the bed with my head in my hands. I survey the room I've shared with Zara for the past week. It's as though half its soul has been ripped out. Where moments ago our possessions were wrapped around one another in a tangle of familiarity, now only Zara's remain, lonely and forlorn. I stare at the carpet. When I get on the train tomorrow, it will mean the end for us, Zara and me. I'll miss her. Meredith too. And Theo?

I haul myself off the bed. All at once, the room feels stifling. I need to get out, breathe some fresh air. My glance strays to the window. Dusk outlines the treetops in charcoal, but at least the rain has let up. Pausing only to pull on my trainers, I return downstairs.

The kitchen blankets me in herb-scented warmth. Classical music, something mellow on strings, trails from the stereo. I flash back to that night, the night before everything changed, when I teased Theo for liking Mozart. No, my fists clench in my sweatshirt pockets, don't think about that.

Theo has his back to me as he doles out pasta from a large saucepan. Meredith is laying the table, Giles uncorking a bottle of wine. The scene strikes me as intimate, elite. Only Zara, curled up on the sofa, acknowledges my entrance. Her tear-reddened eyes meet mine, just for an instant, before she looks away. I make for the patio doors, pursued by guilt and her silent accusation.

"Luke, where are you going?"

Christ, can't he give it a rest? He must know his concerned act is wasted on me. My fingers tighten on the door handle, but I don't turn around. "A walk."

"You should have some dinner," Theo says. "You've hardly eaten all day."

Nice of him to notice. Well, can't have me collapsing on the train tomorrow from lack of food, can we? That wouldn't sit well with his conscience at all. I bite my tongue on a scathing remark. Yanking the door open, I step out into the fading light and fill my lungs with cool, damp air.

My instinct, as I set off through the woods, is to go down to the beach. Then I have a better idea. Theo mentioned a path that leads onto the cliff, promised to take me up there to see the sunrise. An empty promise. Still, there's nothing to stop me checking it out myself. I should be able to find the way, even in the semi darkness. Sure enough, about halfway along the main track, a second path twists away through the trees.

I start along it, leaves whispering overhead. The trail rises at a gentle incline until I hit a gate set into a high fence. Hell. If it's locked, I'll have to turn back, the last thing in the world I want to do. I wrestle with the bolts. The door swings outwards, and I exhale in relief.

Beyond it, the hill climbs steeply, and I shrug out of my hoody, tying it around my waist. Gradually the trees thin to make room for knee-high grass, the ground to my right plunging to meet rocky boulders. Already I've come a long way. I welcome the exercise, welcome the acceleration of my heart rate, the burn in my muscles.

At last, the path levels out. I walk to the edge of the cliff and stare out to sea. The wind, fiercer up here away from the shelter of the trees, lashes my exposed skin. I tilt my face into it, salty air stinging my cheeks. The view must be quite something on a clear day. Now, an expanse of steel-coloured water churns against a backdrop of leaden sky. A line from Mum's favourite Beach Boys song—'Sloop John B'—floats into my mind. I want to go home.

"Luke?"

I stiffen, shoulders hunching in on themselves. My hands, hidden in my sweatshirt pockets, ball into fists. "It's OK, Theo. I'm not going to throw myself off."

"Well, that's a relief." He laughs, an unsteady sound.

Silence stretches between us. I fix my gaze on the roiling sea below and will him to leave, to stop making this harder than it already is.

At length, Theo says, "Zara wants you to know she's sorry. She asked me to come after you, see if I could persuade you to stay."

An incredible weariness steals over me, one that goes far deeper than too many sleepless nights. I should have known. Theo the loyal friend, putting Zara's happiness before his own discomfort.

"I wish you hadn't." My voice is barely audible above the wind. "I wish you'd just let me go."

An endless pause. Then he says, "I can't. God help me, I can't."

He steps closer. The warmth of him brushes my spine before he wraps his arms around me from behind. My breath catches in my throat, but I don't have the strength to pull away. We stand there, Theo nestled into my back, neither of us saying anything as we watch the waves cut themselves to pieces on the rocks below. Slowly, the fact that Theo is really here, holding me, sinks in, and I relax against him.

"OK?" His breath caresses my neck and I shiver.

When I nod, he releases me and takes my hand, drawing me down to sit beside him in the long grass. It's damp from the earlier rain, but neither of us cares. We lean into one another, Theo's arm over my shoulders, mine around his waist, our thighs pressed together. I can't tear my eyes from his face. If I look away, even for an instant, I'm terrified he'll dissolve like sea spray on the breeze.

"Theo." My brain fumbles to catch up with what's happening. I'm wary of breaking the spell, but I have to know. "Why are you here, really?"

He tilts his head. "You know why. Right from that first evening, you knew. Didn't you?"

"I thought I did." Anger blasts through my sense of unreality. "But then you completely froze me out. Giles and Meredith turned up, and it was like I wasn't good enough for you anymore."

"What else could I do? Christ, Zara and I have grown up together. She's one of the most important people in the world to me. I had to fight this, had to at least try."

"But I thought—"

"Luke," Theo rubs my upper arm, "I wanted you the moment you showed up looking like you'd just crawled out of bed."

My laugh snags in my throat. "Maybe I should go for that look more often. Zara said you were flirting with me."

"Course I was. How could I not? But it was allowed, because I knew nothing could come of it. Then, when you looked at me that night and I saw some of what I was feeling in your eyes…" Theo shakes his head. "It scared the hell out of me. All I could think was what have I done? He's Zara's boyfriend, off limits. I can't do this."

"So why are you here now? Why didn't you just let me go?"

"I should, I know that. It would be the right thing to do."

I swallow, forcing the words past the constriction in my throat. "Theo, I need to know. If you're not sure about this, if you're going to back out on me—"

"I won't."

"Because I'd rather you told me now, before—"

"Luke, I won't back out on you."

This time Theo's kiss is gentle and slow, sweet in a way that makes my insides ache. My arms go around him, and he pushes me into the grass. Chill wetness seeps into the back of my T-shirt, but it scarcely registers beside the heat of Theo's body on mine, the firm softness of his mouth. I hook my leg over his, anchoring him against me.

Things get kind of fuzzy after that. Once, an image sneaks into my mind—Zara as I'd left her, curled up on the kitchen sofa, chewing her lip while she waits for Theo and me to return. Then it's gone, the guilt buried beneath the intensity of now. Minutes stretch into an eternity as we lie there, each learning the feel and taste of the other, exploring one another's faces with our lips and eyes.

At last, Theo props himself up on one elbow to gaze down at me, expression dazed. "So?"

"So…" I blink a few times, reorientating myself.

He glances along the path in the direction of the cottage. "This is…awkward."

The guilt creeps up on me again, settling in my gut. We shouldn't be doing this. I should put a stop to it before Zara gets hurt. But I can't. Even while my head tells me this is wrong, my heart accepts there's no turning back.

"We'll have to tell her." Panic squeezes my windpipe, strangling the words. I'm not ready for this. Whatever my feelings for Theo, I'm not ready to announce them to the world, to deal with what this means.

"Hey." Theo rests his forehead against mine, his eyes soft with understanding. "We don't have to say anything, not right away."

"That's really OK with you?"

"You need time to adjust, I get that. We both do."

Overcome with gratitude, I slide a hand to the nape of his neck and kiss him. When we next draw apart, the sky has darkened to ash.

Theo scrambles to his feet and extends a hand to help me up. "Come on, surfer boy, or we'll be walking home in the pitch-black."

We begin the descent along the cliff path and through the woods. Neither of us feels compelled to speak; our frequent glances and sheepish smiles say it all. We don't acknowledge the explosive nature of what we're doing. Sooner or later, Zara will have to know and things will get messy. But not yet. The spark between us is too new, too fragile. For now, we need the chance to nurture it, to cup it in our palms and see whether it has the power to take hold.

Chapter Nine

IPod, sunglasses, change of clothes... I roll my supplies up in a towel, singing Metallica's 'Nothing Else Matters' under my breath.

"Someone's in a good mood." Zara crams a stack of magazines into her beach bag, her smile tentative. For the first time since we've known one another, wariness hovers between us, and beyond a brief hug the previous evening when I announced my decision to stay, Zara hasn't tried to touch me. She must know she nearly pushed me too far and isn't sure where we stand.

"Happy about anything in particular?" she asks.

Hmmm, let's see. I discovered last night that I love kissing your cousin and can't wait to do it again. Probably not what she wants to hear. I turn from the hope in her expression and glance out of the window for inspiration. Yesterday's drizzle has given way to translucent sunlight. It reflects off the distant splashes of water, making them sparkle like polished glass.

I shrug. "Nice day. Perfect surfing conditions."

"I should've known. And I thought it might have something to do with deciding to spend the rest of the summer with your lovely girlfriend." Zara's flippant tone almost succeeds in masking her disappointment. She swings her bag over one shoulder. "Ready?"

"You go on. I'll be there in a minute."

I kneel by my backpack and rummage through the contents, pretending to search for something. I need Zara to take the hint.

"Luke," she hesitates by the door, "I know I said this before, but I really am sorry about yesterday, for behaving like such a brat."

"Don't worry about it." I'd wanted to reassure her, to tell her whatever she needs to hear so she'll leave, but my voice comes out curter than I intended.

Zara gnaws at her bottom lip. "So, you and me, are we OK?"

I suppress a sigh; getting frustrated won't help my cause. Instead, I look Zara straight in the eye and say the one thing that will satisfy her. "We're good. Let's just take things slow, all right?"

"All right." Her shoulders relax. "I'm glad you decided to stay."

"Yeah, me too." It isn't exactly a lie. All the same, as Zara retreats onto the landing, shame elbows me in the conscience. It's short-lived, however. The moment her footsteps have faded, I grab my towel bundle and slip along to Theo's room.

He's on his knees, delving through the jumble sale of clothes under his bed. When I tap on the open door, he scrambles up, flip-flop in hand, and smiles at me. "Hey there."

"Hey, yourself." The warmth in his eyes does something weird to my insides. I advance into the room and make to shut the door behind me.

Theo shakes his head. "Bad idea."

I'm unsure whether his caution stems from anxiety over how the two of us being alone in here might look to the others, or, and this seems more likely, the fear that we won't be able to resist continuing where we left off last night. Either way, he has a point.

I leave the door ajar and flash him my famous come-and-get-it grin. "You didn't invite me in here to ravish me, then."

"Behave," Theo flicks his towel at me, "or you won't get your present."

"You have a present for me?"

"That's what I said."

Curious, I sink onto the end of the bed, a little self-conscious in the wetsuit that clings to my thighs and upper arms. While Theo gathers his stuff together, I try not to stare at the rumpled sheets where Theo had slept, the hollow in the pillow where his head must have rested, but I can't help it. I imagine Theo lying there, imagine pressing him into the mattress the way he'd pushed me into the grass on the cliff top.

I cast about for a distraction. My gaze lands on the bedside cabinet, on the photograph of a young woman in a silver frame. Probably in her mid-thirties, she's dressed in jodhpurs and a man's shirt, her cloud of golden-brown hair tumbling around an unmade-up face. With those soft eyes and the smile that is half shy, half amused, she's the image of Theo.

"My mum." Theo follows the direction of my interest.

I glance over at him. "You're a lot like her."

"So I'm told." Sadness pulls at his mouth. "That photo is all I have left of her."

I frown, uncomprehending, and Theo looks down at his hands as he rolls up his towel. "Dad went a bit crazy after Mum died, handled it worse than any of us. He loved her even more than his precious horses, and that's saying something. The first weekend Clemmy and I came home from school after the funeral, we discovered he'd thrown out all Mum's things—clothes, photos, books, her collection of paintings…everything. It was like she'd never lived there."

Anger sears my throat. "He had no right. How could he do that?"

"He said it was too painful, being reminded of her wherever he looked. He wasn't in his right mind. If he had been, he would have made sure he saved something for Clemmy and me. As it was, if I hadn't taken this photo to school with me, I'd have nothing."

"Your mum didn't leave you anything?"

Theo hesitates, but only for a fraction of a second. "Like I said, this photo is all I have." He straightens with an air of finality. "So, want your present?"

"Can't wait." I noticed Theo avoided answering my question, but let it go.

He rummages in the top drawer of his bedside cabinet and retrieves a paper bag, which he tosses to me.

I peel back the sticky label holding the bag shut and peer inside. A delicious sweetness fills my mouth with saliva.

"I bought it that day in Tintagel," Theo says. "Stupid, really. I knew I couldn't give it to you, not then."

Almost reverently, I withdraw the slab of fudge and break off a chunk. It's the pale gold of caramel inlaid with darker gold nuts. Maple and walnut. "You remembered."

His smile is rueful. "It was one of the first things you ever said to me."

I can't speak. The realisation that, even while he was doing his best to freeze me out, Theo cared enough to buy this for me, means more than anything he could have said.

I pop the fudge in my mouth and hold the paper bag out to Theo.

We eat in silence, eyes fixed on one another. There's something strangely erotic about the moment. As Theo licks the sweetness from his lips, I remember kissing him up on the cliff, wonder how it would be to kiss him now, tasting of fudge. Theo's gaze lingers on my mouth and understanding leaps between us.

"Hey, Theo, you coming or not?" Giles shouts up the stairs, and the spell is broken.

***

Out on the water, paddling my board through the oncoming swell, I marvel at myself. This whole situation feels unreal, as though it's happening to someone else. I just don't do things like this. I don't get all snarled up inside because of a smile, a simple glance, don't obsess over the last time we were alone or fret as to when we'll be able to do it again. Christ, I don't kiss other guys.

Once I'm outside, I turn my board and get into position. As I wait for the wave to hit, I half expect to be assailed by a rush of disgust, a sense of wrongness. It doesn't come. Maybe it hasn't sunk in yet, what I'm doing. Maybe I need the chance to process it all. Whatever the reason, there's no regret, no uncertainty, nothing but the heady feeling of being alive.

The wave shifts beneath me. I'm on my feet, soaring over the glittering surface, the sun a warm hand on my back, a breeze filling my mouth with the tang of brine. I'm at one with the ocean, the surf pounding through my bloodstream.

High on exhilaration, I paddle out again. My gaze drifts to the beach, to the figure standing on the shore.

131

Even from this distance, I know it's Theo. I can almost feel the heat of his eyes on me, dark as they'd been when he watched me lick the fudge from my lips.

The wave takes me by surprise. Distracted, I catch it too early and catapult backwards off my board in a spectacular wipeout. I resurface, the leash pulled taut around my ankle, spluttering and blinking salt water from my vision. Well, that will have given Giles his entertainment for the morning. I can't bring myself to care.

The instant I rejoin the group, Giles smirks at me. "What was that little manoeuvre you pulled off back there?"

"The off the board aerial flip," I deadpan, and Theo and Zara snort with laughter.

"That was your fault," I tell Theo a while later. We're making our way through the woods to the cottage for lunch, the two of us dawdling, letting the others go on ahead.

Theo looks innocent. "Nothing to do with me. I was skimming pebbles, minding my own business."

"You were watching me. It put me off."

"Hey, if you're losing your touch, surfer boy, that's hardly my fault."

I barge him with my shoulder, and he stumbles off the path. He laughs, shoving me back.

"Why?" I ask. "Think you can do better?"

"Perhaps. My instructor once told me I'm a fast learner," Theo darts me a sidelong grin, "or was he just chatting me up?"

"Maybe a little. Fancy taking the board out again sometime, show me what you're made of?"

"Wouldn't that be boring for you?"

"No." I hold his gaze, serious now. "I'd like it."

"Me too." Theo glances towards the others, still engrossed in their discussion, then rests a hand on my hip. It's an intimate gesture, charged with danger, and the warm firmness of his palm burns through my shorts.

***

The following days are scattered with moments like that—shared glances whenever no one's looking, a brush of fingers when Theo passes me a beer, frantic kisses stolen in shadowy corners of the cottage. It isn't enough. Sometimes it feels as though nothing will ever be enough. I'm an explorer stranded in the desert with only a single bottle of water, forced to savour each precious drop because there's no telling how long it will have to last.

And when we can't escape the others, we talk. Lying on our backs in the sand, traipsing around some site of alleged historical interest from Meredith's brochures, we talk.

"Anyone would think you decided to stay to be with Theo," Zara says one evening. She's applying lip gloss in front of the bedroom mirror, and she tosses me an amused glance over her shoulder.

Despite her light tone, she has to be feeling excluded. Giles and Meredith, too. The happiness filling me up leaves no room for guilt. At times I feel I'm getting to understand Theo inside out; at others, it seems as though a cat's nine lives would be too short to learn everything there is to know.

"Do you ride?" he asks me.

We're eating steak and ale pie at an oldie-worldy village pub, the sort of place where the locals gather around the open fire on winter's nights to chat about their dairy herds and the latest football results. Most of the scrubbed wooden tables are occupied, and Theo has to lean towards me to be heard without raising his voice. The others are deep in conversation, making plans for the following day.

I flash him a crooked grin. "I can if you want me to."

"I mean horses, you idiot." His knee bumps mine under the table. "Never ridden a horse?"

"Nope. I begged Mum for a pony when I was about four, but she said it would have to share my room so I decided against it."

Theo shakes his head. "Seventeen and never set foot in a stirrup? Shocking."

"Whereas I'm guessing you were practically born in the saddle, your dad being a trainer."

The moment the words are out, I want to swallow them with my mouthful of mashed potato. In all the subjects we've covered, he hasn't mentioned his dad once, not since the night he told me about the rift between them.

Theo merely shrugs. "Pretty much. I might have ended up a jockey if I weren't so tall. Still, I've got to ride out some of the best horses in the country over the years, the next best thing to racing them myself."

I picture him mounted atop a black stallion, back straight, hands tight on the reins, muscular thighs gripping the flanks. Lucky horse.

"He's an incredible rider," Zara says, breaking into the conversation. "You should see him hunt. Best rider on the field by a mile. No one can touch him."

An unpleasant sensation, like an ice cube touching on a sensitive tooth, jolts through me. I look at Theo. "Please tell me you don't hunt."

"I used to," his eyes hold a trace of defiance, "before it was made illegal."

I stare down at my half-eaten pie. We've disagreed before, argued over whether politicians should send their kids to private schools, and whether *Star Wars* or *The Godfather* are the best films ever made, but this is the first time I've uncovered something about Theo I don't like. I can't match what I know about him, his gentleness and sense of fair play, with the idea of him standing by while hounds rip a fox apart.

"Hey," Theo nudges my foot with his, "don't go all ignorant townie on me."

"You what?" I drop my knife and fork with a clatter. "So because hounding some poor animal to death isn't my idea of a good time, that makes me ignorant? It's barbaric."

"Tell that to the farmers. I'm sure they think it's pretty barbaric when they wake up to find their chicken coop splattered with feathers and guts."

"They should've made sure the fox couldn't get in. It's hardly the foxes' fault. They're just doing what they have to do to survive."

"And hunting was what we had to do to keep down the fox population and protect our livelihoods. I wouldn't expect you to understand."

"Why's that?" I glare at him. "Because I'm a...what was it? An ignorant townie? No, Theo, all that means is that I'm not so blinded by some ancient tradition that I can't tell right from wrong. OK, so farmers have to keep down the fox population, I get that. What I don't get is why it has to be turned into some sick sport. Let the farmers shoot them and have done with it."

Theo rolls his eyes. "Great, so then we'd have a load of wounded foxes staggering around the countryside, dying slow and painful deaths. Does that make you feel better?"

"Oh, I'm sorry. I didn't realise you had the fox's best interests at heart. And there was me thinking it was just about stuck-up people having a laugh."

"Luke, it's the best way. Everyone knows it."

"Yeah, well, maybe you should've tried telling that to the fox when he was being torn to shreds. I'm sure it would've been a huge comfort to him."

"Will you two shut up?" Giles says. "People are staring."

We fall silent, avoiding one another's gaze. Caught up in my conviction, I hadn't realised how our voices had risen. Giles shoots us a look. It's an expression I've seen a lot on him these past few days, irritation mixed with incomprehension and something else. I don't speak to Theo for the rest of the meal. Can't even bring myself to look at him.

While he and Giles are at the bar ordering another round of drinks, and Zara has gone to the loo, Meredith slides into Zara's vacated seat. "I'm glad you decided to stay."

I arch an eyebrow, and her mouth quirks in amusement. "It's much more interesting with you around. That was a good fight you gave Theo."

"But you're still going to tell me I'm just a city boy with no understanding of how things are done in the countryside, right?"

"Hardly, seeing as I was brought up in London. As far as Giles and Theo are concerned, I'm an ignorant townie like you." Meredith fixes me with her wise gaze. "You won't win this one. You'll never convince a country boy that hunting's wrong, just as he'll never convince you it's right. You can only agree to disagree."

I continue to ignore Theo on the drive home. Back at the cottage, we gather all the bottles of liqueur—Bailey's, Kahlua, Amaretto—from the drinks cabinet in the dining room and stay up drinking into the early hours, seated around the kitchen table.

When we finally stumble up to bed in a haze of alcohol, I find myself alone with Theo. He pushes me up against the wall, his breath hot on my lips. "Ignorant townie."

"Fox murderer." I barely get the words out before he kisses me. His mouth crushes mine, rough, demanding, our bodies fusing in the darkness, and I realise none of it matters.

**

Mid-afternoon basks the cottage in drowsy stillness. I exchange a nervous glance with Theo, and we make to duck into the woods.

"Hey, wait for me."

We stop short. Theo adjusts the board on his shoulder and shoots me a look. My own frustration stares back at me from his expression. Only a moment ago, we left Zara fast asleep on a lounger, and with Giles and Meredith upstairs in their room, we'd seized our chance.

Zara runs to join us, a little breathless. "You guys taking the board out?"

"Yeah." I keep my tone casual. This would have been the first time we'd got to be truly alone since the night on the cliff. The board is more of a prop than anything else, our excuse for giving the others the slip.

"Cool." Zara grins. "I'll come and cheer you on."

I resist the urge to grit my teeth. "I'm just giving Theo another surfing lesson. It won't be much fun for you."

"I don't know. Watching Theo fall off the board last time was pretty entertaining."

I appeal to Theo for help. He's staring off into the trees, clearly not trusting himself to speak. Well, what can we say?

We start along the path to the beach. Zara walks between us, her arm looped through mine, chatting away with blithe unconcern. I answer her, outwardly relaxed. It amazes me, this trait I've discovered within myself, the ability to smile and pretend everything's normal. Not something I'm proud of. It isn't that I don't care about Zara, that this will hurt her. I just don't care enough to stop.

Theo's quiet as we make our way through the woods. Fortunately, Zara seems oblivious to his strain. I know it's eating him up, going behind Zara's back, putting on an act in front of his friends.

When we hit the beach, Zara takes the towels from me and spreads them over the sand. Theo and I strip down to our swimming shorts and head into the sea, studiously avoiding eye contact. Barely suppressed tension thickens the air between us.

With the surf lapping about our waists, I relieve Theo of the board. "Want to paddle?"

He shakes his head and I don't press him. We strike out in silence, me on the board, Theo keeping pace with me, until the waves are behind us. Finally, as I hold the board steady, I let myself meet Theo's gaze.

"Christ." His voice is ragged, his expression dark in a way that has me burning up despite the coolness of the surf. "This is killing me."

"I know." I swallow against the gravel in my throat. With Theo this close, the need to touch him is unbearable. Under cover of the water, I reach out to lay a hand on his thigh.

He jerks away. "Don't."

I flinch. Eyes averted, I fold my arms on the board. I shouldn't have done that. It was reckless, stupid. Still, his rejection stings.

"Hey." Theo bumps my shoulder, his tone softer. When I look up at him, he grimaces. "Sorry. It's just, if you do that again I'm going to kiss you, Zara or no Zara, and…well." He doesn't need to finish.

I manage a twisted smile. "S'all right."

We drink each other in, our longing as palpable as the current dragging at our limbs. I rouse myself with an effort. "Let's have you up on this board before Zara wonders what we're doing out here."

The lesson isn't a success. Too tense to concentrate on keeping his balance, Theo takes tumble after tumble. It's torture, having Theo this close and yet being unable to hold him, and my usual patience deserts me.

"Shit." When Theo topples off the board and practically into my arms, it's all I can do to shove him away. "Concentrate, will you?"

Theo winces, and it cuts straight through my frustration to the remorse underneath. I turn away, trying to regain my composure, and see Zara standing at the water's edge. She waves for my attention, before pointing behind her into the trees. I give her the thumbs up to show I've understood. My eyes find Theo's. The look that passes between us is almost physical. We wait just long enough for Zara to reach the fringe of the woods, and then we're moving, fighting and splashing our way back to shore.

Theo drops the board to the sand, careless of damaging it, and tackles me. We collapse onto the towels Zara left spread out for us, my fingers gripping Theo's hair, his tongue invading my mouth. I taste salt, the lingering sweetness of strawberries. We roll over and over, devouring each other, the slick wetness of our skin sliding together, his hardness rubbing mine through our shorts.

I grind against him, bite down on his lower lip. Theo makes a sound partway between a grunt and a moan. He pushes me onto my back, mouth shifting to my neck, his teeth scraping along my collarbone.

"This all right?" Theo's breath singes the hollow of my throat, his hand trailing over my stomach, pausing at the waistband of my shorts.

"Yes. Fuck." I arch into his touch. My voice sounds alien to my ears, hoarse, desperate. I need this, need to feel his hands on me.

Instinct takes over. I don't hesitate, don't stop to think. I tug Theo's shorts down his hips, wrap my fingers around him. He's warm against my palm. Warm and smooth and hard in a way that has me grasping him tighter.

"Luke." Theo raises his head, his eyes darker than I've ever seen them. He kisses me, rough and dirty, his hand reaching inside my shorts.

His touch sends electricity zinging through my entire body, and I gasp, fireworks exploding behind my eyelids. My world shrinks to a pinprick. I'm aware of nothing but my hands on Theo, his on me, stroking, exploring, the two of us locked into a private universe of sensation. Our breathing comes faster, shallower, our touch growing more urgent.

When I break apart, the violence of it rocks me. My vision goes black. I buck into Theo's palm, sinking my teeth into his shoulder. Theo cries out, burying his face against my neck as he shatters in my hands.

Slowly, reality rights itself. everything swims into vivid focus—dazzling sky, the blinding heat of the afternoon, the siren call of seagulls. I sag against Theo, weak from the intensity of what just happened. And Theo holds me, rubbing my back, simply waiting while the scattered pieces reassemble.

Theo runs his fingers through my hair, matted with seawater and sweat. "OK?"

"Mmm hmmm." My smile is lazy, a little shy. I smooth my fingertips over the bite mark on his shoulder. "Sorry."

"Don't be." His answering smile glimmers with amusement and something primal.

I lay my head on his chest; the steady rhythm of his heartbeat drums against my cheek. We stay like that, our legs entwined, the sun blazing down on us, drying the stickiness from our skin.

I trace my thumb over one of his nipples. "When did you know?"

"That I'm gay?" He continues combing my hair with his fingers. "I'm not sure. I suppose a part of me always knew, deep down. Knew I was different. When the boys in my house at Eton passed round the forbidden copies of Playboy someone managed to smuggle in, I couldn't see what the fuss was about. Still, I didn't think much of it, just thought I was a late developer, until I fell for my games master."

"Seriously?"

"Yup. Mr. Williams, a brooding Welshman with the most amazing body I'd ever seen. He was a champion swimmer, competed in the Commonwealth Games."

I smirk. "I wondered how you got into swimming."

"Funny. I'll have you know I won my first race when I was seven. Although," a grin hides behind his words, "I might have been a teensy bit more dedicated once Mr. Williams came on the scene."

"You don't say." I dart him a mischievous glance. "So, let me guess. You seduced him with your prowess at backstroke and ended up having hot sex in the school changing room."

Theo snorts. "Only in my dreams. Turned out Mr. Williams had a wife and two kids. Not that this dampened my fantasy. I spent way too long in the shower after every practice, making sure I was the last to leave, certain it was only a matter of time before he declared his passion and screwed me senseless on one of the wooden benches."

"And I thought you were such a nicely brought-up boy. I'm shocked."

"No you're not."

The grin he flashes me goes straight to my groin. I kiss him, experience the adrenalin rush as he opens up to me, sucks my tongue into his mouth.

Some time later, he asks, "How about you? Have there been any guys?"

I roll onto my back and stare up at the sky. I've never told anyone about my crush; to say it aloud would've been to make it real. Confiding in Theo, though, feels natural. "Only one. Max, our rugby captain. When I made the squad a couple of years back, he shook my hand to welcome me to the team. It was…"

I can't find the words to describe that moment. I'd met Max Harper's incredible eyes, all too aware of his fingers grasping mine, warm and strong, his palm callused from weekends spent working at his family's auto repair garage. I got this plunging sensation in my stomach, the kind of feeling you get when you drive too fast down a dip in the road, a feeling I wasn't supposed to have towards another boy.

Theo props himself up on an elbow, studies my face. His expression tells me he understands. "That must've been terrifying."

"Pretty much." By lunchtime, I looked so ill that Dean frogmarched me to the nurse's office. I felt grubby, exposed, convinced everyone would take one look at me and know the truth.

"What did you do?" Theo swipes a fly off my shoulder.

I cast him a wry smile. After the nurse sent me home, I crawled into bed and fell into an exhausted sleep, waking hours later from the most intense wet dream of my life. I stayed home for the rest of that week, until I calmed down enough to remember my classmates weren't telepathic and that I didn't have a sign spelling out 'homo' in flashing, neon letters above my head.

I shrug. "Got over it, I suppose. Told myself it was just some weird phase."

"How about Max? Wasn't it awkward being on the team with him?"

"Only until I discovered he's the biggest arsehole on the planet."

Theo laughs, and warmth blossoms in my chest. It's hard to imagine feeling closer to anyone than I do to Theo in this moment.

"What about Francis?" I ask. "Was he your first?"

His features tauten, the shutters clanging into place. "I'd rather not talk about it. Do you mind?"

"No worries." I look away, don't want him to see the hurt. It felt right, asking about Francis, given everything we'd shared, but it was stupid.

"Hey." Theo cups my chin, tilting my face to his. He kisses me, an apology in the gentle pressure of his lips.

I pull him down on top of me, run my fingers through his hair. Being here with Theo, the two of us the only ones on a golden beach, the waves crashing in time with my pulse, nothing has ever felt so right.

Chapter Ten

I shift on my lounger and push the damp hair off my forehead. Even on the undercover patio, it's so hot that sweat glues my back to the cushion behind me. Across the terrace, Meredith turns the page of her book while Giles and Zara argue over Theo's crossword. Fed up with their bickering, I jam my headphones in and crank up the volume on my iPod. With Metallica pounding my eardrums, I hook my arms behind my head and watch Theo swim lengths.

Two days have passed since our stolen hour on the beach. Since then, if Giles hasn't been monopolising Theo in an obvious attempt to push me out, Zara's by my side, sliding her hand into mine, murmuring into my ear. She's respecting my need to take things slow. So far, at least. Yet, even without her putting pressure on me, her very presence makes me feel trapped.

Theo cuts through the water, displaying a power and grace my bulk could never achieve. The temptation to join him drags at me. I resist it. With Theo that close, I don't fancy my chances of being able to keep my hands off him. I have to content myself with drinking him in—the toned leanness of his thighs, the way his shoulder muscles ripple as he moves. That same body had lain against mine, grinding me into the sand, making me aware of every hard inch of him. I roll onto my stomach, before the reaction inside my shorts can draw attention to itself, and rest my cheek on my palm.

Someone tugs the earphones from my ears. I jump, twisting my head to find Zara leaning over me in her bikini.

She perches on the edge of my lounger. "I'm bored. Play tennis with me?"

"Zara," I bury my face in the cushion with a groan, "it's about a hundred degrees out here."

"Don't exaggerate. You're just scared you'll lose." She grasps my arm, attempting to haul me up.

I shrug her off. "Seriously, it's too hot."

Zara's expression falls, but before she can argue, Giles ambles over. "I'll take you on, seeing as Luke's not man enough."

She arches an eyebrow. "Sure you can stand another humiliation? You know I always beat you at tennis."

"Only because I let you. Couldn't upset Theo's baby cousin, could I?"

"Right, you've asked for it. Wait here."

Zara leaps up, dashing into the cottage, and I turn away. My gaze meets Giles's. He regards me, eyes calculating, and I get the strangest feeling, like he's seeing me clearly for the first time and can't figure me out. Nausea oozes into my gut. Did he notice me eyeing up Theo? Does he suspect?

Ultra casual, I stretch and pad indoors, putting distance between us. After the humidity outside, the kitchen drapes me in shade, the oak floor cool beneath my feet. Thirst scratches my throat and I make a beeline for the fridge, welcoming the blast of cold air.

"What do you think you're playing at?"

Coke in hand, I turn to confront Giles in the doorway, my brows raised.

"Don't play dumb, Luke. If you're not careful, you'll end up losing that girl. You do realise that, right?"

I snap the ring on my can, the picture of unconcern. "You'd like that, wouldn't you?"

"Listen here." He glares at me. "You and Theo might be all matey now, but him and me go back a long way. You honestly think I'd want to see someone he cares about get hurt by an arrogant prick like you? You're not good enough to lick the dog shit from Zara's boots."

"Whereas you would make her the perfect boyfriend, is that it?" Spite seeps into my tone. The barb about hurting Zara hit dangerously close to home.

Giles's mouth hardens. When he speaks, his voice is tight. "Look, I'm not trying to start anything. I just want to give you a friendly warning. Treat Zara a bit better, or you can be sure someone else will."

"Don't tell me." I gulp down a mouthful of Coke. "Someone like you. Giles the superstud."

He takes a step towards me. "I could have Zara off you in a second and you'd be nothing but a distant memory."

"Now this I have to see. Go for it, Romeo."

"Pretty damn sure of yourself, aren't you? Reckon you have something I don't?"

"Oh," my mouth crooks in a wry grin, "I don't doubt it."

Giles advances, fists raised. I set my Coke can on the worktop behind me, every muscle tensed for a fight. I want this, have been egging him on since the day he arrived. I imagine slamming my knuckles into his handsome face, bones crunching at the force of the blow. Fortunately, for the sake of Giles's perfect nose, Zara chooses this moment to reappear.

"Ready for a beating?" she asks, grinning. She's wearing a baggy T-shirt over her bikini and has tied her hair up under a baseball cap.

With a final dirty look in my direction, Giles turns to her, expression bland. "Let's see if you're still so cocky after the first game, shall we?"

"Not cocky. I just have confidence in my ability to thrash you. Want to umpire, Luke?"

I shake my head. "Gonna stay in here out of the heat for a bit."

The two of them exit through the glass doors. I follow their progress from the window as they cross the lawn, ribbing each other, shoulders bumping. I look away, and my eyes land on Meredith. She's watching them over the top of her book. How much of my conversation with Giles had she overheard? With her back to me, face hidden, it's impossible to tell.

I lean against the worktop to finish my Coke, unease gnawing at me. Giles wouldn't take my challenge seriously, not with Meredith here. All the same, I shouldn't have goaded him, especially as everything he said was true. I am treating Zara badly, far worse than he realises, and however Theo and I try to soften the blow, she's going to get hurt.

I lose track of how long I stand there, immersed in my thoughts. Of its own accord, my focus strays to Theo, now floating on his back. Sod it. I toss my empty can in the bin and head outside, strolling over to kneel in the grass.

Theo swims over and rests his folded arms on the side of the pool. "Hey there."

He smiles at me, and I let out a breath, one that has been trapped inside for hours. My tension eases a fraction. "Hey, yourself."

A look stretches between us, a look fraught with the strain of holding back. My gaze settles on his mouth.

Theo flicks water at me. "Stop it."

"Stop what?"

"Looking at me like that when you know I can't do anything about it. Not here." He lays a hand on my leg. Fire sparks from his touch and licks up the inside of my thigh.

I have to swallow before I can get the words out. "No one's watching. We could always go somewhere else."

"We could, huh?"

"If you like."

Theo gives me a slow smile. His hand slides farther up my leg, and I lean towards him, helpless to prevent myself. Distantly, I'm aware how close we are. Too close.

"Gotcha!"

Theo snatches his hand from my thigh. I jerk away, almost ending up on my back in the grass. I put out an arm to steady myself and glance up. Zara lowers my phone, clearly having just snapped a photo.

One look at me, and she collapses in a fit of giggles. "Luke, your face."

"What do you expect, sneaking up on us like that?" I haul in a lungful of air. My heart batters itself against my ribcage. Is this how it feels to have a cardiac arrest?

Zara flops onto the grass beside me. "I didn't sneak. You two were just too busy plotting to notice me."

I inhale, my heart rate slowing. It's OK. She didn't see anything. If she had, I'd be getting my face slapped.

"So," Zara grins at me, "what's the big secret?"

"Wouldn't you like to know?" My voice puts on a good show of sounding normal. I glance at Theo. He's visibly shaken, fingers gripping his upper arms as though braced for an assault.

I return my attention to Zara. I need a distraction, or she'll realise something's up. "What're you doing with my phone? Thought you were playing tennis."

"There's gratitude for you. I went to get a drink, saw you had a text."

"Right, thanks." I extend my hand for the phone, but she holds it out of reach.

"In a minute. Let's see the picture first."

If it had been the deciding tackle in a rugby match, I couldn't have moved so fast. Zara laughs, trying to squirm away from me, but I pin her and wrestle the phone from her grasp.

"Not fair." She struggles to sit up, flushed and pouting. "It's my pic."

"Actually, it's on my phone, which I'd say makes it mine."

I scan the text, which is from Mum, and then, because I have to know, bring up the most recent photo. It takes every gram of self-control to keep my expression neutral.

"Let's see it then." Zara shifts to peer over my shoulder.

I adjust my grip, shielding the screen. "No, it didn't come out."

"How do you mean? Show me."

"Really, there's nothing to see." I slip the phone into my pocket. "The, uh, camera doesn't work properly."

"That's because your phone belongs in a museum." Zara sits back on her heels, tucking a few loose strands of hair beneath her cap. "You're the only person our age who doesn't own a smart phone. At least I'll know what to get you for your eighteenth."

She's kidding; it's evident from the teasing sparkle in her eyes. Yet, the throwaway comment, the easy acceptance that we'll still be together come November, knocks the wind out of me.

"Hey, Zara," Giles hollers from the tennis court, saving me the trouble of answering. Seems he does serve some purpose, after all. "You playing, or do you want to forfeit the match?"

"In your dreams," Zara yells back. She scrambles to her feet, grinning down at us. "Better go before he gets too full of himself."

Relief gifts me the ability to smile. "That's it. You show him."

Zara gives me the thumbs up. Then she's gone, racing across the lawn.

My shoulders sag. That was close. I turn to Theo. He avoids my gaze, ashen beneath his tan. Without a word, he gestures for me to pass him the phone. I hesitate, but only for an instant before laying it in his palm. Theo handles it with extreme caution, as though disarming a bomb. When he brings up the photo, the remaining colour drains from his face.

"Shit." His voice shakes. "Shit."

I say nothing, simply wait while he absorbs what's on the screen. My camera might not be top of the range, but it captured the two of us in perfect detail—our faces mere inches apart, the intimacy of Theo's hand on my thigh, my eyes shadowed with desire.

"Shit." Theo says again. Finally, he looks at me. "If she'd seen us—"

"But she didn't." I keep my tone even.

151

Theo appears not to hear me. He yanks his fingers through his hair until it sticks up in wet spikes. "How could I be so stupid? We'll have to be more careful."

"Theo, calm down. Zara didn't see a thing." I reach out, intending to touch his shoulder, but he slaps my hand aside.

"Are you crazy? Anyone would think you were trying to get us caught."

His anger punches me in the gut. "Would that really be such a bad thing? She'll have to know sooner or later."

"But not like this. Not by accident."

"Then let's tell her. I know we said we wouldn't, but this sneaking about is doing my head in."

Theo hesitates.

"What?" My voice has an edge to it. "Ashamed of me, or something? This is fine as long as no one actually knows about it?"

Theo hurls my phone into the grass. "This isn't all about you, Luke. Don't you see what a difficult position I'm in here? Imagine if it were Dean. Imagine how you'd feel if you'd fallen for his girlfriend and were going behind his back."

"It wouldn't happen." The words leave my mouth before I can think them through. I could cut out my tongue with a hacksaw.

Theo turns away to hoist himself from the pool, although not before I glimpse his face, pale and stricken.

"Theo, I didn't mean—" but he's already walking away towards the cottage.

On my knees in the grass, I watch him disappear inside. *Well done, Luke, that was really helpful.* I rub my brow, massaging the beginnings of a headache. I hadn't meant that how it sounded. Fact is, Dean and Yasmin have been together since they were fourteen. The idea of me cheating with her behind Dean's back, of her even looking at anyone else, is inconceivable. To Theo, though, already racked with guilt, it must have seemed like I was confirming his worst opinion of himself.

With a sigh, I push myself to my feet and wander back to the patio, dropping into the chair beside Meredith.

She lowers her book. "All right?"

I shrug. It isn't as if I can tell her the truth, but neither do I seem able to summon a lie. I rest an elbow on the table and cup my chin in my palm. I knew the night I decided to stay that it wouldn't be easy. I just never imagined it would be so hard.

"You mustn't take it personally, you know," Meredith says.

I tilt my head to find her knowing gaze on me. With a jolt of apprehension, it occurs to me that she could have been watching us, could have made the connection where Zara hadn't.

"Theo's been doing this a lot," she continues, "since the breakup with Francis. Sometimes he just needs some space."

There he is again, the inescapable Francis. In my mind, he's starting to take on the form of a villain in a crime thriller, shadowy but always lurking in the background. It shouldn't annoy me, her assumption that Theo is upset over him—it's the obvious conclusion to jump to—but it does.

"He's so much better," Meredith adds. "Coming down here has really helped. Still, it's bound to knock him back now and then."

A sick feeling settles in the pit of my stomach. I look away, addressing my question to the table. "Because Francis meant that much to him?"

"Not just Francis, but what he represented. Did Theo tell you about his dream?"

"To open a gallery?"

"Exactly. Theo loves horses, but art is his passion, same as for Giles and me. It's his world, the one thing he's always trusted to be his comfort. Like surfing is for you, I imagine."

"I get that, but what does this have to do with his ex?" I can't bring myself to say his name again.

"Francis is an artist," Meredith says. "An incredibly talented one. Theo was a fan of his work even before we knew him. He dragged Giles and me to an exhibition of his paintings one evening. That's how they met."

I fixate on a groove in the wooden tabletop. Maybe, if I concentrate hard enough, I can process the words without feeling their sting.

"So, you see," Meredith continues, "Francis became tangled up in the dream. He and Theo used to talk constantly about how they would make the gallery a success. And then Francis left, taking part of Theo's dream with him. To Theo, it was the ultimate betrayal."

I trace the groove with my finger. I'm beginning to form a picture in my mind—the handsome artist and his admirer, the instant attraction, the shared dreams. It makes a horrible kind of sense, Theo falling for an artist. For the first time, I have to wonder what the hell he can possibly see in me. "Did you like him?"

"Sorry?"

"Francis. Did you like him?"

"Oh." Meredith fiddles with the book in her lap. "Yes, I liked him. We all did. Francis is one of those people it's impossible not to like."

I have no response to that. After a while, Meredith returns to her reading, and I get up and go inside. I find Theo upstairs, stretched out on his bed. He's still in his swimming shorts, water dripping onto the sheets, his gaze on the photo of his mother. There's so much sadness in his expression that it shoves my doubts aside.

I sit on the edge of the mattress, a pillow's length of space between us. "I'm sorry."

"No," he gives me a tired smile, "I'm sorry. I'm not very good at this. New situation for me, I suppose."

"Hey, you just stole my line."

Theo's laugh is unsteady. He reaches out and rests a hand on my hip. "Really, I'm sorry. You have far more to get your head around. You're a lot stronger than I am."

I scoff. It doesn't seem that way to me. With everything that's happened since the evening on the cliff, I feel like the emotional equivalent of a car crash.

We fall quiet. Zara's laughter, carefree and unaware, bubbles up through the open window. Theo winces, and his eyes drift back to the photograph on his bedside cabinet. He looks less sad, more wistful.

"He'll come round," I say, "your dad."

"Probably, but it'll never be the same. He might not be so keen for me to take over the business anymore." His dry tone doesn't entirely conceal the pain behind it.

"Well, maybe you'll get to open that gallery of yours, after all."

"Maybe. Mum would like that, I think. I get my love of art from her. Did I tell you that?"

I shake my head, interested. It's almost as though this is a follow-on from my conversation with Meredith.

"Yeah. Dad's never had any time for it, doesn't understand why people pay a fortune for something that serves no real purpose. Mum was really proud of her collection, though. Our walls were covered with paintings by her favourite artists—Hockney, Reynolds, Constable—as well as some up-and-coming talent that caught her eye."

I don't miss the use of past tense, and remember what he told me before. "Your dad didn't get rid of the paintings. Not all of them."

Again, that fleeting pause I'd noticed when I asked him whether his mum had left him anything. "Yes, they're all gone, which I suppose means it's down to me to start a new collection." He rolls onto his side to face me. "So when I open my gallery, will you be applying for the job of chief hanger?"

"Not if you care about them being hung the right way up."

"Trust me, with some of the abstract stuff, it doesn't matter."

I raise an eyebrow. "And you call yourself an art lover? Shame on you."

"I know, I know. Meredith says I'm a philistine, but I like to know what I'm looking at, rather than searching for meaning in a load of splodges."

Theo grins at me, a grin of comradeship, and I can't help grinning back. I feel incredibly close to him in this moment. Perhaps now is the time to start laying some ghosts to rest. I take a deep breath. "Francis was an artist, wasn't he?"

Instantly, his expression closes. "Who told you that?"

I avoid his eyes, pulling on a loose thread in the hem of my T-shirt. Maybe I shouldn't have brought it up. But I'd needed to, needed to place the mysterious Francis, this guy who came before me, in some kind of context I can deal with.

"Luke, who—?"

"Meredith mentioned it, just in passing. You met at one of his exhibitions, right?"

"I'd rather not talk about it."

"Why?" I look at him. "It must've been tough, the breakup, but keeping it to yourself isn't going to help."

"Luke, drop it." There's a warning in his voice, but I can't let it go. This is too important.

"Come on, this is me you're talking to. You honestly believe I'd think less of you because your boyfriend cheated on you, or whatever?"

"I said drop it."

I flinch from the vehemence in his tone. "All right." Hollowness drags at my insides, but I stand, working to keep the hurt from showing on my face.

"Luke," Theo sits up, extending a hand to me, "I didn't mean to snap. I just—"

"Don't want to talk about it. Yeah, think I got the message." And before my bitterness can spill over, I turn and walk from the room.

***

"Did you ever meet Theo's ex?" I ask Zara a while later.

Intent on applying mascara in front of the mirror, she glances at my reflection, to where I'm crouched on the floor by my rucksack. "Francis? A few times when I went up to Oxford to see Theo. Why?"

I sift through the muddle of clothes, more to avoid her eye than anything. I'd put my boxers and jeans on in the bathroom after showering, as I have every day since Theo kissed me on the cliff. It isn't like Zara hasn't seen it all before, but being naked in front of her now wouldn't sit well with me.

I dodge the question. "What was he like?"

"Nice. At least, I thought he was—funny, charming, totally swoonworthy."

Christ, Zara, don't hold back. I glare at the mess of T-shirts and socks overflowing from my bag. She has no way of knowing how her every word is like an elbow to the chest. Still, she makes the guy out to be Casanova incarnate.

"It's no wonder Theo fell for him so hard," Zara says, driving the boot in further, "and why he was a complete wreck when the relationship ended."

As well as shutting himself off whenever I mention his name. My gut clenches, but I aim for mild curiosity. "And you really have no idea why they broke up?"

"Like I said, he won't talk about it, but... Wait, how come you're so interested?" Zara's voice grows suspicious. "You haven't asked him about it, have you?"

"Not exactly. I may have mentioned it once...or twice."

"Luke, you promised."

I'm aware of her accusing stare, a pistol jammed against my spine. I *had* promised. But that was when the idea of Theo having an ex meant nothing to me. Feels like a long time ago.

All I say is, "You don't think it's time he talked about it? It can't be good for him, bottling it up."

"And you don't think I've tried?" Zara whirls to face me, mascara wand clutched like a grenade in her hand.

"What would you like me to do, Luke? Force feed him truth potion? Tie him to a chair and torture it out of him?"

She slaps her palm onto the dressing table in frustration. Frustration at herself, I realise, for being unable to help Theo when he needed her.

"Sorry." I drop my gaze. "I didn't mean... Sorry."

Zara takes an audible breath. When she speaks again, she sounds calmer. "You don't know what it was like. After he and Francis split up, Theo sort of went inside himself. For weeks, he just shut himself away in his room. He wouldn't see anyone, stopped going to lectures, probably would have starved to death if Giles and Meredith hadn't made him eat."

As I listen, anger bubbles in my stomach, a burning hatred towards this guy I've never met.

"He refused to talk to anyone, even Giles. I went up to see him as often as I could, tried to get him to open up. We all did, but he wouldn't. He still won't."

Which means what? Foreboding, slimy and cold, cramps my gut. "I don't get it. You remember when Jack caught Emma cheating with some college guy? He couldn't wait to tell the world what a bitch she was."

"That's Theo for you. Too loyal for his own good. I tell you, though, if Francis dares come near him when I'm around, I'll cut off his balls and force them down his throat."

"You think he might?" The thought of Francis has awakened a protectiveness in me I've never experienced before.

Zara turns back to the mirror, roots around in her make-up bag. "All I know is that Theo's still hung up on him, and if Francis does beg him to take him back..."

She doesn't finish the sentence, doesn't need to. It's as if she's putting my own fears into words. My fingers close around something, a sock, squeezing it in my fist. Is Zara right, and Theo's still hung up on Francis? That would explain his reluctance to talk about him. And where do I fit into this little scenario? Am I just a diversion? A substitute to tide Theo over until he gets back with Francis?

No. I release my grip on the sock, let it return to the depths of my pack. I can't allow myself to think like that. The way Theo looks at me, the hungry urgency of his kisses... It has to mean something. So he was in love with Francis, but that was in the past. Francis isn't here now, and there's no reason to think he ever will be again. That should be enough. I need it to be enough.

The doubts are still there; I can sense them lurking in the dingy alleyways of my mind, ready to accost me when my guard's down. I ignore them and comb through my bag in search of something suitable for a night out. The black shirt, when I unearth it, is somewhat crumpled after being confined to the bottom of my rucksack, but it'll do.

As I button it, Zara appraises me from where she's perched on the bed, buckling her sandals. "You look nice."

"Thanks." I run a hand through my hair. It's as dishevelled as always, and the shirt is definitely on the wrong side of creased.

"Seriously, you should dress up more often." Zara comes over to me and slides her arms around my waist.

I stiffen. It's a tiny movement, the merest tensing of my shoulders, but she feels it.

"Luke," Zara releases me and steps away, hurt flashing in her eyes, "what's going on with us? Be honest."

Be honest. Does anyone truly understand what they're asking when they say that? Zara certainly doesn't. I almost tell her, almost come right out and say it. Only the thought of Theo stops me. This isn't just my secret to share, and he stands to lose a hell of a lot more than I do.

I massage the bridge of my nose. No get-out clause materialises from the snarl of my thoughts, no easy half-truths. The pretence is starting to wear me down. "We should go. The others will be waiting."

For several long seconds, Zara studies me in silence. I'm fobbing her off, and we both know it. At last, she turns her back on me.

"Fine." The single word slaps me across the face. In a violent motion, she snatches her clutch off the dressing table and stalks from the room.

Chapter Eleven

The others are waiting for me in the hall when I get downstairs.

"Let's go to Edesia," Zara's saying. "I feel like living it up."

Giles throws me a scathing look. "Not sure they'll let your boyfriend in."

"Giles, how about you give it a rest?" Theo snaps, and I'm not the only one who turns to stare at him.

Giles shrugs, but an expression akin to hurt flickers in his eyes. "I only meant that Edesia has a dress code, and Luke doesn't exactly look the part."

"He looks fine." Theo's gaze brushes me; the heat behind it melts some of my tension. "So, we're going to Edesia. Everyone agreed?"

"And then clubbing," Zara says. "We have to go clubbing."

"Right. And how are you proposing we get you and Luke in?"

"This isn't Brookminster, Theo. Someone's bound to let us in somewhere."

"We'll see," Theo says, and I know this is his way of trying to make things up to her.

A horn beeps twice from the driveway, bringing the discussion to a halt, and I follow the others outside to the waiting taxi. Zara leaps into the back beside Giles, no doubt to avoid having to sit next to me. Meredith raises an eyebrow, but slides into the passenger seat without comment. I'm about to climb into the middle row, when a touch on my shoulder stops me.

"Sorry." Theo's breath caresses my ear.

I swallow, fighting the urge to drag him back into the cottage and up to bed. I smile at him, a smile of forgiveness, and open the car door for him.

Giles and Zara do most of the talking on the journey to the restaurant. I barely listen, hyperaware of the foot of space separating Theo's thigh from mine, his hand resting on the seat between us. I keep my own hands on my knees, and try to prevent Zara's words about Theo still being hung up on Francis from invading my mind.

After Giles's snide remark about dress codes, Edesia is pretty much as I imagined. It has a carpet so thick I could happily stretch out on it and fall asleep, and the sort of soft lighting that makes everyone appear better looking than they are. Nice if you like that kind of thing. Zara's obviously in her element, flirting with the handsome young waiter who leads us to a corner table.

I slide onto the velvet banquette, which is far comfier than our sofa at home with its worn cushions and sagging springs, and smile at Theo as he prepares to slip in after me.

Zara grabs his arm. "Oh no, you're sitting next to me. Otherwise you'll just talk to Luke and ignore me all night."

She drags him to the other side of the table. Theo shoots me a helpless look, but pulls out the chair beside hers, leaving Meredith and Giles to join me on the bench. I turn away from him to give the waiter my drink order. It isn't Theo's fault; he couldn't exactly have refused. All the same, resentment simmers in my chest.

Once the waiter has left, I pick up my menu, partly to avoid Theo's eye, but mostly so I don't have to see Zara's satisfied expression. She's pissed me off and she knows it. I glare at the menu, which is written in what I take to be French. Since I opted to study Spanish, it may as well be Martian.

"What's this meant to be?" I demand of Meredith, indicating something that says, "Bar Poele a la Thai."

She looks to where I'm pointing. "Pan-fried sea bass."

"Why don't they just say that?"

"Because then they wouldn't get away with charging so much. Is that what you're having?"

"Don't think so." The ghost of Francis still hovers on the fringe of my consciousness. Unease roils in my stomach, sapping me of my appetite. "Is there any such thing as a steak in this place?"

Meredith takes the menu from me and leafs through it. "Here, this is what you want. Entrecôte De Boeuf Sauce Poivre."

"You sure?"

"Sirloin in a creamy pepper sauce. Trust me."

"Fine, but if I end up with octopus or something, you're swapping with me."

At that moment, the waiter returns to deliver our drinks and take our orders. When he comes to me, I try to remember Meredith's pronunciation, but Giles's sneer tells me I've made a complete hash of it.

"Don't they teach French in state schools these days?" he drawls once the waiter has gone.

I swallow a mouthful of my Coke. "Only kissing."

Zara giggles, before remembering she's supposed to be mad at me and turning it into a cough. I glance at Theo.

His gaze snags mine, and I flash him a wink. In that instant, it doesn't matter that we're in a room full of people; there may as well be no one there but the two of us.

"Theo! Oh my God, is that you?"

A girl of around twenty descends on our table. In an off the shoulder black dress and a gold comb holding back her blonde hair, she exudes class.

Theo's face lights up. "Tabitha?"

"It is you." The girl hugs him, laughing. "I knew it was, but Mummy and Daddy thought I was hallucinating. I can't believe it. And Giles and Zara too." Tabitha releases Theo to smile around at us. "And who else do we have here?"

"This is Meredith, my good friend from Oxford, and that on the end there is Luke, Zara's...boyfriend." Theo fumbles the last word, but no one but me appears to notice. "Guys, this is Tabitha. Our families met here on holiday...six years ago, was it?"

"Seven," Tabitha says. "Definitely seven."

"Right. And we've been friends ever since," Theo finishes.

"Nice to meet you, Meredith." Tabitha smiles at her, before her gaze settles on me. "Wow, Zara, you've found yourself a real looker, haven't you? Hi, Luke."

"Hey." I take in Tabitha's arm, draped in an overly possessive way across the back of Theo's chair, and coolness steals into my tone.

Theo shoots me a puzzled look, then returns his attention to Tabitha. "Come and eat with us, or do you have to be with your parents?"

"Oh, they won't mind. I'll just go and tell them what I'm doing." After enveloping Theo in another hug, she weaves her way through the diners to talk to a couple seated at a table on the far side of the restaurant.

I stare after her, eyes narrowed. She really is stunning, and moves with the confidence of someone accustomed to having guys drool all over her. The strength of my antagonism knocks me off balance.

"See something you like?" Zara hisses at me under cover of Theo and Giles's exclaiming over the miracle of seeing Tabitha.

"Not particularly." I avert my gaze.

Tabitha rejoins us just as the starters arrive. She slides into the seat beside Theo's—the seat that should have been mine—and instructs the waiter to fetch her food from her parents' table. Clearly carrying her own plate would have been beneath her.

"So, are you down here for the summer?" Giles asks.

"I wish." Tabitha spears a forkful of foie gras. "Actually, I'm just visiting Mummy and Daddy for a couple of days. That's why it's so amazing to bump into you like this. I leave for Thailand tomorrow. A friend of mine has a villa on one of the islands."

"Let me guess. This friend just so happens to be male, filthy rich, and has his own helicopter and private yacht."

"Giles, as if I would. You know my heart has only ever belonged to Theo."

Theo grins. "For a few weeks every summer, anyway."

A lump of potato skin—sorry, pelures de pomme de terre—lodges itself in my throat. I force it down with a mouthful of Coke. *Lighten up, Luke, for Christ's sake. They're joking; any idiot can see that.*

Tabitha's brown eyes dance. "Stop taking the piss. I may have half of London in love with me, but none of them can compare to you. Besides, it was decided that first

167

summer. You promised to marry me if I let you ride on my new jet ski."

"You did, you know," Zara says. "I was there."

Theo laughs. "Looks like that's settled then." He attempts to catch my eye across the table, but I turn away.

I scarcely notice when the waiter removes my starter and replaces it with the main course. Tabitha takes charge of the conversation, flirting outrageously with Theo, quizzing Giles and Meredith about Oxford, asking Zara about her plans when she leaves school. She even tries to talk to me about surfing, although it's obvious she's out of her comfort zone. Tabitha has this way about her, a way of expressing interest in whatever we have to say, that casts everyone under her spell. Everyone except me.

And the worst thing? Beneath the plummy accent and air of entitlement, she's genuinely nice. The objective part of my brain can appreciate she's just the sort of girl I go for—bubbly, outgoing, good fun—and I hate everything about her. It wouldn't be so bad if she'd just keep her fucking hands to herself. Every time I risk a peek, Tabitha has her arm draped around Theo's shoulders, or else she's leaning into him, laughing over one of Giles's supposedly funny stories.

I glare at my barely touched steak. A pain like cramp twists my gut. What's wrong with me? It isn't as if I believe Theo's attracted to Tabitha. Girls have never done it for him; he said as much on the beach. Tabitha can crawl all over him if she likes, and it shouldn't matter. But it does. For some reason my brain grapples to understand, it matters like hell.

I'm the only one who doesn't order dessert.

"You OK?" Meredith leans in to murmur in my ear.

I nod, but she continues to watch me, her expression anxious and thoughtful.

"So, where are you guys headed next?" Tabitha asks, spooning up a dollop of white chocolate soufflé.

"Zara wants to go clubbing," Theo says, "if we can find somewhere that'll let her and Luke in without ID."

A wicked smile creeps across Tabitha's face. "This really is your lucky night. I happen to know a rather sexy bouncer at Indigo's. I'll get them in, no problem."

On our way out, Tabitha leads Theo and Zara over to say hi to her parents. From a distance, I watch Theo shake hands with a tall man in a dinner jacket, before an older version of Tabitha wraps him in a hug. He laughs at something the woman says, completely at his ease. Well, why wouldn't he be? These are people from his social circle. Unbidden, my mind replays the moment by the pool when Zara almost caught us, Theo's expression of horrified panic. Obviously he doesn't want to hurt her, neither of us do, but what if it goes deeper than that? What if, deep down, he knows I'll never be accepted in his world and so there's no point rocking the boat?

"You're very quiet tonight," Meredith says.

"I expect this isn't really his scene," Giles drawls. "A bit too upmarket. Right, Luke? You'd probably prefer a Happy Meal from McDonald's."

I fling him a disgusted look, but otherwise ignore him. I don't have the emotional energy to spare for Giles right now.

"Are you sure *you* wouldn't, Giles?" Meredith asks. "Because it seems to me you're the one acting like a child here."

Giles's face tautens. Mouth set, he turns his back on us and folds his arms in huffy silence. I give Meredith a grateful smile, but she merely shrugs.

Just as she promised, Tabitha gets us past the bouncers and into the club without difficulty. Cool dusk gives way to suffocating gloom. Strobe lights flicker over the dance floor, casting everything in a purple haze. I draw in a breath. The air burns my throat, and I can almost taste the combination of alcohol and sweat on my tongue. Within seconds, the heat has pasted my shirt to my skin. Music batters my eardrums, vibrates inside my chest, and my head throbs in time to the beat.

Tabitha's connections also snare us a table. As we get settled in, ordering drinks, draping jackets over chairs, Theo's arm grazes mine. Our eyes lock. Even in the midst of all these people, I can distinguish his scent, warm and musky and intoxicating. A crazy impulse seizes hold of me. I imagine steering him onto the dance floor, imagine him grinding against me in the concealing darkness. My heart picks up speed. Do I dare? In the crush of bodies, would anyone even notice?

Hands grasp my hips from behind. "All right if I borrow Luke for a bit?" Tabitha calls to Zara over my shoulder.

"Feel free." She grabs Theo by the hand. "Come on, let's show these country bumpkins how it's done."

I watch them go, resentment a fist-sized stone in the pit of my stomach, until they become lost in the crowd. Tabitha squeezes my hips, giving me a little push towards the dance floor. I curb the reflex to slap her hands away. It's easier to go along with it, and I allow myself to be guided into the sea of gyrating couples. I glance around, but there's no sign of Theo in the chaos.

"Come on," Tabitha moves against me, shouting to be heard over the music, "show me your stuff."

I grimace and sort of sway on the spot. I'm an awkward dancer at the best of times. Whatever grace I'm able to muster when riding my board, deserts me the moment I set foot on a dance floor. Normally, on nights out with Dean and the lads, it doesn't matter. Right now, I'm nowhere near drunk enough.

"Have you and Zara been together long?" Tabitha asks.

"Not that long, no."

"Well, you're a sweet couple. Be sure to hold on to her."

I nod, still scanning the throng. Please, someone, get me out of this.

Tabitha must sense I'm not getting into it. After only two tracks, she says she's parched and suggests we stop for a drink. Relieved, I follow her back to our table, where Giles and Meredith are seated with their arms crossed, not looking at each other. We get there just as Theo and Zara arrive, flushed and laughing.

"Phew!" Zara pushes her damp hair off her forehead. "It's been a while since we did that." She extends a hand to me. "Your turn."

Her smile offers part forgiveness, part apology. Maybe the idea of me dancing with Tabitha has ignited some possessiveness in her, or maybe it's merely her natural good humour. Zara isn't the type to hold a grudge.

I can't bring myself to accept the olive branch. "Dancing really isn't my thing."

"My turn, then." Giles stands with a triumphant smirk in my direction.

Zara raises her eyebrows at me, asking my permission. Like she needs it. I shrug, and she allows Giles to pull her away.

171

Once they're out of sight, I turn to Theo and take a determined breath. I can do this. I'll just make it sound like a joke. No big deal. But before I can open my mouth, Tabitha slides her arm around Theo's waist.

"Come on, Fiancé," she says, and apparently forgetting all about being thirsty, propels him into the writhing mass of bodies.

I slump into the seat across from Meredith and gulp a mouthful of Jack Daniel's and Coke. My gaze scours the dancers for a glimpse of Theo, but he's nowhere to be seen. Meredith stares into her wineglass, twisting the stem around and around between her fingers. In the strange half-light, her expression is enigmatic, unreadable. Guilt muscles in on my despondency. It's my fault she isn't the one tearing up the dance floor with Giles. If I hadn't goaded him this afternoon, if Meredith hadn't felt compelled to stick up for me, if I'd accepted Zara's invitation to dance…

They're gone for what feels like hours. I've long since finished my drink, although I've been trying to make it last. Occasionally, Meredith glances over at me, but neither of us says much. Images keep invading my mind— Theo and Tabitha dancing together, their bodies close, flirting, having fun. Suddenly, I can't sit still any longer.

The need to move, to be doing something, overwhelms me. I lean across the table to be heard over the noise. "Want to dance?"

Meredith looks at me, eyebrows raised. "Thought it wasn't your thing."

"Changed my mind. Dance with me?" Somehow, I dredge my lazy smile up from the depths of my soul.

Clearly it isn't up to par, because she shakes her head. "Sorry, Luke. Whatever game you and Giles are playing, I'm not getting involved."

I grimace, but don't attempt to deny it. Instead, I gesture to her empty glass. "At least let me buy you another drink."

Meredith regards me, perhaps searching for an ulterior motive. "All right. Thanks."

Glad to have a purpose, I fight my way through the club. A scrum greets me at the bar, but I don't mind the wait. It's better than sitting around.

"What can I get you?" The pretty barmaid smiles at me when it's my turn, her West Country burr obvious even above the music. She has a nice smile, open and friendly.

I place my order, try to return her smile, but my face refuses to cooperate. Drinks in hand, I start to shoulder a path back through the crowd.

That's when I see them.

They're dancing together on the fringe of the dance floor, Tabitha standing on tiptoe, saying something in Theo's ear, something that makes him laugh. I halt, transfixed, dimly aware of the people flowing around me. Theo didn't tell me he could dance, not like this. I can't look away, am captivated by his fluid grace, the blatant sensuality of his every movement.

And it should be me out there.

Rage, dark and ugly, surges up inside me, choking the air from my lungs. Tabitha's way too close, arms hooked around Theo's neck and her hips thrusting against him, just as I'd pictured myself doing. My hands curl so tightly around the glasses I'm holding, it's a wonder they don't shatter. I swear, if she were a guy, I'd punch her fucking lights out. Oh, but that wouldn't be appropriate, would it? No one's supposed to know Theo and I are together.

"What's wrong?" Meredith asks the moment I rejoin her. "You look…" She breaks off.

I hate to think how I must look. I can scarcely see for the black spots obscuring my vision. My hands shake as I set the drinks down, and liquid sloshes onto the table. Without a word, I turn to leave.

"Where are you going?"

"Outside. Need some air. Headache."

Deaf to Meredith's anxious questions, heedless of the curses from those I shove and elbow aside, I stumble out into the night. I'd fully intended to just start walking, to walk and walk until I'd put a thousand miles between myself and Indigo's, but a face full of cool air slaps some sense into me. I content myself with wandering a short way along the road, where I lean against the display window of a charity shop.

All around me, the street hums with the usual Saturday night revelry—girls in high heels weaving along the pavement with their arms around each other, couples engaging in drunken arguments, a guy throwing up in the gutter. No one takes the slightest notice of me.

I close my eyes, ball my hands into fists. They're trembling. I've never felt so out of control in my life. I'm not one of those guys, the ones who get aggressive after a few drinks. That isn't me. Just for a moment though, watching Tabitha climb all over Theo, I couldn't have said what I was capable of. It scared me shitless.

"There you are." Zara's voice slices into my thoughts. "Meredith said you seemed upset. God, you look awful."

I open my eyes, focusing on her with an effort. "I'm fine. Just a headache." I barely recognise the words as mine, they're so stiff and cold.

Her expression falters. "This is about Giles, isn't it? You're mad at me for dancing with him."

"You can dance with whoever you like, Zara. I don't own you."

"Please, Luke, don't be like that. You know it didn't mean anything."

"Zara, I don't give a—"

"Everything all right?"

Christ, not him, not now. As Theo joins us, all I can see is him dancing with Tabitha, her hands on him. Emotion rises like bile in my throat.

He glances at Zara, before his gaze settles on me. "Luke?"

"He's upset with me," Zara says, and she sounds close to tears. This only makes me angrier.

"I'm not upset." I slam a fist into the window behind me; it shivers ominously. "I have a headache, OK? That's all."

"OK, OK." Theo talks to me as though soothing a frightened horse. I can feel him studying me, but I refuse to look at him. "Wait here while I get the others and call a cab."

"No," I shake my head, frustrated, "that isn't what... You guys carry on. I'll stay out here."

"Don't be an idiot," Theo says, and disappears inside before I can argue.

We wait in silence, Zara eyeing me with a mixture of anxiety and suspicion, me feigning interest in the people who pass us on the street. I can't help hoping Tabitha will make a scene, show herself up to be nothing but a spoilt little rich girl, but of course she doesn't.

"Hope you feel better soon," she says and gives me a hug, which I don't even attempt to return. Releasing me, Tabitha smiles around at the others. "It was great to see you all."

"And you," Theo says. "Have an amazing time in Thailand."

"You know I will. And you enjoy the rest of your holiday. Oh, there's a cab. I'm going to grab it before someone else does." With a final airy wave, she hurries away, high heels clacking along the pavement.

On the ride home, Theo presses his thigh against mine in the dark back seat of the taxi. I flinch from the contact and stare out of the window, seeing nothing, immune to his confusion. If he really doesn't know what's wrong, I'm sure as hell not going to tell him. Let him figure it out on his own, him with his expensive education.

Back at the cottage, Meredith blanks Giles and heads up to bed. He watches her go, guilt eating at his expression.

Theo lays a hand on his shoulder. "Talk to her."

Giles nods. Without a word to any of us, he follows Meredith upstairs.

I move ahead of Theo and Zara into the kitchen, making straight for the glass doors.

"Where're you going?" Zara demands from behind me.

"Out."

"Luke," Theo says, "it's three in the morning. You should take something for the headache, get some sleep."

I know he's right. He's always right, always so grown up, so fucking responsible. My blood reaches boiling point and bubbles over, crackling and snapping in my ears. I fling him the dirtiest glare I can summon and step out into the night, pulling the door shut behind me. Then I'm striding for the woods, walking as fast as I can without running. I wind my way along the path, pitch-black save for the occasional splash of moonlight. Tree roots do their best to trip me, branches clawing at my face, but I don't stop. I don't stop until I reach the beach.

When I emerge from the trees, the waves roar in welcome. There's something primal about the sound, something angry. It's as if they're part of me, the external embodiment of my turmoil. I can almost be fooled into believing they understand, even while I don't understand myself. I don't understand anything.

I run to meet them, snatch up a fist-sized pebble and hurl it out to sea. It arcs through the air before the darkness devours it. I imagine it tumbling into the water, being dragged under by the current, helpless and insignificant in the vastness of the ocean. I throw pebble after pebble, hurling them as far from me as I can, until my shoulder throbs. How long before it stops hurting? How long before I don't care?

"Luke!"

My heart plummets. Why couldn't he just stay away? Without glancing around, I begin walking along the shore, walking fast.

His footsteps pound the sand behind me. "Luke, wait. Talk to me."

I grit my teeth, but don't slow down. If I ignore him, maybe he'll give up and leave me the hell alone.

"Look," he tries again, "you're clearly upset with me. At least tell me what it is I'm supposed to have done."

"Like you don't know." I swing to glare at him. "Does she always have that much trouble keeping her hands off you, or was tonight a special occasion?"

He blinks. "Who? Tabitha?"

"I didn't see anyone else groping you."

"I'm clearly missing something here. You know I'm not interested in Tabitha, not in that way."

"But does she know that? Does she?"

His silence says it all.

"No," I can't keep the scorn out of my voice, "I didn't think so."

"Luke, that's not fair. You know I only came out to my dad last summer."

"Did she kiss you?"

"I'm sorry?"

"I said, did she—?"

"Oh, for crying out loud." Theo throws up his hands. "She kissed me once, on the cheek. What does it matter? It doesn't mean anything."

"It means something to me, Theo." The shout wrenches itself free of my throat. "But you never stopped to think about that, did you? How it made me feel, having to watch her climb all over you, in front of everyone? You didn't give a shit."

I turn my back on him and stumble away, kicking aside unsuspecting pebbles and lumps of driftwood unfortunate enough to get in my path. I'm shaking, shaking so hard I can scarcely walk straight.

"Luke!"

"Fuck off, Theo."

"What, so you think this is easy on me? Do you?" For the first time, his voice holds real anger. "How about putting yourself in my position for a moment."

I keep moving, in no mood to listen.

"Go on, Luke. You think I enjoy watching you and Zara together? The way she touches you? You share a bed with her, for Christ's sake. What do you think that's like for me, lying there, wondering, imagining? You think that's easy?"

I round on him. "And whose fault's that, Theo? Remind me. We're sneaking around like what we have is something shameful, something that needs to be hidden away, and why? So you won't have to get some guts and tell Zara the truth."

It's impossible to see his reaction in the moonlight, but I hear it, hear his sharp intake of breath as though I've struck him across the face.

The rage seeps from my body. I sink onto the sand, bury my face in my arms. "Fuck, Theo, I'm sorry. It's just so…hard."

He sits beside me, laying a tentative hand on my back. "Why don't you tell me what this is really about?"

I lower my arms and stare into the waves rolling onto the shore a few feet from us, their crests dusted with silver.

"Come on," Theo rubs my back, "help me out here."

"I…" The confession gets tangled up in my tongue. I trace a figure of eight in the sand with my finger. "I wanted it to be me."

"You wanted what to be you?"

I force myself to meet his eyes. "I wanted to be the one wrapped around you on that dance floor. I wanted everyone there to look at me, to know I was with you."

"Oh." Theo hesitates, his expression thoughtful. "Listen, what you said before about me stalling over telling Zara—"

"Theo, I—"

"No, I deserved it. Maybe I am putting it off—Christ, the last thing I want to do is hurt her—but I'm thinking of you, too, believe it or not." His mouth softens into a smile. "Coming out, that's a big deal. People's perception of you will change overnight, and not always in a good way. You'll get some who'll look at you like you're scum just for holding my hand in public, and some who'll do a lot worse. It's tough, Luke. I didn't know if you were ready for that. Are you?"

I return my gaze to the water. Theo's right. Once I let the world in on my relationship, there'll be no going back. And what about my mates? To them, I've always been the authority on girls, the one with the come-and-get-it smile who can be relied on to know exactly what to say to get them eating out of my hand. All that will change.

But surely they won't just turn their backs on me. Dean and I have been friends too long, been through too much. From being laid up with chicken pox and losing our baby teeth, to stressing out over exams and tasting our first beer, we've done it all together. I've shared everything with him. Well, almost everything.

A snippet of conversation stirs in my memory, something Dean said to me on the phone the day I arrived in Cornwall. "Did Zara's cousin get out the pink hair and rainbow flags to welcome you?"

A sick sensation grips my stomach. He was joking. He was. Still, there's no escaping it. I'll be Luke the queer. Luke the poofter. Luke, who had most of the girls at school in love with him, but instead went and fell for another guy. Will he hate me for it? Feel disgusted? Betrayed? One thing's for sure. He'll never view me in the same light again. Am I ready for that? Truly?

Theo touches my cheek. "We can do it, you know. We can go back right now and tell them. Tell Zara."

"Really?" I melt into the warmth of his palm. "You'd do that?"

"If it's what you want."

I swallow against the lump in my throat. That he's prepared to do this, despite my behaviour tonight, makes me feel humbled, childish.

"I'll have to go, won't I, once Zara knows? You two will need time."

"I expect so."

"Do you want me to?"

"What do you think?" Theo leans in until our foreheads touch, his gaze intent on mine.

I put my arms around him as his come around me. We stay like this, simply holding each other, Theo's breath caressing my lips. This is all still so new, so intoxicatingly strange. I've hardly begun to explore my feelings, to understand what they might mean. Leaving now would be impossible.

"We'll wait," I murmur against his mouth.

He draws back slightly, studying me. "You sure?"

"Yes." I take his face in my hands and kiss him. "We'll wait."

Chapter Twelve

By the following afternoon, I'm seriously beginning to regret my decision.

No one surfaces much before lunchtime. Woozy and hungover, we seek refuge in the shade of the terrace, alternately reading and dozing and drinking gallons of ice-cold water. I'm sprawled on a lounger, attempting yet again to make some headway with *A Game of Thrones*, when Zara insists on dragging me off for a walk.

"We need to talk," she says once we're out of earshot of the group. "About last night."

"It's too hot to talk." Away from the undercover patio, the sun stabs at my eyes and aggravates the pounding in my skull. "Anyway, there's nothing to say. I told you, I had a headache. Now, can we drop it?"

"Not until you admit you're upset with me for dancing with Giles."

"You'll have a long wait."

"For pity's sake." Zara kicks out at the grass. "Why are you acting like you don't care?"

"Erm, let's think. Maybe because it's the truth?"

"I don't believe you."

"That's your problem, not mine." Christ, anyone would think she wants me to get all possessive on her.

"Luke, please." Zara grabs my arm, her eyes imploring. "I'm trying to apologise here. If you would just meet me halfway."

"You know, Zara, I'm starting to wonder whether you only danced with Giles in the first place to try and get my back up."

"So you admit it. You were jealous."

That does it. I wrench myself free and turn away from her. "Look, believe what you like, OK? I don't give a shit."

Zara rounds on me, hand raised. For a moment, I'm sure she's about to slap me. Instead, she delivers a sharp elbow to my ribs and stalks back towards the cottage. I huff out a frustrated breath, kneading my sore eyes with my palms. Girls. Sometimes they're as hard to fathom as the concept of infinity.

By the time I climb the steps to the upper terrace, Zara has pinched my lounger, the one next to Theo's. She blanks me as I pass, her head bent over a magazine. Both Theo and Meredith shoot me anxious glances, but Giles can't hide a satisfied smirk.

I ignore the lot of them and go inside, pulling the door shut behind me. It's cool and wonderfully quiet in the kitchen. I flop onto the sofa, lean my throbbing head against the cushions, and close my eyes. I can feel the situation slipping from my grasp. I'm not sure how much longer I'll be able to keep this up. Sooner or later, Zara will push me too hard and I'll snap. I'll blurt it all out, to hell with whether Theo is ready, whether either of us is ready.

I brush the hair from my sweaty brow. Was I wrong last night to say we could wait? Maybe we should've just got it over with. I try to imagine it, to imagine how today might have played out. Zara would still be fuming with me, albeit for a different reason, and I'd be packing my bags, preparing to go home. An ache tugs at my gut. Despite everything, all the rows and sneaking around, I'm glad I'm here. In a weird way, the realisation comforts me, gives me strength.

The soft grind of the glass door prises my eyes open. Meredith slides it to and sits on the sofa beside me. "OK?"

"Not really." I hook my arms behind my head, propping my feet on the coffee table. I don't feel the need to lie, not about all of it.

She nods. "You and Zara both looked pretty upset."

"Yeah, well, Zara thinks I'm pissed off at her for dancing with Giles last night."

"And are you?"

"Course not. I've told her a hundred times, but she won't let it go. I mean, does she want me to be jealous, or what?"

"Of course she does." Meredith's tone implies this should have been obvious. I frown at her, and she rolls her eyes. "Listen, it's none of my business, but you haven't exactly been all over Zara since Giles and I arrived. Dancing with Giles was probably Zara's way of testing whether you still care."

I study my feet on the coffee table. I do care about Zara, just not in the way Meredith means, the way that would have me riled up with jealousy over her dancing with someone else, the way I felt when I saw Theo and Tabitha.

"I wish she'd back off a bit, that's all." Probably not the response Meredith's expecting, but an honest one.

She regards me, expression thoughtful, but doesn't comment. My attention drifts to the terrace. Zara is leaning over Theo, showing him something in her magazine. Theo catches my eye and offers me a wry smile. My heart swells. Theo's smiles can do that, render everything else trivial, insignificant. Before I give myself away, I avert my gaze and find Giles watching Meredith and me from behind his book. He isn't smirking anymore.

"What's happening with you and Giles?" I ask. Although they were on speaking terms when they came downstairs this morning, there was something off between them, a politeness that hadn't been there before.

Meredith shrugs. "Giles knows I'm unhappy with him."

"For dancing with Zara?"

Her mouth twitches. "For being such a prick to you. There's no excuse for it, and I told him so."

Gratitude warms my chest. Meredith hardly knows me, not really. For her to stick up for me against the guy she loves means a lot. I touch her shoulder and can almost feel the ferocity of Giles's glare. "Thanks, but I don't want to make things awkward between you two. I can take care of myself."

I flash her my most confident grin. Yet, even as the words leave my mouth, I'm not entirely sure they're true.

***

I wander onto the patio, hair damp from the shower, my muscles pleasurably sore after an afternoon on my board. Theo's waiting for me.

"Come for a walk?" he asks.

I smile at him and we start over the lawn, heading for the woods. It's two days since the disastrous night out, two days since we were last able to talk alone. Zara's seen to that, sticking to Theo like chewing gum, seizing every opportunity to make me feel excluded. But for the fact that she's currently upstairs washing her hair, she would have insisted on coming along, if only to spite me.

"Don't mind us, will you?" Giles calls out from where he and Meredith are lighting the barbecue. "We'll just slave away here. You go off and have fun."

Theo glances over his shoulder at him. "We won't be long, but Luke needs to see this."

"Well, don't blame me if you end up with cold steaks. And you're on clearing-up duty."

Theo gives Giles the thumbs up and urges me forward with a brief touch on my arm. When I look back, Giles is still watching us, his expression hard to decipher. Then the trees swallow us and obscure him from view.

Patches of sunlight slip between the leaves, flickering and dancing like fireflies. The air, laden with the earthy scent of leaves trampled into soil and the salty freshness of the sea, cools my skin.

I nudge Theo's shoulder with mine. "So, where're we going?" Not that it matters. He could be taking me to visit the local sewage works and I wouldn't care.

He grins at me, his face mysterious in the half-light. "There's something I promised to show you."

I don't press him. Simply being with Theo, the two of us alone with the wind in the trees and the nearby rush of waves, is enough. Besides, when Theo leads me off the main path and onto the narrower track, I have a good idea where we're headed.

After a while, I say, "Giles really doesn't like me, does he?"

"Oh," Theo runs a hand through his hair, "I wouldn't say that."

"You're kidding me."

"No, really. He isn't sure what to make of you, that's all. You're an unknown quantity. He just hasn't learned to trust you."

I suppress a grim smile. Giles doesn't trust me one bit. He's made that clear from the moment he arrived, and if I'm being completely honest with myself, he has good reason. But there's more to it than that; his hostility feels personal.

"I suppose Giles is a bit protective of me," Theo says, "and of Zara too, although he has a funny way of showing it. Zara had a thing for him once."

"Yeah, she told me." That seems like forever ago.

"Well, I think Giles kind of got used to Zara looking up to him. You're nothing like any of the boys she's been out with before, and you're the first one she's ever invited to the cottage. It's my guess Giles sees you as a threat."

I laugh. "If only he knew."

Theo's mouth quirks up at the corners, but anxiety pinches the skin between his brows.

"What?" I ask. "You think he suspects?"

"No, I don't think so. I mean, I'm pretty sure he would've said something."

"Yeah, to tell you to stop fooling around with riffraff like me."

"I happen to like riffraff."

I punch Theo on the arm. "Watch it, rich boy."

He chuckles, pausing to unbolt the wooden gate. As we climb the hill, Theo takes my hand, his grip firm and warm. "Sorry Zara's giving you such a hard time. This can't be much fun for you."

"It's OK." I squeeze his hand. "We have thick skins, we riffraff. Besides, this sort of makes up for it."

We continue the ascent in silence, letting our entwined fingers speak for us. Everywhere is so quiet. It still amazes me, the quiet, the utter lack of human activity. And then we crest the hill and emerge into a burning, orange sunset. Without a word, Theo walks me to the edge of the cliff and steps away, giving me the space to take it all in.

Last time I came up here, it was almost dark, the view hidden behind a veil of clouds. Now, though... Now I can see everything. It's spread out below me, shimmering like a painting when the paint is still wet, a brilliant expanse of green headlands and blue-grey water, the sky streaked with every shade of fire. The sun feels so close, close enough that I could reach out and touch it. I picture myself riding the waves, my board beneath my feet, surfing right into the heart of that inferno.

I pull my phone from my jeans pocket and snap some pictures. No photo, not even one taken by a professional, could ever do this view justice. It doesn't matter. I turn the camera on Theo, catching him off guard, and take a close-up of his startled face. He retaliates, retrieving his own phone and aiming it at me. We snap endless pictures, both of each other and of the scenery. Perhaps, if we commit this moment to memory, we can make it last forever.

Side-by-side, we stand at the cliff edge and watch the sun sink lower on the horizon. I lace my fingers through Theo's. "Thanks."

He doesn't need to ask what for. With his hands on my shoulders, he turns me to him and kisses me. I sink into it, pull his hips into mine, moaning into his mouth when our tongues meet. I'm not sure how we end up on the ground, but we do. We're in the grass and Theo's sucking my neck, grazing the skin with his teeth, and my hands are all over him, sliding beneath his T-shirt, forcing their way down the back of his jeans. Theo gasps. His breath burns the skin of my throat, sending a shock wave through my entire body. I free my hands, reach down to fumble with his zip.

"Nah uh." Theo takes hold of my wrist, pinning them over my head. His words caress my lips. "Wait."

He silences my protests with his mouth, kissing me with a hunger that saps the oxygen from my lungs. Then he's moving lower, fingers releasing the button on my jeans, drawing them and my boxers down over my hips. He takes me in his mouth, the warm wetness of his tongue sliding against my skin, and I cry out. Can't help it. My head falls back, eyes fluttering shut. I arch my hips, hands tangled in the grass, and let the world drop away.

***

Despite his threat, Giles has kept the steaks warm for us. Not that we would have cared. He may as well have served barbecued slug for all the notice we take.

"You were gone a long time." Giles's tone is casual, but that strange expression, the same one I glimpsed earlier, lurks behind his eyes.

Theo fiddles with his fork. "Luke wanted some pictures."

"I would've shown…" Zara says, before she remembers she isn't speaking to me.

I eat on autopilot, barely tasting the food, my mind still up on the cliff. Conversation eddies around me like water. I lean back in my seat and stare up at the sky. My body feels light, almost weightless, as though I could float away on the breeze.

This is when Giles butts in, reminding Theo and me— out of the goodness of his heart, I'm sure—that we promised to clear up. He's making a point, punishing Theo for abandoning him to the barbecue, punishing me for being the cause. I begin stacking the plates, too much on a high to let him get to me.

Giles must sense as much, because his face hardens. "Watch what you're doing with those. They're not your cheap IKEA brand, you know."

"You don't have to worry," I assure him. "I'm incredibly good with my hands."

I wink at Theo. He ducks his head, although not quickly enough to hide his blush, and escapes into the kitchen with a fistful of glasses. I heft the pile of plates and follow. When I half turn, sliding the door shut with my elbow, my gaze connects with Giles's. This time, I have no trouble reading his expression. Concern.

"Luke." Theo smothers a laugh. "You can't do that."

"Do what?" My tone is innocent, though the grin I flash him is anything but.

"Say things like that. It isn't helpful."

I only smile and begin loading the dishwasher. Theo bends to help, removing the plate I've just put in and replacing it the right way round. We keep stealing glances at each other. I can't stop staring at his mouth. I remember the heat of it, can feel his smooth hardness against my tongue, my senses filled with the musky taste of him.

We reach for the cutlery holder at the same time. Our fingers collide, his eyes snaring mine. The temptation is too strong. It overwhelms me, shoving caution aside. I lean forward and kiss him.

I know we're in trouble a split second before Theo stiffens. A faint noise sounds behind me just as a breeze stirs the hairs on the nape of my neck. The steak solidifies like concrete in my stomach. Slowly, fist clenched around my handful of forks, I turn.

Meredith is framed in the doorway. She stares at us, gaze flitting from one to the other, her expression blank with shock. No one speaks. The silence is almost tangible, thickening the air between us until it has the consistency of lukewarm soup. Meredith moves first. In two long strides, she crosses the kitchen and snatches her sweatshirt from where it's draped over the back of a chair. Then she's gone, sliding the door shut behind her.

I swear under my breath. Theo says nothing. He simply takes the cutlery from my grasp and continues stacking the dishwasher.

"Shit." I press a palm to my forehead. "Theo, I'm sorry."

He shrugs. "They had to know sometime."

"But I shouldn't have… It was stupid."

"Yes, well, not much we can do about it now. We'll just have to face the music." He swings the dishwasher door to with a click. His face is pale but set. Without looking at me, he squares his shoulders and heads onto the patio.

I follow, braced for Zara's hysterics and recriminations, Giles's smugness at being proved right about me all along. There's none of that. Besides the fact that Meredith refuses to meet our eyes, everything is just as we left it. I spend the rest of the night waiting for the guillotine to fall, my insides twisted into a cat's cradle of nerves. Yet, Meredith goes to bed a while later and she hasn't breathed a word.

Zara and Giles head upstairs soon after, leaving Theo and me alone. I look at him across the table that separates us. I want to touch him, to smooth the tension from his shoulders and kiss the lines from the corners of his mouth, but all at once the distance feels too great. Our intimacy of earlier, the easy pleasure we'd taken in one another on the cliff, has evaporated.

"I'm sorry." I don't know what else to say, just that I have to say something, anything, to fill the void. "This is all my fault."

"No." Theo shakes his head. There's no condemnation in his tone, and yet it's obvious from the shadows behind his eyes that he wishes tonight hadn't happened.

***

Nothing puts things into perspective like a session on the surf. I emerge from the water, body humming with adrenalin, the late morning sun warm on my skin. Between them, the sea air and exhilaration have cleared the fog of a restless night from my brain. So Meredith knows. This is hardly the end of the world. Like Theo said, people had to find out sooner or later. We might have wanted more time, time simply to enjoy each other before the tsunami hit, but I messed that up. The main thing now is that Zara doesn't hear it from anyone else.

I carry my board back to our usual spot at the base of the cliff. Immediately, my gaze goes to Theo, who's knocking a beach ball about with Zara and Giles. Though he's laughing, the smudges beneath his eyes reveal the strain he's under. Zara and Giles ignore me as I pass, which is expected. Theo glances my way, but only for an instant. Since last night, he has avoided being alone with me. I try not to mind.

I wander over to where I've left my stuff and begin packing my board away. Stretched out on the blanket, Meredith's attention remains fixed on her book. Like Theo, she's barely acknowledged me since the previous evening.

After zipping up my board bag, I lean over and touch her on the shoulder. "Walk with me?"

She raises her head to consider me, expression cool. I'm sure she's about to refuse. Instead, she lays aside her book and gets to her feet. Without waiting for me, she turns and starts walking along the beach. I scramble up and fall into step beside her. In my periphery, I catch Zara and Giles watching us. I return my attention to Meredith. Even with her face averted, I can feel the disapproval emanating from her in waves. It leaves me oddly tongue-tied. Several times I open my mouth to speak, but no words come.

At last, she lets out an impatient sigh. "You know, I've already had this conversation once today."

"Oh." I nudge a pebble with my toe. Theo must have talked to Meredith while I was out on my board.

"I told Theo not to worry," Meredith adds. "Your secret's safe with me."

I frown at her, unsure if I heard right.

She looks at me directly. "That's not to say I like it. If you must know, I think Theo's behaving appallingly. I would never have believed it of him."

"Whereas you have no trouble believing it of me? Thanks."

"Luke, that wasn't what I meant. I don't know you well enough to judge. Anyway, that's different. You and Zara have been together...what, a few months? Theo's known her all his life. He's probably closer to her than he is to anyone else. I don't get how he can go behind her back like this."

I glare at her, that weird protectiveness resurfacing. "You think this is easy on him? You think he doesn't care what this will do to Zara? It's crucifying him. If you know Theo at all, you have to realise that."

"Luke," Meredith holds up her hands in a placating gesture, "you don't have to defend him to me, really. I'm not blaming him. He can't help how he feels about you. It's the dishonesty I don't like. Zara has a right to know, that's all I'm saying."

"Yeah." The anger bleeds out of me and my shoulders slump. "Yeah, I know."

***

After lunch, a grim-faced Giles snatches up his car keys, announcing that he and Meredith need some alone time. Once they've gone, Zara retrieves a battered Scrabble board from the kitchen dresser and challenges Theo to a game. She doesn't invite me to play, even though I'm sprawled on a lounger mere feet away. I'm starting to feel like the unpopular kid at school, the kid no one talks to for fear that the stigma will rub off on them. Then, with Zara intent on choosing her letters, Theo catches my eye, and I'm reminded I'm not on my own. We're in this together.

I roll onto my stomach, chin cradled in my arms, and pretend not to watch Theo's hands arranging and rearranging the letters in front of him. He's soon ranking up ridiculously high scores with words I've never heard of, while Zara attempts to outwit him with a shameless display of cheating.

"Zara," Theo's tone swings between exasperation and amusement, "what exactly is a judex when it's at home?"

Zara rolls her eyes. "Someone who has retired from professional judo, of course. Everyone knows that."

"Is that right?"

"Absolutely. Look it up if you don't believe me."

"I intend to," Theo reaches yet again for the dictionary, "but I'm introducing a new rule. Every time you make up a word, I'm deducting twenty points from your score."

"What? No! You can't just go making up rules."

"Watch me. Unless you'd rather admit defeat now and declare me the champion."

Zara grumbles, but takes her word off the board and pushes her letters around on the table in search of a new one.

I get up and wander over to the pool, sliding into the cool water. I float on my back and close my eyes against the blinding blue of the sky. Conversation drifts over to me from the patio, easy, companionable. I try not to resent them for it. Theo owes this time to Zara, I know that. It might be the last they get to spend together before everything falls apart.

I lie there, thoughts rippling around me, until Giles and Meredith get back. A while later, the smell of charcoal fills the air, accompanied by the chink of bottles. In a heavy kind of daze, I drag myself out of the pool and head inside to shower.

When I emerge fully dressed from the bathroom, Zara's sitting on the edge of the bed. From her determined expression and folded arms, it's obvious she's been waiting for me. I hesitate in the doorway to the en suite, heart trampolining into my throat. Did he tell her?

"Luke." Zara sucks in a harsh breath, and then the words burst out. "How long are you going to keep punishing me?"

I blink at her, uncomprehending, and push the wet hair off my forehead. This isn't the line I expected her to take. After all, she's the one who's been ignoring me.

"For the other night," she adds. "With Giles."

"I've already told you. I really don't—"

"And it's no use saying you don't care, because you obviously do."

"Zara," I grit my teeth, fighting for patience, "I'm getting a bit sick of this conversation, to be honest."

"You're getting sick of it?" She leaps to her feet, takes a step towards me. "*You* are? How do you think I feel? I've apologised over and over, but you won't talk about it."

"That's because there's nothing to talk about."

"Then why are you being like this? So bloody difficult."

I laugh. "You have a very screwed-up way of seeing things, Zara. I'm not the one who's been behaving like a spoilt brat. Is this what you do when Daddy won't buy you a new pair of shoes? Well, it might work on him, but you're wasting your time with me. I don't give a—"

Zara slaps me hard across my still damp cheek. It stings. A lot. I steel myself not to react. Without glancing at her, I cross the room to the window.

"Luke." All the anger has drained from her voice. She sounds shaky, close to tears. "Luke, I'm sorry."

I turn to face her, the bed between us. "Yeah, me too."

"I shouldn't have hit you."

"I dunno. I probably deserved it."

Her laugh is part sob, part hiccup. She dashes a hand across her eyes. "I wish you'd talk to me. There's clearly something wrong, and if it isn't Giles—"

"It isn't."

"What then?"

I stare down at the bedspread and trace the pattern with my gaze, anything to avoid looking at Zara. Once again she has given me a cue, a perfect opening to confess, and once again I'm powerless without Theo. If he has any hope of holding on to his relationship with Zara, he has to tell her himself.

At length, Zara breaks the silence. "Luke, if I ask you something, will you promise to tell me the truth?"

A calmness settles over me. She knows, or at least suspects. Maybe that's a good thing. It might make it easier on everyone.

"I promise." Sorry, Theo, but I have no choice.

Zara inhales, psyching herself up. "Are you… Is there something going on between you and Meredith?"

"What?" I gape at her.

She shrugs. "You're always going off with her, and you said yourself you think she's pretty."

"Zara, I think lots of girls are pretty. It doesn't mean I want to go out with them."

"Just answer the question."

I look her straight in the eye. "No, there's nothing going on between me and Meredith."

Zara studies me for a long time. Eventually she sighs, some of the tension leaving her shoulders. "OK. I'm going to have a shower."

As soon as the bathroom door clicks shut behind her, I'm hurrying along the landing. Theo's in his room, thank Christ, and he's alone. He's sifting through the pile of books on the bedside cabinet, but his expression is distant, unfocused.

I close the door and move to sit next to him on the bed. "We have to tell her."

"I know."

"Soon, Theo. It's getting impossible."

"Luke, I know." He glances at me, irritation flashing in his eyes. When he catches sight of my cheek, his face softens. "What happened?"

"Impossible, like I said." I try to smile and feel it twisting out of shape.

Theo reaches out, touching the spot where Zara slapped me. "I'm sorry."

"S'all right."

"No, it isn't. I shouldn't have forced you into this position, not for this long. I'm going to sort it out, I promise." He squares his shoulders, features unusually hard. Yet, the pain beneath his bravado cuts me up inside.

I lay a hand on his thigh. "Want me to be there? For moral support, or whatever?"

Theo places his hand over mine. He's tempted; I can see it in his eyes. After a pause, he shakes his head. "No, it's OK. This is something I have to do on my own."

Chapter Thirteen

"I wish you'd tell me what's going on between you two."

"Giles, there's nothing going on. I already told you that."

"Hardly nothing. Going off for walks on the beach, having cosy little chats. What am I supposed to think?"

"You're being ridiculous."

"Am I? You're always sticking up for him, taking his side against mine."

"Well, maybe if you didn't feel the need to get at him at every opportunity…"

Their voices waft through the kitchen window to where I'm seated alone on the patio, Giles's rising with frustration, Meredith's resolutely calm. I rest my elbows on the table and do my best to tune them out. Apprehension has my stomach all knotted up, and the shouting grates on my nerves.

He must have done it by now.

I stare across the lawn to the trees, dark and impenetrable in the gloom. Overhead, clouds have imprisoned the sky behind a forbidding wall of grey, and the morning air crackles with tension. Mind you, any storm will seem like an April shower compared with what's coming.

Theo looked awful at breakfast, almost ill, pale and tired with dark rings around his eyes. Still, when he asked Zara to go for a walk along the beach, his expression was determined, his voice steady. I watched them from the kitchen window until they entered the woods, then came and sat out here to wait. That was fifteen minutes ago now, the longest fifteen minutes of my life.

The scrape of a chair jolts me from my thoughts. Giles settles into the seat beside me. "We need to talk."

I arch an eyebrow. This guy really knows how to pick his moments. I'm starting to believe he does it on purpose.

Giles glares at me. "I don't know what your game is, but if I find out there's something going on between you and Merrie—"

"Giles, if you can't keep hold of your own girlfriend, that's your problem, not mine."

"What the fuck's wrong with you? You're so insecure you have to have the whole world in love with you? Is that it?"

"Yeah, must be. Is it working? Going to stop pretending and declare your undying passion?"

Giles clenches his fists on his knees, seconds away from punching me. The thought is oddly gratifying.

"Look," he controls himself with an effort, "I know you don't give a damn about me, but what about Theo?"

I look away. Nothing he has to say about Theo can have any relevance now. My mind drifts, wondering how he's bearing up, how much of a rough time Zara's giving him. I wish he'd let me go with him to share some of the blame.

"For Christ's sake, Luke. I can't work out whether you're totally insensitive or just plain blind. You must realise Theo has a thing for you."

So, Theo was right; Giles has guessed at least part of it. The question is, how much?

"What if he has? With respect, Giles, it's none of your damned business."

"It is when my best mate's being made a fool of. Do you think I haven't seen the way you act around him? You're leading him on, making him hope for something that'll never happen. It isn't fair."

He's so wide off the mark it's funny. It's on the tip of my tongue to tell him so, purely for the satisfaction of seeing his expression. I bite back the impulse. He'll know soon enough. Everyone will.

My gut twists. Once Theo and Zara get back, nothing will ever be the same. I'm ready for this. I am. Hell, part of me wants to shout it from the crest of a ginormous wave. But it's a big deal, like Theo said, and telling Zara is merely the beginning. I imagine confiding to Dean about Theo, then the news spreading to Max and my other teammates, the rest of my form, the entire school. My heads spins. Maybe because home feels so far away, it's only just dawning on me what I'm up against, what this will mean.

"Luke, are you even listening to me? If Theo gets hurt because of you—"

"He won't." I let out a breath and turn to meet Giles's gaze. "You have my word."

His eyes narrow. "He'd better not. I don't think he could handle it, not after Francis."

That name again. The unease I've come to associate with the mention of Theo's ex, uncoils like a snake in my gut. "Zara said Theo hasn't talked about it, not to anyone."

"He hasn't. Whatever that bastard did, it's too painful, and if you ask me, Theo's still in love with him."

I wince. His words strike me right where I'm most vulnerable, and he doesn't even realise it. Not that it's true.

Theo wouldn't be putting his relationship with Zara on the line otherwise.

"Tell me, Giles," I say, "are you really concerned about Theo? Because it seems to me this has more to do with the fact that you don't like us hanging out. You think I'm not good enough for him."

He snorts. "Is that what you think? I don't like you because of your background? Luke, I don't like you because you're an arrogant shit."

Well, that told me. I have to give him points for honesty. Still, it takes one to know one, I reckon. I'm about to say as much, when the sound of voices echoes from the woods. Even from this distance, I recognise Zara. She's sobbing.

"What the…?" Giles powers to his feet, eyes raking the tree line.

This is it. I stand. My entire body feels heavy, weighed down with cement. He did it. Until this moment, I wasn't sure he would, couldn't allow myself to believe.

Zara's sobs grow louder, tinged with hysteria, and a second later she and Theo burst from the woods. But something's wrong. I leap down the patio steps and run to meet them, Giles half a pace ahead. Theo has Zara in his arms, cradling her like a baby, and the front of his T-shirt is drenched with blood.

***

Numb with shock, I sit in the back of Theo's Golf and hold Zara's towel-swathed foot on my lap in an effort to prevent the broken glass from sinking deeper. Theo wanted to take it out, but Zara cried harder, pleading with him not to touch it. Through her tears, hostility forgotten, she begged me to go with her to the hospital. This, more than anything else, told me what I needed to know.

Theo drives to the local Accident and Emergency with a reckless disregard I wouldn't have thought him capable of. More than once, I glimpse the flash of a speed camera as we zip past. I try to quell the emptiness eroding my insides, to concentrate on Zara, her ashen face averted from the possible sight of blood.

Luckily, the A and E department is quiet at this time on a weekday morning, and the motherly receptionist promises we'll be seen within half an hour. With Zara busy filling out the necessary forms, I pull Theo into an alcove beside the drinks machine.

"You didn't tell her."

Theo drags a hand through his already dishevelled hair. "Don't look at me like that. It isn't as if I didn't try."

"Isn't it?"

"What, so you think I was going to back out on you? It was hard to find the right moment, that's all. You know Zara, how difficult it is to get a word in sometimes. Anyway, she'd taken her shoes off to paddle, and I'd just said there was something I needed to tell her... Well, you know the rest."

"Yeah," I can't keep the bitterness out of my voice, "I know."

Hurt flickers in Theo's eyes. "This isn't my fault, Luke."

He's right. I know it, deep down, but I blame him all the same. Without another word, I return to Zara and take the seat beside her.

The doctor, a plump Asian man with a kind face, calls us in a few minutes later. After removing the glass and cleaning the cut, he beams at Zara. "Only a scratch. A couple of stitches and you'll be good to go."

Zara manages a weak smile, but reaches for my hand. Apparently, she's as freaked out by needles as by the sight of blood. In the short time it takes for Doctor Singh to stitch her up, she keeps a painful grip on my fingers, eyes squeezed shut. Once her foot has been bandaged, she's given a pair of crutches, prescribed some painkillers, and told to keep her weight off it as much as possible.

We're quiet on the drive back to the cottage. Zara leans against me with her head on my shoulder, exhausted by her ordeal.

"Oh, I just remembered," she says when we're almost home. "Theo, before I cut myself, you were going to tell me something."

Theo's knuckles whiten on the steering wheel. "It wasn't important."

I glare out of the window. So, I'm not important. That's nice to know. I'm being unreasonable. Theo can't kick her when she's down. But even while my brain accepts the reality of this, the hollowness devours another piece of my soul.

Zara slides her hand into mine and nuzzles her cheek against my shoulder. "Sorry I've been such a bitch. Can we start again?"

I hesitate. If Theo hasn't the heart to tell her the truth, maybe I should. At least it would be over and done with. Theo must read the intention in my expression, because he catches my eye in the rear-view mirror and shakes his head.

I slump in my seat. "All right."

Zara exhales in obvious relief and squeezes me in a one-armed hug. The look I shoot Theo over her head contains all the betrayal and resentment in the universe. In that moment, I almost hate him.

***

The storm finally breaks during the night. We wake next morning to rain lashing the windows and the angry growl of thunder.

"Someone find the cards," Zara says after breakfast. "I'm in the mood to win at Black Lady."

She has installed herself on the sofa in front of the kitchen fire, her injured foot propped on a pile of cushions, and is deriving far too much enjoyment from having us all wait on her.

At once, Giles leaps up from his armchair to rummage in the dresser drawers. The look he shoots me, where I'm huddled over a mug of coffee at the table, makes it clear he's unimpressed by my performance in the caring boyfriend department. I can't work out whether he's doing it to spite me, or if it has more to do with the continued friction between him and Meredith. Either way, Giles has thrown himself into the role of chief entertainer and nursemaid with disgusting enthusiasm.

"Are you two playing?" Zara asks, while Giles shuffles the cards.

Meredith declines, scarcely raising her head from the book she's reading. Since her argument with Giles the previous day, she has been even quieter than usual.

"Luke?"

I feel Zara's eyes on me and glance up with an effort. "Sorry, have a bit of a headache."

Theo's gaze rests on me, full of regret and understanding. He knows I'm avoiding him, have been since we got back from the hospital.

Zara deals the cards, and the three of them are soon immersed in their game. I cup my chin in one hand and stare out at the storm. The raindrops hurling themselves against the windowpane remind me of myself; they have as much hope of cracking the glass as I do of getting through to Theo.

I can't pretend any longer. The more I think about it, the more sense it makes. Zara, Meredith, Giles...they're all right. Theo is still in love with Francis. I've suspected it from the outset. In my heart, the doubts have always been there. It's why he refuses point blank to talk about him, why he's so reluctant to bring the world in on our relationship. OK, so he said he was about to tell Zara yesterday, and maybe he would have done. I suppose I'll never know. But here's what I do know. It was a good twenty minutes after they left when Zara cut herself, plenty of time for Theo to have brought up the subject if he'd really wanted to. But he didn't. He didn't because whatever he feels for me, it isn't enough.

"Queen of Spades!" Zara slams her card down on the table. "That's a fifty-point penalty to Giles. Oh dear, Giles, you're really off your game today."

"Actually, I think you'll find I have everything under control."

"What, by losing catastrophically?"

"There's more than one way to win, you know."

It's a measure of how depressed I am by my own thoughts that I view Giles's smugness as a welcome distraction. I cast my mind back to the times I've played

Black Lady with Dean's family. It's kind of like Whist, only the aim is to lose tricks rather than win them. Every time you win a trick containing a heart, you score penalty points, and if you land the Queen of Spades, it's a full fifty. The winner is the player who has amassed the least points by the end of the game.

But there's another way to win, I remember. If you accumulate all the penalty cards, the entire suit of hearts plus the Queen of Spades, you have the choice of wiping your own score or doubling the scores of the other players. Of course, it's a risky strategy. Fail to win just one penalty card and you set yourself up for a huge total.

Zara's eyes widen. "No way. You can't do it. He can't, can he, Theo?"

"I don't know." Sprawled on the rug by the coffee table, Theo examines his cards. "He's let us in on what he's up to, so he must think he can."

"Well, he can't." Zara sets her jaw. "I'll stop him."

Giles's grin is a challenge. "I wouldn't bet on it."

"I would."

"How much?"

"Anything you like."

"Anything?" His gaze narrows. "OK then. If I win, you have to kiss me."

Zara snorts. "You've got to be joking."

"What if I am? If you're so sure you can stop me—"

"I am."

"Well then, we have a deal?"

Zara laughs, but catching my eye, she shakes her head. "No deal."

"Which rather proves my point?" Giles smirks, flicking his cards with a thumb. "I won that trick, so it's my lead."

Engrossed in their game, none of them notice Meredith gather her book and slip from the room. Nor do they seem aware of it when, a few minutes later, I get up and follow.

Meredith's in the sitting room, curled in an armchair by the fire. Though she has her book open on her knee, she isn't reading. When I take the chair across from her, she gives me a half-hearted smile. I recall that afternoon, years ago it seems, when she sought me out with sympathy and hot tea. I'd been intent on leaving then. Perhaps I should have. It would've saved me a whole lot of grief. Instead, I'd let myself believe Theo wanted me, that we could make it work.

"I'm sorry," I say. "If I've made things awkward between you and Giles."

Meredith shrugs. "Not your fault."

"It sort of is. He's only doing this, flirting with Zara, to get at me."

"Poor Giles. He has no idea he's wasting his time."

"Don't you care?"

Meredith closes her book and traces the title with a finger. "I care. There just isn't much I can do about it."

I frown into the empty grate. How can she be so calm? It's as though she knows she won't be able to hold Giles, so isn't even going to try. I can't work out whether she's weak, or just so much wiser than the rest of us.

"You all right?" Meredith asks.

"Yeah," I say, then sigh. "No, not really."

She considers me with that directness of hers. "Theo will tell her, you know. Zara."

"Will he?"

"If that's what he said. Just be patient with him."

"You don't think…" I can't get the words out.

"Think what?"

I swallow. "That he might still be in love with Francis."

Meredith falls quiet. Her expression, somewhere between pity and discomfort, puts me in mind of a coach about to break the news to his most dedicated player that he'll never be good enough to make the first team.

"Francis isn't here," is all she says.

***

It's after lunch when Theo succeeds in cornering me.

I'd wandered into the kitchen in search of my iPod. I was desperate to go for a walk, to escape the stifling confines of the cottage, but the rain was still pouring down in sheets and I would've been drenched in seconds. With my earphones in, I could at least tune out the world for a while.

Zara and Giles were deep in conversation when I walked in, seated close together on the sofa and speaking in low voices.

"Giles, we… Oh hi, Luke." Zara sounded falsely bright, the way people do when you interrupt them talking about you.

I ran my gaze over the work surfaces. "Have you seen my iPod?"

"Bedside cabinet, top drawer. I found it on the floor the other morning and put it away so it wouldn't get lost."

"Thanks." Turning to leave, I'd glimpsed their expression, Zara's flushed and sort of guilty, Giles's defiant. Bet they'd been having a nice little chat about me, about what a shitty boyfriend I am.

Whatever.

I have my foot on the bottom stair when Theo emerges from the shadows of the hallway and grabs my arm. "We need to talk."

I try to wrench myself free, but he tightens his hold. I could fight him, force him to let go. Somehow, I don't have the energy. Avoiding his gaze, I allow Theo to draw me into the dining room. As soon as he has the door shut, he releases me, and I hug my arms to my chest. It's partly a defensive gesture, partly protection against the chill of the room.

"I know you're mad at me," Theo says, "and I'm sorry."

I cross to the window and stare out at the rain-washed driveway. "Are you?"

"What's that supposed to mean?"

"You tell me."

Theo says nothing. I hear him take a step towards me, then stop. He must sense I'm not in the mood to be touched. I glare at the puddles forming on the gravel. The constriction around my heart makes it hard to breathe.

"Luke," Theo's tone is wearier than I've ever heard it, "I get why you're angry, I do, but it wasn't my fault. You must see that."

"Maybe. All a bit convenient, though, wasn't it?"

"Convenient? I'm not following you."

"No?" I swing to face him. He's leaning against the foot of the grand dining table, forehead creased. "You don't think Zara picked the perfect moment to step on that glass? It completely let you off the hook, after all. You weren't just a tiny bit relieved?"

Theo rocks back, mouth open. "I can't believe you actually said that. You seriously think I'd want Zara to get hurt?"

I shrug. "All I'm saying is that it gave you an excuse not to tell her. I mean, you've made it pretty obvious you don't want to."

"Of course I don't." Theo pushes himself away from the table, his eyes blazing. "What sort of sadistic bastard do you think I am? You honestly expect me to enjoy telling one of the people I care about most in the world that I've gone behind her back, betrayed her trust in the worst way possible? Well, I can't. If I could turn back the clock, change things so I wouldn't have to hurt her like this, I would. Sorry if you think that makes me weak or cowardly or whatever, but there it is."

His words drop between us, boulders hurled over the edge of a cliff. They slam into me with a force that is almost physical.

"Well, thanks for that." My voice comes out raw, harsh. "Thanks a lot. So nice to know where I stand."

"That wasn't..." Theo shakes his head, impatient. "For Christ's sake, grow up."

"You what?"

"You heard. You're acting like a spoilt child."

I laugh, though I've never found anything less funny. "Can you hear yourself? The upbringing you've had, and I'm the one who's spoilt?"

"No, I said you were acting like it. It might help if you actually listened."

"So I'm thick as well as spoilt. Still, what do you expect? I don't have rich parents who could afford to send me to Eton."

Theo looks down at his hands. He draws in a long breath, controlling his temper with a visible effort. "This is pointless."

"Yeah." I can't hide my bitterness. "It always has been, hasn't it?"

Slowly, he raises his head to meet my gaze. "What're you saying?"

"I dunno. That I'm sorry, I suppose. For not being what you want. I've tried, I've tried so fucking hard, but it's no use. I'm not Francis."

Theo regards me, his face expressionless. It's as though he doesn't even recognise me anymore. "No, you're not."

I recoil. I'd known it was coming, had done all along. Yet, hearing it from Theo, seeing the truth in his eyes, is like having my gut scraped out with a fillet knife. Without a word, I bolt for the door.

"Luke—"

But I'm already in the hall, stumbling away from him up the stairs. I don't bump into any of the others, which is lucky; one look at my face and our deceit would have come crashing down like a tower of toddler's building blocks. In my room, the door safely closed behind me, I sink onto the edge of the bed and drop my head in my hands.

I don't remember the last time I cried. Even when I was seven years old and fell off the monkey bars, fracturing my arm in two places, I remained stoically dry-eyed throughout the trip to the hospital. The nurse who plastered me up gave me a red lollypop and called me a brave soldier. I don't feel brave, not right now. Tears burn behind my eyelids and stick in my throat. I grit my teeth, palms pressed against my eyeballs, willing them back.

So that's it. We're Over, Finished, nothing but a memory to be filed under the heading *Experiences Never to be Repeated*. Really, it was doomed before it began. I just hadn't wanted to see it. I fell for Theo, for his gentleness, his beautiful smile, and my feelings had blinded me to the truth. I let myself believe I was irresistible, that I could exorcise the ghost of Francis. Giles was right about me: I am an arrogant shit.

A soft knock filters through my misery. I look up, blinking the dark spots from my vision.

Meredith pokes her head into the room. "Giles and I are going to the supermarket. Need anything?"

At least those two are talking again. That's one less thing for me to feel bad about. I shake my head, not trusting myself to speak.

Meredith studies me, her eyes full of understanding, but all she says is, "Theo's coming with us. Will you keep Zara company?"

I nod once. Meredith casts me a final sympathetic glance, then retreats. I wait until the front door bangs shut, before dragging myself to my feet and down the stairs. Numbness weighs on me, like when someone punches you in the leg, only the sensation has spread to my entire body.

The moment I drop onto the kitchen sofa beside her, Zara tosses her magazine aside with obvious relief. "Everyone's abandoned me. How mean is that?"

"Good job you have me then, huh?" I attempt a smile; it feels more like a grimace.

Zara looks at me with concern. "How's your head?"

"Not too bad. I'll live." Probably. I might go around with an ache inside me for the rest of my life, but I won't die from it.

She slides her hand into mine, interlacing our fingers. It's a comforting gesture, reassuring. I don't pull away.

"Thanks for giving us another chance," she says.

I squeeze her hand. She has no idea how close I came yesterday to dashing her hopes once and for all, putting an end to this whole charade. If not for Theo... I thrust the thought away.

"I've been impossible to be around," she adds, "I know that, but I really care about you, Luke. I want this to work."

"I know you do." It's the most I can offer her. If I could only have fallen for Zara, how much simpler my life would be.

She kisses me, her mouth soft and tentative, then draws back with a smile. "Want to play Twenty-One?"

"Sure." I reach for the cards on the coffee table. Anything to pass the time between now and forever.

After winning fourteen games in a row, Zara flings down her cards. "This is no fun. You're not even trying."

"Sorry. Guess my brain isn't up to it." I push myself to my feet. "I'm going to make a cup of tea. Want one?"

"Go on then. Oh, and can you pass me the rest of my fudge? I left it on the worktop somewhere."

I unearth it half hidden behind the toaster. The sight of the small paper bag rams me harder than any tackle I've suffered on the field. All at once I'm remembering that morning in Theo's room, the softness in his eyes when he said he had a present for me, the way he'd licked the fudge from his lips.

"Luke?" Zara prods.

"Here." I snatch up the bag and toss it onto her lap, careful to keep my face averted.

I'm filling the kettle at the sink when the doorbell chimes. I exchange a look with Zara, her expression revealing my own confusion.

"That can't be them already," she says, "but who else?"

"Only one way to find out." I put the kettle on to boil and head into the hall where I pull open the front door.

A young man, maybe mid-twenties, blinks at me through the rain. He offers me a cautious smile. "Hello there."

"Hi?" It comes out sounding like a question. Arms folded, I regard him.

The stranger rakes me with eyes that are the most brilliant turquoise I've ever seen. Even with his dark hair plastered to his forehead, he's striking. "And you are…?"

He's half a head shorter than me and slight to the point of fragility. Still, some protectiveness has me shifting to block the doorway. "I could ask you the same thing."

But, of course, I already know. There's a weird inevitability about it, Him turning up here, today of all days.

"How rude of me." He holds out his hand, smile growing apologetic. "I'm Francis, Theo's ex. May I come in? I need to see him."

Chapter Fourteen

"Sorry to gatecrash like this." Francis settles in an armchair by the kitchen fire, slender legs crossed, elegant hands curled around a steaming mug.

I let him in. What else could I have done? OK, I could've told him to get lost, told him Theo would rather eat rotting sea urchins than spend a single second with him, and slammed the door in his lovely face. I was tempted. Fuck, every instinct screamed at me to do it, to send Francis packing once and for all. It would have been the easiest thing in the world, and Theo would be none the wiser.

But I had no right. The decision as to whether or not to see Francis rests with Theo, and Theo alone. So I let him in.

Fists aching from the urge to knock him flat onto the driveway, I'd moved aside and led Francis along to the kitchen. I even made the bastard a cup of tea. No one can say I haven't been brought up properly. Not that Francis needed me to show him where to go. It was painfully obvious he knew his way around just fine. Handy for Theo having this place, the perfect romantic getaway.

"What're you doing here?" Zara asks now. She regards him through narrowed eyes, although her initial shock has worn off, helped along, it seems to me, by his display of concern over her injury.

Francis looks between us, his gaze direct. "I have to see Theo. This has gone on long enough."

"You really hurt him," Zara says. "I mean, really hurt him. He was in pieces."

"You think I don't know that? You think I haven't spent every second of every day since we broke up wondering how to put things right?" He leans forward, pleading for understanding.

I study him from my perch on the corner of the kitchen table, searching for any sign that he's playing us. Nothing. As far as I can tell, his regret is genuine.

"What happened?" Zara's tone softens. "Theo won't talk about it."

Francis examines the contents of his mug. "Perhaps I shouldn't say, not if Theo hasn't. It was all so stupid, a misunderstanding that got out of hand. I would never have set out to hurt him, I swear." His voice cracks.

"We believe you," Zara reaches out to touch his arm, "but how come you've waited so long? If it was a misunderstanding, you need to sort it out."

"I tried, of course I did. Phone calls, texts... I even wrote Theo a letter. Anything to get him to hear me out. I went to Oxford several times. If I could just see him face-to-face, I knew we might have a chance. But Giles and Meredith were like bodyguards, wouldn't let me near him. No way I was giving up that easily, though."

"How did you know he was here?"

"I went to his house. His dad didn't exactly invite me in for a cup of tea, but he told me where to find Theo, and that was all I cared about." Francis lifts his head, expression earnest. "Is there any hope he'll see me? Any at all?"

Zara pats his arm. "I'm sure he will. He's been miserable these past couple of months. It's obvious he still cares about you. Right, Luke?"

I flinch. *What're you asking me for?* I want to fling at her. *You're the one who's known him all your life. I'm just his plaything, a distraction to amuse him over the summer. How should I know how he feels? I thought I did, but I don't.* I stare down at my hands, balled into fists on my thighs.

"I dunno. Maybe." The admission clogs like wet sand in my throat.

There's a pause. I glance up to find Francis surveying me, his expression curious, assessing. After a moment, his shoulders relax.

"Thanks for saying that." He directs his smile at Zara, before turning it on me. "And thanks for not leaving me out in the rain."

"Everything will work out," Zara assures him. "You'll see."

I say nothing. My face feels stiff, a clay mask that will crumble to dust if I so much as twitch a muscle. Does Francis have any idea how much I wish I'd left him on the doorstep? From the appraising look he gave me, I'd wager he does, or at least suspects.

Confident now that Theo won't turf him from the cottage on sight, Francis falls into easy conversation with Zara. He asks her about school, and has her in stitches over the antics of Lord What's-his-name of Wherever, who, if half of what Francis says is true, belongs on a psychiatric ward. Every so often, his gaze rests on me with that mixture of curiosity and puzzlement. It's as if I'm a piece of contemporary art, fascinating but indecipherable.

And I can't take my eyes off him. Even while despising him, despising myself, I find it impossible to tear my gaze away. It isn't just that he's incredible to look at, although that's part of it. What he has is less tangible than beauty.

It's in the deceptive languor that barely conceals a vibrant energy, the rich expressiveness of his voice, the way his face comes alive when he laughs. I hate him, hate him for being what Theo wants, and yet he's more mesmerising than anyone I've ever met.

No wonder Theo's hooked on him. I never stood a chance, not really. This time with Theo, the spark I'd been so sure was beginning to catch and grow into something bright, unstoppable, was all for nothing.

The front door slams.

My head snaps up at once. Zara breaks off mid-sentence and her gaze connects with mine, anxious and a little afraid. Francis pushes himself to his feet, body rippling with tension. Our eyes converge on the doorway.

Theo appears first, a carrier bag in each hand. When he sees me propped against the table, he hesitates, biting his lip. Though he's pale and drawn, he offers me an awkward smile. I should say something, anything, to warn him.

But it's too late.

Theo turns, searching for Zara, and looks straight at Francis. If I hadn't seen it, I wouldn't have believed it possible for him to get any paler, but he does. It's like watching a vampire suck every last drop of blood from his face. The carrier bags slip from his fingers, thudding to the floor with the clang of glass on glass. Theo doesn't seem to notice. He simply stares at his ex, features blank with shock.

Francis opens his mouth, but before he can speak, Giles materialises in the doorway with Meredith at his shoulder.

"Theo, what's up with you today? That's my wine you're..." Spying our visitor, his face hardens. "What the fuck are you doing here?"

Francis arches an eyebrow. "Ah, the faithful guard dogs."

"Get out." I thought Giles hated me, but the icy loathing in his voice as he addresses Theo's ex is something else altogether.

Francis only shrugs. "I'm going nowhere. Not until I've talked to Theo."

"That's where you're wrong, Buster. Either you walk out of here on your own, or I throw you out. It's up to you."

"What? So you own this place now? Face it, Giles. You're not throwing me anywhere."

"Watch me." Giles glares, moving to stand shoulder-to-shoulder with Theo.

A grim smile pulls at my mouth. Forget all the shit he's given me this summer. Right now, I could kiss him. Meredith, hovering in the doorway with a bulging carrier bag, snags my eye as if to say, "See? Not so bad, is he?"

Francis extends his palms in a conciliatory gesture. "Look, I'm not here to make trouble. I just want to talk to Theo."

"And what if Theo doesn't want to talk to you?"

"Then I'll go and never bother you again, but I need to hear it from him. I have to be sure this is what he wants. You can't make that decision for him, Giles. Does he even know I came to Oxford, that you and Meredith refused to let me see him?"

This gets a reaction. Theo shoots Giles a startled look, but then his gaze returns to Francis, an insect drawn to a Venus fly trap.

"You didn't tell him." For the first time, Francis sounds angry. "You had no right to keep that from him, either of you."

Giles explodes. "We had every right. Do you have any idea what you did to Theo? You destroyed him, and if you think we were just going to let you come crawling back so you could hurt him all over again—"

Theo lays a hand on his friend's shoulder. "It's OK, I'll handle this." He meets Francis's gaze head-on. "Why are you here, really?"

"To see you." Francis stares into Theo's eyes and it's like he's transmitting his very soul across the space between them. "Can we talk, in private?"

Theo hesitates, but only for a second. There's no standing up to a look like that. "Fine. You have five minutes."

He pivots and makes for the door, Meredith stepping aside to let him pass. I turn away. I can't stop Theo from going, but that doesn't mean I have to watch. Francis hurls a triumphant smirk at Giles, and then he's gone.

The door has barely shut behind him when Giles erupts. "What the fuck is Theo playing at? He should have let me chuck the bastard out in the rain."

"That's not fair," Zara says. "Francis drove all this way just to talk to Theo, and he did seem genuinely sorry."

"Oh, that's all right then. So what if he messed Theo up for months? None of it matters so long as he's sorry."

"Giles, don't you dare act like I don't care about Theo. I care about him every bit as much as you do."

"Really? You have a funny way of showing it."

Zara tries to push herself off the sofa, but winces when she puts weight on her injured foot. She subsides onto the cushions with a glower. Meredith rolls her eyes and carries her shopping over to the worktop, where she begins unpacking it in her quiet, methodical way.

Giles starts to pace. The squeak of his trainers and the periodic banging of cupboard doors filter through to me, distant, insignificant, like the sounds you hear when you're half asleep. My mind is elsewhere, with Theo and Francis, wherever they are. I can visualise them, alone together, Francis on his knees, face rent with regret and pain. And Theo will forgive him. How can he not? He'll look at Francis with that softness, the softness I've come to think of as mine. Then he'll kneel down in front of him, take Francis in his arms, and…

"And you." Giles gets in my face, arms folded across his chest. "What exactly were you thinking?"

I blink, attempting to clear my head. "Huh?"

"You, letting him in like that. The moment you knew who he was, you should've told him to drive off the nearest cliff."

For once, we're in complete agreement, although I'd rather saw off my own balls with a breadknife than admit it. "Maybe I thought Theo should have the chance to decide for himself. You ever consider that?"

"Oh, but I was forgetting." Giles's lip curls in a sneer. "You've known Theo for all of a few weeks and you're already an expert."

"Right, whereas you know everything about him? That's bullshit. He hasn't even told you what happened between him and Francis, and you still think you have the right to dictate his life? You have no idea what went on."

"No, but I saw what it did to him, and unlike everyone else here, I actually care enough never to want to see him hurt like that again."

My fist comes up. I pull it back and prepare to swing, to land Giles one right on the jaw.

Meredith forces her way between us. "Giles, stop it. You're not the only one here who cares about Theo. Plus, Luke does have a point."

"Yeah, I should've known you'd take his side. So you think we should just let Francis come swanning back in and break Theo all over again?"

"You don't know that's what will happen. He might be truly sorry, like Zara said, and," Meredith casts me a glance that's full of apology, "if Theo's still in love with him, don't you think we should give him the space to try and work things out?"

Giles scowls around at the three of us, but he's outnumbered. His shoulders sag, and he expels his breath in a long sigh. "I don't trust him, that's all."

Meredith says something commiserating, but I'm in no mood to listen. I've heard as much as I can take. I push off the table and make for the exit.

"Where're you going?" Giles asks. There's a trace of something that could be regret in his tone.

I ignore him, yanking open the kitchen door, and escape into the hallway. No one comes after me. I'm grateful for that. At the foot of the stairs, I lean my pounding forehead against the cool paintwork of the wall and close my eyes, taking refuge in the quiet darkness behind my eyelids. If I've been through a shittier day than this, I can't remember.

I don't mean to eavesdrop, that's the God honest truth. I only intend to pause for a moment, to collect myself before slipping up to my room and my iPod, where I'll be able to blast my eardrums with Lamb of God's *Ashes of the Wake* until I forget my own name.

But the door to the dining room is half open, and Francis's voice, raw with passionate intensity, drifts out to where I'm standing just outside. "It's the only thing that makes sense, Theo, we both know it."

I freeze, the air stuck in my throat, waiting. Theo says nothing. Gripped by some sadistic urge to torture myself, I edge nearer the door.

When Dean and I were about eight, we slipped upstairs to his parents' bedroom while they were preoccupied decorating the lounge, and unearthed the forbidden DVD of *28 Days Later*. We watched it on Dean's ancient fourteen-inch telly, both of us glued to the edge of the bed, rigid with fear at the horror unfolding. I wanted to pull a pillow over my head, to crawl under the duvet and hide, but pride stopped me. I wouldn't be the first to crack. That's how it is now. I know I won't like what I'm about to see, and yet I have to look.

Theo has his back to the window, so I can't make out his expression. Mere hours earlier, I'd stood in that very spot, confronting him, pouring every poisonous drop of frustration and spite into the void that separated us. Now, as I watch, transfixed, Francis steps closer, captures Theo's face between his palms, and kisses him.

Theo doesn't move, not right away. It's as though Francis's touch has turned him to stone. Then, in slow motion, like a statue come to life after an eternity, unable quite to believe his luck, he reaches up and lays his hands on his ex's shoulders.

It shouldn't be a shock. Deep down, the moment I found Francis waiting on the doorstep, I knew how this would play out. Still, it is. Seeing Theo with Francis, witnessing with my own eyes what everyone has been telling me all along... He may as well have set a sword on fire and plunged the white-hot blade into my gut.

A gasp hitches in my throat. It's barely a sound, a sharp intake of breath, like when someone barges you in the school corridor, but it's enough. Theo shoves Francis away with a force that sends him stumbling backwards. Francis steadies himself against the table and turns to study me. Though his mouth quirks in evident amusement, his eyes are slits of ice.

"Zara's boyfriend, huh?" He raises his eyebrows at Theo, before returning his attention to me. "Is there a problem?"

"No problem." My voice comes out flat and faraway. I look past Francis, straight into Theo's anguished face. "I just wanted to know you were all right, but I can see you are."

"Luke," Theo takes a pace towards me, hands outstretched, "it isn't—"

I turn and flee. Theo calls after me, but he can have nothing to say that I want to hear. Without pausing to think, I wrench open the front door and spill out into the storm. Drops the size of bullets pelt my cheeks, the bare skin of my arms. In an instant, I'm drenched, my jeans and T-shirt clinging to me like cellophane. It doesn't matter. I would've braved an Arctic blizzard, anything to escape Francis's smirk and the crushing weight of Theo's guilt, the depth of his betrayal.

Clouds, thick and black, race each other across the sky, taking the last of the daylight with them. I break into a jog, head bent, hands clenched against the pain, and skirt the edge of the cottage. When I round the corner, a shadowy form looms out at me from the gloom of the undercover patio. I stumble to a halt. My heart vaults into my chest. Then the shape solidifies into something unthreatening, familiar. My surfboard. I let out a sigh of relief. It's like glimpsing a friend in a crowd of hostile strangers.

I don't stop to think. I yank open the board bag's zipper and pull out my board. Slick with rain, my hands fumble with the fins, but I work fast. Any hesitation and my common sense will butt in, inform me what I'm about to do is crazy. I can't allow it, can't afford to. This is the one thing that has the power to help me forget.

I hoist the Spitfire onto my shoulders and run, the souls of my trainers slipping on the sodden grass. When I enter the woods, I slow down, but only a fraction. More than once, my foot connects with an exposed root and I almost go down. Dimly, I'm aware of my board bumping and scraping against bark. I'll regret this later, curse myself for my carelessness when I inspect the damage, but the alarm bells are a distant ringing in my ears.

The instant I lurch from the trees and onto the beach, the elements re-launch their assault. A fierce wind drives me backwards, hurling rain and clumps of wet sand into my face. I barely notice, oblivious to everything but the sea. A huge steel-grey vortex, indistinguishable from the swirling clouds above, it batters itself in a frenzy against the shore. The sheer force of it, the angry ferocity, unleashes a tendril of fear in my heart.

Don't stop. Don't think.

I drop my board to the sand and strip to my boxers. My clothes are too wet to offer any protection from the chill and will only drag me down. My mind flashes to the wetsuit I left back at the cottage. No time to worry about that now. Frigid pellets ping off my back and shoulders. I'm shivering, but scarcely feel the cold. I take a final look at the wall of water ahead of me, imagine riding it as though on the back of a blue whale. Then I hoist my board up once more and race to meet it.

The first wave hits, a thousand icy needles to my shins. The shock snags the air in my lungs. I grit my teeth and wade deeper. The sea is like a living thing. At every step, it tugs me this way and that, having its fun with me before swallowing me whole. The beginnings of panic gnaw at my stomach. I'll never make it. This is madness, far more advanced than anything I've ever attempted.

Quelling the voice of reason, I push forward. Once up to my waist in freezing water, I lower my board on to its heaving surface. Wave after wave crashes over me, threatening to tear the Spitfire from my grasp.

"No you bloody don't." Somehow, saying it out loud lends me strength. Jaw set, fingers clamped in a death grip on the edge of my board, I haul myself on and start to paddle.

It's like declaring war on the Atlantic. I battle through enemy lines, sometimes losing ground, but always ploughing onwards, ducking through wave after charging wave, the ocean determined to force me into retreat. My arms and legs scream with the effort. It takes all my resolve to keep going, not to give in. Through the pain and exhaustion, I imagine I hear someone shouting my name, but it's only the howling wind, the furious roar of the surf.

Finally, I'm through. Not that it's much calmer even out here. The swell dips and bucks beneath me, a thoroughbred intent on throwing off an inept rider. I lie flat against my board, heart thudding, muscles on fire, and try to catch my breath. What am I doing? I'm a strong surfer, but waves this big, this powerful, will test my skill to the limit. Moreover, if anything goes wrong, if I get into difficulty, I'm on my own.

Mum's face, serious and trusting as it had been the night before I left for Cornwall, wavers in front of my eyes. "Never, ever go out on your board without someone being close by. Promise me."

And I promised. Guilt crushes my ribcage. I promised, and now I'm about to break my word in the worst possible way.

I could always cheat, take the easy way out and ride the waves on my belly. It would be the safe thing to do, the sensible thing. It isn't as if I'm trying to impress anyone. Besides, no one will ever know.

I've made up my mind to dispense with the heroics when I glance up and see the wave rushing towards me. Fear rips a gasp from my mouth. A triple header, easily three times my height, the barrage of water advances on me with frightening speed. Adrenaline surges through me. Instinct takes over. My body moves into position, every muscle tensed. I didn't come out here to be carried to shore like a novice. I doubt I'll have the nerve to tackle anything this foolhardy again, and I'm going to ride it like a pro.

I wait, senses alert, every grain of concentration fixed on the waterfall hurtling closer. Before I'm expecting it, before I'm ready, it's there, looming above me, blotting out the sky. I tense, nerve endings tingling in anticipation. Wait… Wait… Wait… Now!

The wave shifts underneath me and I move into action, launching myself to my feet in the single fluid motion that is second nature to me.

The moment I'm up, I know I'm in trouble. I've timed it all wrong, taken off too early. The growing darkness, the roiling sea, my own muddled brain have all conspired against me, skewing my judgement. Worse still, there's nothing I can do to stop what's about to happen.

In the split second before impact, the horrible truth occurs to me. I've forgotten to attach my leash. I cry out, a scream of pure terror. With nothing to connect us, my board slides from under me. I hit the water just as the monstrous wave slams on top of me, punching the breath from my lungs and jarring every bone in my body. I struggle, gag on a gallon of salt water. The riptide is too strong. I reach for the surface, grabbing for my board, a piece of driftwood, anything to cling on to, but my fist closes on emptiness. Then the current has me in its clutches, greedy, uncaring, and is dragging me down...down...down...

Chapter Fifteen

Water. Water all around me. It presses in on my eyeballs, forces its way into my nose and between my lips. I can't breathe, can't see. I'm trapped in a world of impenetrable grey. Waves pummel me, shaking me like a ragdoll, until I don't know which direction is up. I battle for control, stretching for the surface, but for all I know, I'm merely diving deeper.

So this is it. This is how it ends. I'm going to drown. The realisation weighs on me, pulling me down. Panic constricts my chest, and a few precious air bubbles escape into the watery depths. I'm going to drown, right here, right now, and it's entirely my own fault. My body goes limp. I'm too exhausted to fight, the current too strong. I simply lie back in the swell and let it carry me where it will.

At least Giles will derive some satisfaction when they find my bloated body washed up on the beach. I imagine my funeral—Zara's tear-streaked face, Meredith's sadness, Mum's disappointment that I'd broken my promise, her unendurable grief at losing someone she loves for the second time. And Theo, will he attend my funeral? Will he feel bad about my death? I hope he will. I hope he lugs a sack load of guilt around with him for the rest of his privileged life. My heart hurts, though whether from the lack of oxygen or the ache of loss I'm not sure.

Steel bands fasten on my upper arms, yanking me upwards. A moment later, my head breaks the surface and

I'm gasping for breath, retching and spitting as I try to suck air into my starved lungs. All the while the hands keep their painful grip on my biceps, steadying me in the heaving swell.

The tightness around my chest eases, and I blink the water from my vision. Theo's face swims into focus, less than a foot from mine. He looks odd in the gathering darkness, unlike himself, his eyes stony and devoid of warmth.

"Come on." His voice matches the hardness in his expression. "Let's get you out of here."

Theo begins to haul me towards the shore, but I resist, scanning our surroundings in a daze. "My board. Have to find it."

"Forget the fucking board. You want to kill us both?"

His uncharacteristic harshness stuns me into submission. Not that I have the energy to argue, even if I wanted to. I let him take command, his skill and strength evident as he guides us through the surf, one hand supporting my chin to keep me afloat.

The wave I attempted to catch must have brought me farther inland than I thought. After only a few strokes, the comforting solidity of the seabed grazes my toes. We wade the rest of the way, although Theo maintains a firm hold on my arm, probably worried I'll do something stupid like go back for my board.

My board. The miraculous Spitfire I'd saved up for years to buy, and which has given me the best rides of my life. I threw it away, flung it like a piece of rubbish into the sea to be dashed to bits on the rocks. The loss of it stabs at me like a stitch in my side.

By the time we stagger onto dry land, I've recovered enough to try and wrench myself free of Theo's grasp.

He's too quick for me. He shoves me away and I fall hard, all the wind knocked out of me.

Before I can scramble up again, he towers over me, hair plastered to his head and his features contorted with anger. He's fully clothed apart from his trainers, and water streams from his clothes to join the rain pooling on the sand. The sight of him would strike terror into Moby Dick himself.

"What the fuck were you playing at? Are you out of your mind?"

I open my mouth to defend myself—no idea how—but Theo seizes my shoulders and shakes me so violently my head whips back and forth.

"Christ, Luke, do you have some kind of death wish? Is that what this little stunt was about? Thought you'd make a bold gesture and drown yourself like the Lady of fucking Shalott?"

I stare at him. Weakness spreads through me, making me light-headed. I put out a hand to steady myself. I could have drowned. But for Theo, I might be at the bottom of the Atlantic by now, my swollen corpse bumping along the seabed.

He glares at me without pity, fingers biting into my shoulders. "Well, what am I supposed to think? I mean, either this was some pathetic suicide attempt, or you're just a complete idiot. Did you even stop to think how I'd feel when I saw your board gone? If I hadn't come out after you, if I'd been just a minute later... Jesus!"

The furious mask disintegrates. He collapses to his knees and tries to put his arms around me. That single movement shatters the last of my numbness. All the turmoil of the past few hours—the hurt, the anger, the utter humiliation—comes flooding back, galvanising me.

"Don't." I scramble up, backing away from him. "Don't you dare."

"Luke." Theo pushes himself to his feet and reaches for me.

The empathy in his expression is more than I can stand. I shove his hand aside. "I said don't. I don't need your pity, OK?"

"Luke, will you just—?"

"It's all right, Theo, I get it. You don't have to explain. You've done your bit, saving my life and everything, so you don't have to feel bad. Now you can go back to Francis like you obviously want to."

We regard one another through the rain, water trickling down our cheeks like tears. Wind and spray lash my bare skin. I shiver, standing there in only my boxers, and hug my arms to my chest.

"He's gone, you know," Theo says. "Francis. I left Giles to see to it while I came after you."

I shrug. "You didn't have to do that on my account. I'll be out of your way first thing tomorrow."

"I wish you'd stay."

"So that I can watch you snogging Francis at every opportunity? Tempting offer, but I think I'll pass."

"Francis kissed me. It isn't the same thing."

"That's not how it looked to me. You had your hands on his shoulders, Theo. I saw you."

"Then you also saw me push him away. Or did you miss that part?"

"You only pushed him because you knew I'd seen." I brush the rain from my eyes. "Stop playing with me. I know you're still in love with Francis. Everyone warned me. I just didn't want to listen."

"Who's everyone when they're at home?"

"Giles, Meredith, Zara."

"Great." Theo shakes his head. "So my friends are telepathic now? You didn't think to ask me how I felt?"

"That's so not fair. I kept asking about Francis. I asked over and over, but you were too busy feeling heartbroken to tell me the truth."

"Luke."

"Of course, it would've been nice to have a heads up, to know I never even stood a chance."

"Luke, shut up."

I glare at him, too mad to heed the dangerous flatness in his tone. "Still, never mind. Don't you go worrying about me. I'm sure I'll get over it. At least you don't have to pretend anymore. You're free to go off with lover boy like you obviously wanted to all—"

"Shut up, all right? Just shut up."

For the second time that evening, Theo succeeds in stunning me into silence. I scowl at him, resentment churning like the surf inside me.

"You want to know why I don't talk about Francis?" His every syllable is raw with pain. "Because I hate him, that's why. He made me fall for him, then betrayed me in the worst way he could. And you think I'd let him kiss me after that? I'd rather gouge out my eyeballs with a skewer than let him lay so much as a finger on me. So now you know. Satisfied?"

His voice fractures. Theo turns, walking a short way along the beach. He stands with his back to me, shoulders rigid, and stares at the waves prostrating themselves at his feet.

I remain where I am. With his outburst, it's as though Theo has sliced open a festering wound. All the toxic emotions—the rage and jealousy, the suspicion and self-doubt—drain away like poison.

I give him a minute before approaching, my tread heavy with shame. "Theo, I'm sorry. I didn't know."

"Of course you didn't. How could you?" He turns to me, tenderness softening the haunted look in his eyes, and holds out a hand.

I go to him. Theo puts his arms around me, hugging me so hard it traps the air in my chest.

"Thought I'd lost you back there," he says in my ear. "Ever give me another scare like that and I'll kill you."

I let out a shaky laugh and lay my cheek on his shoulder. His sodden T-shirt chills me where it rests against my skin, but nothing can prevent the warmth that flares inside me at his closeness.

"What did he do to you?" I ask, my face buried in his neck.

He rubs my back. "Not now. We need to find your clothes. I didn't save you from drowning only to have you end up with pneumonia."

I raise my head to study his expression. He has a point. Even with our bodies pressed together, our teeth are chattering. Still, I can't suppress the suspicion that he's fobbing me off.

Theo smiles and cups the nape of my neck. When he kisses me, his lips are soft and surprisingly warm.

"Later," He says against my mouth, "I promise."

***

The moment we stumble into the kitchen, shivering and dripping wet, the others converge on us, Zara with the aid of her crutches, and demand to know where we've been. I invent a lie about seeing the enormous waves from my bedroom window and deciding to try and ride them, careful to tone down the part about me almost drowning. It all sounds pretty lame to me, but Giles and Zara, although incredulous that anyone could be so stupid, accept it without question. Meredith, knowing exactly what had driven me to it, rolls her eyes in exasperation.

"But your board." Zara gives me a one-armed hug, heedless of my drenched clothes. "I'm so sorry, Luke."

Giles shakes his head. It's obvious what he's thinking, that I have no one to blame but myself, and he's right. For once, however, he chooses to keep his opinion to himself.

After showering and changing into dry clothes, Theo and I return to the kitchen where someone has lit the fire. Meredith ushers us onto the sofa either side of Zara and presses mugs of hot chocolate into our hands. It doesn't take long for the conversation to turn to Francis.

"I really messed up." Zara sniffs, blinking back tears. "I should never have let him through the door."

Giles shoots me a pointed look. "If I remember rightly, someone else was responsible for that particular screw-up."

"Cut it out, Giles," Theo says. "Luke wasn't to know. None of you were. If this is anyone's fault, it's mine."

Zara bites her lip. "But I shouldn't have trusted him. He spun me this sob story and I just lapped it up."

"Zara," Theo puts an arm around her, "you're hardly the first person to fall for Francis's charm. I'm living proof of that."

Bitterness creeps into his voice. We're quiet for a while, the silence broken only by the crackle and pop of the flames.

"So," Giles says at last, "you going to tell us now?"

Theo nods, playing with a strand of Zara's hair. "You have a right to know after so bravely defending my honour. You all do. Mind if we leave it till tomorrow, though? I'm done in."

He catches my eye over Zara's head, communicating without words. I get it. He doesn't want to tell the others, not until he's talked to me. I give him a swift smile, then turn to stare into the fire before anyone can see how touched I am.

**

Much later, I'm on my way downstairs to fetch Zara's painkillers when Meredith calls out to me. I pause in the doorway of her room. "What's up?"

Meredith's perched on the foot of the bed in her sleeveless pyjamas, unwinding her hair from its plait. She glances over at me, then down at her lap. "I owe you an apology."

"Why?" I grin. "What've you done?"

She doesn't return my smile. Retrieving her hairbrush from the chest of drawers, she turns it over in her hands. "About what happened earlier with your board, I feel sort of responsible."

"Brilliant! I had no idea my stupidity was your fault. That's a real weight off my mind."

"Luke, I'm serious. I shouldn't have implied Theo was still in love with Francis. I was only saying what I believed to be true, but, well, I know it can't have helped. I just keep going over it in my mind, what could've happened if Theo hadn't gone out after you—"

"But he did." I cut her off before she can give voice to the thought. It isn't something I want to dwell on. I lean against the doorframe, hands in the pockets of my hoody. "Forget about it, OK? I certainly intend to. Can't have a black spot like that tarnishing my glittering surfing career, can I?"

This time, Meredith's mouth twitches in a reluctant smile. She begins sweeping the brush through her hair in long, rhythmic strokes.

"Anyway," I add, "I'll be gone soon, so you won't have to worry about my knack for making an idiot of myself anymore."

"You're going to tell Zara?"

"Yeah. Can't put it off forever."

Meredith nods. The brush snags on a tangle and she tugs it free. "Giles and me too. We're flying out the day after tomorrow to spend the rest of the summer with his parents at their villa in Tuscany."

I look at her in surprise. "All right for some. When did you decide this?"

"Earlier, while Theo was out searching for you. Things have been strained between us, as you've noticed. Giles thinks a change of scene will do us good."

"That has to be a positive sign, right? He must want to make this work."

"Yes," Meredith's expression softens, "I really think he does." She replaces her hairbrush on the chest of drawers and glances at me. "How about you? Any plans for the rest of your summer?"

"Not really. It'll be nice to hang out with the lads. Of course, we don't all have boyfriends with handy villas in Tuscany." I grin to show I'm kidding.

Her eyes gleam with amusement. "I'd invite you, only..."

"Yeah, I can just imagine how well that would go down," I say, and Meredith laughs.

"Excuse me."

I hadn't heard Giles approach. I turn to find him right behind me, arms folded, features a concrete mask. With a shrug, I step back from the threshold, allowing him to shove past me into the room. Before I can say goodnight to Meredith, he shuts the door in my face with a decisive click.

I roll my eyes and continue downstairs. Theo is alone in the kitchen, seated in the armchair by the fire. When I come in, he raises his head from the pad he has open on his knees and darts me a quizzical smile.

"Zara forgot her painkillers." I retrieve them from the worktop and fill a glass from the tap. Leaving water and tablets on the draining board, I cross to perch on the arm of Theo's chair. "What've you got there?"

"Oh," he glances down, "just my doodles."

I hold out a hand. "Let me see?"

Theo passes me the sketchpad with an embarrassed smile and I leaf through the pages. The drawings are of the sea mostly—gentle surf tumbling onto sand, huge waves hurling themselves up rocky cliffs.

I raise an eyebrow. "Thought you said you weren't that good."

"No, I said I wasn't good enough to do it professionally."

"Whatever. They look bloody good to me." Even devoid of colour, the sea appears alive, every fleck of foam depicted in minute detail. When I trace the contour of a wave with my fingertip, I'm half surprised it isn't wet to the touch.

I turn to the next page and stop. This one is of me, stretched out on a lounger in my swimming shorts. I have my arms hooked behind my head, and I'm staring up at the sky as though into another world. It's a strange sensation, seeing myself like this, through someone else's eyes. I study the drawing, transfixed by the full curve of my lower lip, the dark hair trailing down my stomach and under the waistband of my shorts, all picked out with the same painstaking care as the waves.

Heat floods my cheeks. "When did you do this?"

"A while ago." Theo toys with a hole in his jeans. "Can't remember exactly."

But I can. With sudden clarity, an image flashes into my mind, an image from the day I'd first taken Theo out on the board—me half dozing in the shade of the undercover patio, Theo hunched over the table, pencil flying over the paper in front of him. Lost in my haze of contentment, I was oblivious to his attention. Imagining his eyes on me, of him taking in every muscle, every curl of my eyelashes, makes me feel kind of jittery.

I rifle through the remaining pages, but they're blank. Maybe Theo didn't want to risk anyone stumbling across the drawing of me. Maybe it's simply that everything has been so crazy. Whatever the reason, that sketch is the last one.

Theo lays a hand on my leg, waiting until I look at him. He gives my thigh a gentle squeeze. "Zara's painkillers?"

"Oh, right." I place my hand over his, let it rest there for a moment. "I'll be down in a bit, OK?"

"OK." Theo removes the sketchpad from my grasp, his smile warm. "I'll be here."

***

"I really am sorry about your board." Zara hands me the empty glass and settles back against the pillows, her expression full of empathy in the lamplight. "I know how much you loved that thing, how long you had to save up for it."

"Yeah, well, it was my own stupid fault." I turn away to set the glass on the chest of drawers. Just thinking about my Spitfire produces a pang in my gut.

"Luke, are you coming to bed?"

"In a while. Still feel kind of wired."

"At least lie down with me for a bit. Please?" Zara pats the bed beside her.

All I want to do is return to Theo, but there's no holding out against the entreaty in her tone. A few minutes won't hurt; I can give her that much.

When I stretch out on top of the covers beside her, Zara nestles into my side, her head on my shoulder. "Still, thank God it was only your board. It could've been so much worse. If you'd actually tried to ride those waves—"

"Well, I didn't." With an effort, I manage not to snap. Exactly how near I came to ending up as fish food is a secret I'd rather keep between Theo, myself, and my nightmares.

Zara presses closer, kissing my neck, her hand trailing down my stomach towards the waistband of my jeans.

I stiffen and catch hold of her wrist. "Zara."

"What's wrong?" She scans my face, sounding hurt.

I take a deep breath. "Not now, OK?"

"But we haven't… Not for ages. Come on." She drops her voice to a throaty murmur, free hand toying with my zip. "You know you want to."

I flinch. Releasing my grip on her wrist, I inch towards the edge of the mattress. "I said not now, all right?"

"Fine!" She spits out the word before rolling away from me onto her back. "I don't get why you agreed to give us another go when it's obvious you can't bear to be near me." Her voice quivers, tears glistening on her lashes.

Shit. For a moment, I let my head fall against the solid wood of the headboard. Zara's upset again, because of me. I reach out to her, but she slaps my hand aside.

"Don't." She swipes at her eyes. "Go, Luke. Just…go."

I hesitate. It would be so simple to take the escape route she's offering, to leave her alone and go to Theo, waiting downstairs for me in the kitchen. But I can't. Confronted with her tears, the trembling set to her mouth, I can't leave things hanging between us any longer. She deserves an explanation.

"Luke?" Zara's glare challenges me to go, even while pleading with me to stay.

I take a deep breath and look at her properly for what feels like the first time in weeks. "This isn't working out, is it?"

She sniffs, focussing her attention on me. "What're you saying?"

So I tell her. Not about all of it—I don't mention my feelings for Theo, or the fact that we've been having a relationship in secret—but the part that relates to her and me. I try to be gentle, to make it clear how much I care about her, even if I don't love her the way she wants me to. In the end, though, I have to be truthful, something I should have done the moment Theo kissed me that morning by the pool.

I expect Zara to protest, break down, beg me to give us another chance. But she doesn't. She simply hears me out, occasionally batting away a silent tear as it trickles down her cheek. Her mute acceptance, so un-Zara-like, is proof that she understands.

"I'll go," I finish, "first thing tomorrow. Pack up my stuff and get out of your hair."

Zara nods, again without protest. If I don't leave soon, we'll end up killing each other. She knows it as well as I do.

"I'm sorry," I reach out to touch her hand, which is clenching and unclenching on the edge of the duvet, "really. If things could have been different…"

She casts me a wan smile. "I had such high hopes for this holiday. We were going to have the best time ever."

"And instead we've driven each other mad." I brush my thumb across her knuckles. "I've been a difficult sod, haven't I?"

"A bit, but it wasn't just you. I've been a stroppy cow."

"You? Never."

Zara raises an eyebrow at me. Her rueful grin mirrors mine. The awkwardness that has stretched taut between us since I realised my feelings for Theo melts away, replaced by a wistful sadness.

"So," Zara says, "with Giles and Meredith off to Tuscany, it'll just be Theo and me. Not that I mind. Maybe I can persuade Bianca and some of the other girls to come down. Ooh," Her eyes light up, "I'm pretty sure her brother's single at the moment. Olly would be just perfect for Theo."

I'm quiet. Her brave attempt to pick herself up, to salvage what remains of the summer, fills me with a mixture of affection and guilt. Once she discovers the truth, pool parties and match-making will be the last things on her mind.

"At least this hasn't been a complete disaster," Zara goes on. "I mean, you and Theo will keep in touch?"

"Expect so, yeah." I drop my gaze, willing myself not to blush.

"And you and me," Zara reaches over to squeeze my hand, "we can still be friends, can't we?"

I suppress a wince. She will insist on putting me in these situations, seeking assurances I'm in no position to give.

"I'd like that." I smile at her, hoping she can read the sincerity there. Of course, once she finds out how I've been going behind her back, the odds of her wanting anything whatsoever to do with me are around a zillion to one.

Chapter Sixteen

"I should've told you before." Theo runs his fingers through my hair. "I was so busy worrying about how I was feeling, I didn't stop to think how it might look to other people, to you."

I lean into him on the sofa. "It's all right. Tell me now."

Theo hesitates, staring into the fire. The flickering orange flames provide the sole illumination in the darkened kitchen. Quiet wraps the cottage in stillness, the sort of stillness that only exists at the dead of night when everyone else is asleep.

Finally, he says, "You already know how Francis and I met."

"At one of his exhibitions, right?"

"Right. I'd been a fan of his work ever since Mum bought one of his paintings. That was before he started making a name for himself. Mum had a real eye for spotting new talent, predicting which artists would make it big. Francis's was the last painting she bought. After that, she was too ill to go out to exhibitions. She still followed what was happening in the art world, though, right up until she died."

Theo breaks off, his expression tinged with sadness. I lay a hand on his leg, offering him what comfort I can.

He gives me a grateful smile. "So, I was already in awe of Francis as an artist, even before I met him. He has this gift for taking something completely ordinary, a park bench, say, and painting it in a way that's totally unique. I swear, I must have stared at his painting on our drawing-room wall, the one of a fallen oak, a thousand times, and still managed to find a detail I'd missed."

"You obviously thought he was something special." My words hold no resentment; I'm simply stating a fact.

"He's an amazing artist, no denying that." Theo's voice, which had grown animated while he described Francis's work, turns weary. "So, when a gallery in Oxford held an exhibition of Francis's paintings last October, the three of us—Giles, Meredith and I—went to check it out. At the time, I was only interested in seeing his work. I mean, I knew there was a chance Francis would be there, but I doubted I'd actually get to speak to him."

"But you did."

"Yeah. He came up behind me while I was admiring a watercolour of a riverbank, asked me what I thought. I was so star-struck I'm amazed I managed to string two words together. I can't remember what I said, but I must have made some kind of sense because he stayed and talked to me for ages."

I have no trouble imagining it—the eager student, all shyness and wide-eyed admiration, and Francis, with that silky charm and mesmerising blue gaze, drawing Theo in and refusing to let go.

"You saw how he is." Theo seems to read my mind. "He was so friendly, so interested in what I had to say, I couldn't help relaxing. Until he asked me out, that is. It's a miracle Giles and Meredith didn't have to pick me up off the floor. This incredible-looking guy, this artist I'd idolised since I was fourteen, wanted to take me for a drink. It was beyond belief."

"Funnily enough, I have no problem believing it." I smile, nudging my thigh against his.

"Shut up." Theo blushes, his expression losing some of its tension. He takes my hand. "Anyway, I won't bore you with all the details. He took me out for a drink after the exhibition, then to dinner the next night, and back to his place the night after that."

"Yeah, reckon I can fill in the blanks."

"Well, let's just say I fell hard for him. He was my first real boyfriend, I suppose. I'd had a couple of relationships at school, if you can call them that, desperate fumbles I was never allowed to talk about. This was the first time I could be completely open about it. Then there's the fact that Francis was my hero. This beautiful guy, the one I'd had a crush on for years, wanted to be with me. It was like a dream.

"Things got serious pretty fast. We had it all figured out. When I left Oxford, I'd open my gallery and Francis would show his paintings there to help me get it off the ground. I thought I had my future mapped out. Looking back, though, the whole thing was doomed from the start."

Theo's eyes take on that haunted look. I tighten my grip on his hand, feel the pressure when he squeezes back.

"The thing about Francis," he says, "is that he's kind of...wild. I don't know how else to put it. You'll find this hard to believe because he seems so confident, so sure of himself, but he's crippled with insecurity, at least where his painting's concerned. Maybe all artists are. It makes him difficult at times. Unpredictable. Oh, not violent, or anything, just wild. He does everything to excess— smoking, drinking, partying. Drugs too, for all I know, although he managed to hide that from me. Knew I'd disapprove, I suppose."

I try to match this new information with the cool young man I met earlier, try to picture him high on coke or throwing up in the gutter. My imagination fails me.

"Worst of all," Theo says, "at least when it came to things falling apart between us, he's a compulsive gambler, an addict. He had this group of friends he met with on Friday nights, his poker club, he called it. Other evenings, he played online. Francis tried to explain it to me more than once, could see it bothered me. For him, he said, there was nothing else like it. Nothing could compare to the buzz he got every time he scooped a big win, which was fine, only—"

"He didn't always win." I study Theo's face, shadowy in the firelight, stroking my thumb over his palm. I'm beginning to see where this is going. It isn't what I expected, and I don't like it one bit.

Theo sighs. "He used to ask me for money. It was just small amounts at first, and he always promised to repay me. Sometimes he did, but overall I gave him more than I got back. Soon he was asking to borrow higher and higher amounts. Dad gives me a generous allowance to live on while I'm at uni, but it got to the point where I was handing most of it over to Francis." Theo's eyes meet mine, his full of shame. "I should have said no. I was just so in awe of him, I couldn't refuse him anything. You must think I'm pathetic."

I shake my head, winding my fingers through his. "You're too decent for your own good, that's all."

"Thanks for that." Theo's mouth crooks in a wry smile. "Anyway, I had to say no eventually. I had nothing left to give him. Francis had already taken that month's allowance. I thought he was going to use it to pay off his debts. Instead, he put it all on a poker game in an effort to recoup his losses. If he'd won, he claimed, he could've cleared his debts and paid me back with interest."

"But he didn't." It isn't a question.

Theo huffs out a long breath. "He lost everything. The following morning, Francis came to me in pieces. He begged me for more money, said the guy who ran the poker club was getting nasty. This guy knew some pretty rough blokes, apparently, and was threatening to have them pay Francis a nighttime visit if he didn't cough up.

"Luke, I'd never seen him in such a state. He was terrified half to death. I would've helped him if I could, but he'd completely cleaned me out. I even phoned Dad to ask for an advance on next month's allowance, but he refused to speak to me."

"Why didn't Francis go to the police? I know he owed money, but that doesn't give anyone the right to threaten him."

"He was scared the papers would get hold of it. The alcohol and all-night parties are common knowledge, of course, but the press love that wildness about him, portray him as a lovable rogue. If they ever found out about the gambling, they'd rip him to shreds."

I frown. "I'm guessing he found a way to pay up, though. I mean, as far as I could see, all his limbs were intact."

"Oh, he found a way, all right." A coldness I haven't heard before hardens Theo's tone. "I was already trying to work out what I could sell to raise the money. As you might have noticed, I'm not interested in designer clothes or flash cars like Zara and Giles. I've always rather had books or art supplies than anything else."

I nod and finger the rip in the knee of his jeans, my smile warm. His total lack of materialism is one of the things I like most about him.

"Still," he says, "I do have a few odds and ends that are worth something—first editions of some of the classics, a watch my dad gave me for my eighteenth. Whether they would've fetched enough to get Francis out of trouble, I doubt it, but I was willing to do anything I could to help him. Well, almost anything." Theo winces. He stares into the fire, but as though seeing something else. "Thing is, I did have one piece that would easily have covered Francis's debts if I'd sold it. It also happened to be the one thing I would never part with."

A cold weight settles in the pit of my stomach. It's as if my subconscious knows what's coming, even if my brain hasn't caught on.

Theo grips my hand so tightly it hurts. "You asked me once whether Mum gave me anything of hers before she died."

"And you told me all her stuff had gone." Again, something about his choice of words strikes me as off.

"It has…now, but she did leave me something. I told you about her art collection, that she had several old masters. My favourite was a Stubbs of a grey mare. She reminded me of Epona, my first pony. Mum knew I'd always loved that painting, and a few days before she died, she said it was mine. If she'd predicted Dad would have a total breakdown and get rid of everything, maybe she would've signed the whole lot over to me. I don't know. All I know is that the Stubbs was the only thing of hers I had, apart from the photo." Theo meets my gaze. "Francis knew about the painting, of course. I kept it locked in a safe at the flat Giles and I share in Oxford, but I showed it to him several times. He was perfectly aware what it was worth. When he got into so much debt, he begged me to sell it."

"Let me get this straight." My voice is deadly calm. "He asked you to sell the painting your Mum left you so he could pay back the money he'd lost playing poker?"

"He wasn't thinking that rationally, to be honest. Francis was literally in fear for his life, half expecting heavies armed with crowbars to bang on the door at any moment. I'm not defending him, Luke," Theo adds when I start to protest. "I'm just telling it like it was. Anyway, I refused."

"How did he take it?"

"Badly. That was the first time we really fought. I accused him of using me for my money. He accused me of not loving him enough, of caring more about a piece of canvas than I did about him."

Anger seeps through the cracks in my composure. "That's emotional blackmail, Theo. He had no right."

"I know that now." he massages his forehead. "After he stormed out, I spent the whole night wondering whether he might have a point, whether I was being selfish, putting a painting before Francis's life. I hardly slept and couldn't concentrate on my lectures next day. When I went back to the flat that afternoon, I unlocked the safe, planning to take out the Stubbs. I often did that, just sat for a while and looked at it when I needed to think. Made me feel closer to Mum, I suppose. This time, I hoped it might help me figure out the best thing to do. Only..." Theo trails off, unable to find the words. It doesn't matter; the enormity of Francis's betrayal is etched on his face.

"No." I shake my head, more in disbelief than denial. "Please tell me he didn't. No one could sink that low."

Theo drops his gaze. "I knew straight away it was him. Even if we hadn't just argued about it, Francis was the only one who knew the code for the safe. Not hard, considering it was his date of birth. Ironic, really."

"And you let him get away with it?" I wrench my hand from his, rage propelling me to my feet. "He stole—yes, stole—the most valuable thing you own, and you just let him do it? Fucking hell."

"Keep your voice down." Theo casts a nervous glance towards the closed door. He looks up at me, expression resigned. "What could I have done, Luke? Think about it. Francis was my boyfriend. He knew the code for the safe. For all the police would be able to tell, I'd given him the painting, then demanded it back after we fell out. I had no proof. Besides, I kind of blamed myself."

If Francis were to walk through the door right now, I'd kick the shit out of him until the bastard wished the heavies had got to him first. I settle for flopping back onto the sofa and pulling Theo into a hug, my voice fierce against his neck. "It wasn't your fault."

"Wasn't it?" Theo settles into me, touches his forehead to mine. "He's an addict, Luke, and all I did was feed his addiction by giving him money. I should've done more, got him professional help."

"It wasn't your fault." I tighten my arms around him. I don't care how many times I have to say it. I'll go on saying it until he believes me. "And we'll get your painting back, whatever it takes."

"I don't think there's much chance of that. With his connections in the art world, Francis would've known just how to get rid of it without leaving a trace."

"Valuable paintings don't just vanish into thin air, Theo. It's out there somewhere, and we'll find it."

Theo's eyes lock with mine. He swallows. "Thanks, Luke."

"What for?"

"For being here, and listening to me run on. For not calling me a gullible idiot, even though I deserve it."

My laugh gets tangled up in my throat. I shift onto his lap, kneeling astride him, and press my lips to his. The kiss is deep, probing, and expresses my feelings far better than any words could.

Theo draws away slightly. He cradles my face, thumbs tracing my cheekbones. "Won't Zara wonder where you are?"

"No. I told her. Not about us," I clarify when his eyes widen, "but she knows it's over."

"How did she take it?"

"All right. Better than I expected, anyway. I think she knew it was coming."

"Poor Zara." Theo strokes my back. "You'll be going home then?"

"Said I'd pack up my stuff tomorrow. Today, I suppose."

"Where does she think you are now?"

"Spare room." I flash him my come-and-get-it grin. "Can I stay with you tonight?"

Theo gulps. "I'm not sure that's the best idea. If we get caught—"

"We'll be careful." I lean in, teasing his lips with mine. "Please?"

Theo's moan is half surrender, half entreaty. His hands trail down my spine, settling on my hips. Even through my jeans, heat darts to my groin at the contact. This time the kiss is hard, bruising. Theo's tongue fills my mouth, devouring me, his touch urgent on the inside of my thighs. I grind into him, sucking on his tongue, greedy, wanting.

With a groan, Theo nudges me backwards. We tumble onto the rug, pulling our T-shirts off over our heads. We fall on each other, skin sliding against skin, our hands and mouths everywhere, breath coming quick and harsh.

Theo nibbles a path along my collarbone; the gentle graze of his teeth sends desire rippling through my whole body. I thrust against him, the friction almost painful. I'm hot all over, burning up. Any second, I'll either burst into flames or shatter into a million red-hot fragments. Fingers clumsy with haste, Theo fumbles with my zip, tugging my jeans down over my hips, while I work to free him of his. When his erection rubs against mine, Theo kisses me again, swallowing my cry of pleasure, expelling his into my mouth.

My brain shuffles into the passenger seat, giving my body control of the wheel, letting it go where it wants. In a single movement, I roll Theo onto his back and straddle him. I take us both into my hand, gasping when his smooth hardness makes contact with my palm. Slowly, my gaze on his face, I trail my fingers along the silky length of his shaft.

"Luke." Theo's breath hitches. "Christ."

He adds his hand to mine. The warm tightness of his fingers rips a sound from my throat part way between a growl and a whimper. I throw my head back, knuckles crammed into my mouth to stifle the noise. We move against each other, locked into a frenzy of caresses and exploration, discovery and desire. It's needy, frantic, all the frustration and misplaced anger of the past days spilling out in an unstoppable rush that leaves us weak and shaken.

***

"Ever wish you could control time?" Theo nuzzles his cheek in my hair, his tone drowsy. "Just freeze it so you could live in a single moment forever?"

We're wrapped around one another on the sofa, the dying firelight playing over our skin. I have my leg draped across him, my head nestled on his shoulder.

"Like now?"

"Like now." Theo's arm tightens around me, and I melt into him. More than anything, I wish I could halt time in its tracks, stay here with Theo in the protective darkness, no need for explanations or condemnation.

Theo rubs my back. "Thought what you'll do when you get home? About telling people, I mean, or not telling them, as the case may be."

"Not really." I turn my face into his neck. Actually, I've done a pretty good job of not thinking about it. Whenever I let myself imagine broaching the subject of Theo with Dean and the other lads, my stomach ties itself in knots and it becomes difficult to breathe.

"You know it's up to you, don't you?" Theo says. "Whatever you want to do, tell people or not, is fine with me."

Gratitude warms my chest. Perhaps I don't have to come out, not right away. I contemplate hiding the truth from my best mate, lying to him whenever Theo visits or I go to Oxford to see him, passing him off as a friend. Pressure squeezes my temples just thinking about it. "I don't want this...us to be a secret. I'm sick of sneaking about behind people's backs."

"OK," Theo sounds cautious, "but you don't have to decide now. You might feel differently once you get home."

I nod. Fact is, I know I'll feel differently once I'm with Dean, when I'm forced to look him in the eyes, but I meant what I said. I'm fed up of pretending, of acting like my relationship with Theo is something shameful. I won't do it anymore.

"How about you?" I ask. "Going to try and patch things up with your dad?"

"Nope. I've been open with him, done my best to keep in touch. Now it's up to him. If he wants to talk to me, he knows where I am." His offhand tone only partially masks the bitterness behind it. I have the urge to track down his dad and demand to know what he thinks he's playing at, turning his back on his own son.

I lay a hand on his hip, his skin warm under my palm. "I'm not going to help your cause, am I? Even if I were a girl, I'm guessing your dad wouldn't think I'm exactly suitable."

"Honestly, I couldn't care less." Theo covers my hand with his. When I look up at him, his eyes hold mine. "I wish you didn't have to go."

"Me too."

"If there was any other way...but I need to try and sort things out with Zara, if it's at all possible."

"Really, I get it." I attempt a smile. "Do what you have to. I'll wait."

Theo brushes his fingertips along my cheek, his own smile soft in the half-light. "I love you, Luke Savage."

A grin creeps over my face. His words expand inside my chest, until it feels somehow both full to bursting and lighter than a helium balloon. It isn't as if no one has ever said this to me before; I just didn't understand what it meant, not then. Unable to speak, I answer him the only way I can. I kiss him, slow and deep and searching. Theo sighs into my mouth, hands sliding down to grip my inner thighs, gently drawing me on top of him.

***

A sharp inhalation invades my consciousness. My eyes inch open, and I squint against the sunshine pouring through the glass doors. I struggle to sit up, but Theo's weight pins me to the cushions.

"Luke?" He stirs against me, pushing himself up on one elbow. His eyes find mine, bleary and confused.

I can't respond. My attention is riveted over his shoulder, on the figure standing in the middle of the kitchen floor. My horror must be visible in my expression, because the flush drains from Theo's cheeks and he twists to look behind him. That's when he sees her, Zara. She has her hand over her mouth, shocked gaze taking in the scene—the two of us wrapped around one another on the sofa, our clothes strewn across the rug. Then she looks at me, and that single glance brings the charade of the past weeks crashing down around us.

Chapter Seventeen

"How long has this been going on?"

I expect her to lose it, to scream at us, pelt us with every piece of china she can lay her hands on. Part of me wants her to; anger would be easier to deal with, put us on a familiar footing. It might even make me feel less like the complete shit I am.

But Zara does none of those things. Propped against the table to keep the weight off her bandaged foot, she confronts me across the kitchen, her expression a calm mask I don't recognise. She takes no notice of Theo standing awkwardly beside me. Neither does she seem aware of Meredith seated in the armchair in the corner, or of Giles perched on the arm, both of them following the exchange, separate but concerned. She remains focused on me, arms folded, waiting.

I appeal to Theo, but he keeps his head bowed, not looking at me. He hasn't looked at me, not once, since the moment Zara walked in on us tangled up in one another on the sofa.

I sigh and turn back to Zara. "I don't see how this will help."

"I said how long, Luke. I need to know."

I massage my temples, brain scrambling for an answer. How long has it been? Two weeks? Longer? So much has happened in that time. "It was that night, the one before I was planning to leave. You sent Theo after me to persuade me not to go."

"Oh." Zara shows no surprise. Well, she's already suffered the ultimate betrayal. It can't exactly get any worse. "So, when you decided to stay, it wasn't for me at all. It was never about me, none of it."

My instinct is to look away, to escape the hurt in her eyes, but I don't. I owe her that much.

"I'm sorry." These are the only words I can dredge up. The fact that they're true makes them no less worthless.

Zara disregards my apology and continues in the same even tone. "So, it's been going on all this time. Did you think I had a right to know at any point, or were you happy just to let me carry on believing you and me had something?"

Her voice wobbles. She presses her lips together, holding on to her control with a visible effort.

"Zara," Theo's face twists as though someone's waging a tug-of-war with his intestines, "we wanted to tell you. I was going to, once Luke went home and it was just you and me, I swear." He makes as if to put out a hand to her, then thinks better of it.

Other than a slight tensing of her shoulders, Zara blanks him, keeping her eyes fixed on me. I glance at Theo again, a silent plea for help, but he either doesn't notice or pretends not to. What's he thinking? I wish I knew. I'm starting to feel invisible, like I don't exist for him anymore.

"Luke?"

I stamp out my own feelings and concentrate on Zara. This isn't about me. "It's true. Theo was going to tell you once I'd gone. He thought it would be easier that way."

"Easier?" She glares at me, and I'm almost relieved to see the spark rekindle in her eyes. "Like you cared about making things easier on me. If you did, you wouldn't have gone behind my back in the first place. Want to know what I think? I think the only reason you're owning up now is because you got caught."

Theo recoils but doesn't attempt to defend our actions. Neither of us do. The way we've behaved, sneaking around in secret, stringing Zara along…there's no justification for it.

Meredith speaks up, addressing Zara. "You're wrong, you know. They were going to tell you. They were just waiting for the right time."

I meet Meredith's gaze. She doesn't have to do this, put her neck on the line for us, but it means a lot. My gratitude must be evident because she raises her eyebrows in a gesture that says, "Well, what else could I do?"

"Whoa." Giles pushes himself to his feet. He and Zara gape at Meredith as though she's morphed into a troll. "You knew about this?"

She stands too, staring them down. "It was an accident. I wasn't meant to find out, no one was, not until they'd told Zara."

"But when you found out, you didn't think to mention it? You didn't think Zara deserved to know what was going on?"

"Giles, it wasn't my secret to share. Theo and Luke had the right to tell Zara when they were ready. I'm sorry," Meredith says to Zara, "really."

Zara blinks, seeming dazed.

Giles turns away from Meredith in disgust and hones in on Theo. "I'm not completely blind. It was obvious you had a thing for Luke. You, though," he looks at me directly for the first time that morning, "I never would have believed it."

I shrug. Not much I can say to that. Before meeting Theo, I wouldn't have believed it of myself.

"So, basically," when Zara unearths her voice, it trembles with the beginnings of hysteria, "everyone suspected what was going on except me. You must all have been having a right laugh. Poor, clueless Zara, actually gullible enough to believe anyone gives a damn about her."

"Hey, that's not fair," Giles says. "You think I would've kept quiet if I'd known? Unlike some people." He shoots Meredith a dirty look.

Zara ignores him and crosses the room in a few strides, barely cringing when she puts weight on her injured foot. She halts in front of me, hands on hips, jaw set. "Do you know what's really funny about all this?"

I shake my head.

"I stuck up for you, that's what, against Giles. He kept telling me you were bad news, that I could do so much better, but I refused to listen. Then, when we were alone in here yesterday afternoon and he tried to kiss me—"

"Don't." Looking beyond her, I see what Zara, who had her back to the others, hasn't noticed. Meredith falls back a step, as though from the force of Zara's confession, the colour bleeding from her face.

"What's up, Luke?" Zara spits. "Don't like hearing about me kissing someone else? It's all right for you to go around sticking your tongue down other guys' throats, but not for me? Well, you don't have to worry because I didn't let him, and do you know why? I actually told Giles it wasn't fair to you." She lets out a humourless laugh. "God, I'm such a—"

"Merrie, wait!"

The panic in Giles's voice has Zara spinning on her heels. Meredith, however, behaves as though she hasn't heard him. Already fumbling with the sliding door, she slips outside and pulls it shut behind her.

Giles starts forward, then changes his mind. Zara gnaws her lower lip, her expression stricken with the comprehension of what she's done. In silence, the four of us watch Meredith walk away along the path, back straight and head held high, until she vanishes into the trees.

As soon as she's gone, Giles swings to glare at Zara, mouth working. If I weren't so mired in my own misery, I might feel a twinge of sympathy for him. I brace myself, readying for the explosion, but it's Theo who rounds on Zara.

"That was out of line." He doesn't shout, but if I were Zara, his cold anger would cut me far deeper. "I know you're mad at me, and you have every right to be, but that's no reason to take it out on Meredith."

The last of Zara's self-control shatters. I see it happen, like a guitar string wound too tight until it snaps.

"I'm out of line? Me?" She advances on Theo, features contorted with fury. "That's rich coming from someone who's been having it off with his best friend's boyfriend. I mean, how dare you, Theo. How fucking dare you!"

"Zara—"

Before Theo can finish, Zara slaps him hard across the face. The sound cracks the air like a burst balloon. I wince, but save for the flicker of his eyelids, Theo gives no indication he even felt it.

"I hate you!" Zara draws back her hand for another attack. "You hear me? I fucking hate you."

She makes to hit him again, but I step in and catch hold of her wrist. "Hey, that's enough."

"Get. Off. Me." Zara struggles, blasting me with the full force of her rage. "Don't you dare touch me ever again. You can save that for your precious boyfriend."

Her voice breaks. The tears spill over, pouring down her face. The fight drains out of her and I loosen my grip. Wrenching herself free, Zara shoves past me and stumbles from the room.

***

I spend the rest of that nightmare day cramming my belongings into my rucksack before retreating with my stuff to the spare bedroom, where I fall in an exhausted stupor onto the bed. The mattress is bare, devoid even of pillows. It doesn't matter; I won't be getting any sleep.

I don't know how long I lie there, staring out at the darkness gathering beyond the window with my back propped against my rucksack, before Meredith tracks me down. "Just wanted to say goodbye."

Concern rouses me from my desolation. She looks awful, her eyes bloodshot in her drawn face. "Where will you go?"

"Theo's driving me into Bude. I'll book into a B and B for the night and catch an early train tomorrow."

"Will you be OK?"

She offers up a sad smile. "I expect so, in time. How about you?"

"I expect so," my smile matches hers, "in time."

Alone again, I return to watching the sky and let the torpor settle around me. Gradually, night draws a black veil across the glass, but no one else comes to find me. Why should they? Zara loathes my guts, and Giles has never made any secret of the fact that he doesn't trust me. A wise move, so it turns out.

And Theo... Does he hate me, too? Probably, if the way he's been avoiding me is anything to go by. I can't blame him. I was the one who instigated things last night, the one who'd flung caution overboard and let the current sweep it away. In doing so, I've stomped all over Theo's hopes of salvaging his relationship with Zara, and he might never forgive me for it. The knowledge weighs like a sack of cement on my heart.

***

I open my eyes to moonlight bathing the room and a dull pounding in my head. I swallow. My throat feels dry as though I'd inhaled half the beach. I need a drink. Grimacing, I stretch the soreness from my muscles and haul myself to my feet. My legs shake beneath me, and I support myself against the wall for a moment, listening. Silence smothers the house in stillness. Hopefully the others are in bed, although I doubt anyone's getting much sleep.

With the moon to guide me, I creep from the room and down the stairs. In the kitchen, a waft of cool air strokes my face and I pause. The sliding door stands ajar. So I'm not the only one up. I hesitate, but only for a second. Then I'm across the room, peering into the darkness. I have to know.

He has his back to me, poised at the edge of the pool, hands in his pockets. He's nothing but a silhouette outlined in silver, and yet I know it's him. I would recognise him anywhere. Perhaps, more than my thirst, he's what brought me downstairs. Perhaps, deep down, I sensed he was out here.

Heart hammering, I descend the patio steps and cross the lawn. Theo remains motionless, gaze fixed on the sky, as if hoping a black hole will appear and suck him into oblivion. When I come up beside him, his body tenses. He spares me a fleeting glance, his expression hard to read in the starlight, before looking away.

Pain cramps my gut. I want to reach for him, to collapse into his solid warmth and beg him to tell me it will all be OK. But I don't. His taut posture makes him seem distant, untouchable. I know what he's doing— shutting me out, slamming the door on me and ramming the bolts into place. We've been here before, the first time Theo realised there might be something real between us. That had hurt, but nothing like this.

The silence stretches on, growing wider with every passing second. If I don't speak up soon, the gap might become unbridgeable. "Theo... I'm sorry."

I don't know what I'm apologising for—for screwing up last night, for not insisting we tell Zara sooner, for coming to Cornwall in the first place. Maybe for everything, the whole hellish mess.

Theo expels a breath that comes from somewhere deep inside him. "Me too."

He doesn't look at me, shows no sign of saying anything further. I wish he'd talk to me. When he closes himself off like this, it's impossible to guess at the thoughts swirling inside his head. Still, the guilt must be eating him up.

"I get it." I try again. "You need some space, need to sort things out with Zara, and that's OK."

Even as the words leave my mouth, a part of me hopes he'll ask me to stay, assure me we can see this through together, somehow. For a moment, I think he might.

Theo turns to me, and there's no concealing the indecision in his eyes. Then he shakes his head, averting his gaze. "Thanks."

Neither of us speaks after that; there's nothing else to add. Countless hours of having so much to share that we stumbled over our words, desperate to discover all there was to know, and here we are without a single thing to say. As we stand side-by-side, staring up at the stars, we may as well be at opposite ends of the universe.

**

The following morning, Giles gives me a lift to the station. I ask him to drop me off in Bude where I can catch a bus to St. David, but he insists on driving me the forty minutes into Exeter to meet my train. Maybe his conscience is bothering him. More likely he just wants something to do. Either way, it's good of him.

During the silent drive, I remember the last time Giles offered me an escape route, the day after Theo first kissed me, when Zara had begged me to stay. Perhaps I should have taken him up on it then, got out while I still could. It would have saved us all a whole lot of heartache.

I didn't see anyone else before I left. Zara went to sit by the pool after breakfast, and a while later Theo settled on the patio to read, in sight of her but keeping his distance. I saw them from the spare-room window as I packed the last of my stuff. I took my lead from them and resisted the urge to say goodbye. Easier on everyone that way. Has Theo plucked up the courage yet and joined Zara by the pool? Has he persuaded her to talk to him? I hope so.

Giles makes no attempt at conversation, too absorbed in his own problems to take advantage of this last opportunity to lay into me. When he pulls up outside the station, he continues to stare straight ahead, waiting for me to get out.

I pause, my hand on the door. I should at least say something. "Uh, thanks."

Giles still doesn't glance at me, just nods once.

I open the door and step onto the pavement, reaching into the back seat for my rucksack. About to shut the door, I hesitate again. "I didn't mean for any of this to happen, for anyone to get hurt."

Giles looks at me then, and his eyes hold no condemnation, only weary sadness. "I believe you," he says, and I can tell he does.

My train is already waiting when I negotiate my way to the right platform. I hoist my bag onto the luggage rack and flop into a seat by the window. At least I don't have my surfboard to contend with. There, I knew something positive would come out of that fiasco.

The train is pulling out of the station when it hits me. I shoot up, scrambling in the pocket of my jeans. Fingers clumsy with panic, I extract my mobile and scroll through the contacts.

Nothing.

I repeat the process more slowly, clicking through a name at a time. The realisation squeezes the air from my lungs. Theo's number... I don't have it. We'd meant to swap them before I left, but then things slipped beyond our control. Somehow, we always thought there would be more time.

I stare down at the useless phone in my hand. So even if I want to text Theo, to tell him I'm thinking about him, reassure myself he's there, I can't. And Theo...there's no guarantee he'll want to get in touch, but supposing he does, perhaps once the rawness has healed, he won't be able to. Zara has my number, of course, and she knows whereabouts I live. My shoulders slump. Yeah, I can really see her agreeing to help us. Why should she? Besides, knowing Zara, she will have deleted all trace of me from her phone by now.

In a daze, I return the mobile to my pocket and lean my head against the window. That's it, then. My one hope lies with Zara, and given how Theo and I have betrayed her, this amounts to no hope at all.

**

Three days later, I'm sprawled on my bed, staring blindly up at the ceiling and wishing I were somewhere, anywhere, else. Even with my window flung wide, the afternoon sun cranks up the temperature in my room until it resembles an oven. The air, humid and choked with petrol fumes, adheres to my skin, glueing my tongue to the roof of my mouth. If I don't roast alive, I'll surely suffocate. Neither prospect bothers me all that much.

I reach for my phone, just as I have countless times since I got home, and scroll through the photos. Why am I torturing myself? I'm not sure, other than that these pictures are my one link with Cornwall. With Theo. Without them, this visual proof, my mind could be tricked into believing the summer never happened.

I gaze at the blurry image on the screen. It's the snap Zara took of Theo and me, him in the pool with his hand on my thigh, me leaning in close, our lips mere inches apart. I stare with all my might, willing myself back to that moment. I can almost feel the sun on my skin, feel Theo's touch, warm and firm on my bare leg, his breath caressing my lips.

"I'm off now, Luke." Mum pokes her head into my room.

Dragged from my reverie, I glance at her. "Huh?"

"To work. I'm on the late shift today. I did tell you."

Had she? I don't remember. With a grunt of acknowledgement, I return my attention to the phone still gripped in my hand.

"Luke, love?"

"Hmmm?"

"Please don't think I'm interfering, but are you planning to shower at any point this summer?"

I cast her another blank look. All I want is for her to leave me alone and let me sink back into my stupor.

"It's just that it's starting to smell not too pleasant in here." Mum grimaces in apology. "Think you might be able to rouse yourself to have a wash this afternoon?"

"Yeah, fine." Merely thinking about it, the logistics of hauling myself into the bathroom, of peeling the clothes off my sweat-caked skin and turning on the shower, makes me dizzy with exhaustion. Still, playing along seems the fastest way to end the conversation.

Mum lingers in the doorway, watching me, and her expression echoes some of my own unhappiness. "Luke?"

My stomach twists. Not now. One of the best things about Mum is that she never tries to invade my space or force me to open up. Even though it's obvious something's wrong, she hasn't asked me about Cornwall, or Zara, or why I'm back sooner than expected. She knows I'll tell her when I'm ready. My fingers clench around the phone. Please don't make me talk about this now.

She sighs. "There's some leftover chilli in the fridge and plenty of food in the freezer. Be sure to eat something, OK?"

"OK." I sag into the mattress. Through my relief, I'm hardly aware what I'm agreeing to.

Mum studies me for a moment longer, as though wanting to say more. Then she's gone, pulling my door to behind her. The click of the front door drifts along the hallway, followed by murmured voices. Probably poor old Mr. Okeke, forever searching for his beloved spaniel killed in a hit-and-run ten years ago.

Some masochistic urge draws my attention back to my phone. The picture of the two of us, Theo and me, so blatantly happy and into each other, taunts me from the screen. I can't look at it anymore; it hurts too much. I scroll through my meagre collection of photos, settling for one I took on the cliff. From the angle of the shot, Theo appears to be standing right on the edge, as though about to step backwards into nothingness. He was gazing directly into the camera, lips pressed together to hold in his laughter, eyes soft with tenderness, for me.

Shit. I toss the phone onto the bedside cabinet with a clatter. Shit, shit, shit. Before I can stop them, the tears burn behind my eyelids. I press my palms into my eye sockets, willing them down.

"Wow, you look like crap."

My hands fly away from my face. Dean's lounging in the doorway, freckled and sun-burnt under his fair hair.

A grin tugs my mouth up at the corners. It wavers around the edges, but at least it's there. "Good to see you too."

And it is. I'd wanted to be alone, to burrow into a deep, dark tunnel and hide from the world. Yet, with Dean here, his uncomplicated familiarity filling my room, the painful knot in my stomach loosens.

Dean shakes his head. "You should've told me you were back."

What to say? I fumble for an excuse but come up empty-handed. "How did you find out?"

"Your mum rang me this morning. She said you were in a bad way, asked me to come over." He takes me in, his expression concerned. "So the thing with Zara, it didn't work out?"

"You could say that." Talk about an understatement.

Dean crosses the room, putting a hand on my shoulder. "Sorry, mate."

I nod. In the face of his sympathy, it's all I trust myself to do without breaking down.

Dean must sense I'm in danger of losing it, because he turns away to give me a moment to compose myself. "Hey, these your holiday pics? Let's see."

I look over just as he reaches for my mobile on the bedside cabinet. With a jolt, I realise I forgot to clear the screen. "Uh, no, those aren't…anything."

I push myself onto one elbow, grabbing for the phone, but Dean already has it in his hand. He holds it away from me, grinning. "Come on. It's only fair, seeing as you buggered off for weeks."

I watch, helpless, as Dean examines the photo on the screen, the one of Theo on the cliff. His eyebrows shoot up. "Who's this?" He tilts the phone to show me, but I don't even glance at it.

"Theo." The single word comes out sounding flat. I feel like the air before a storm, heavy and suffused with eerie calm.

"Zara's cousin, right? The queer one."

I flinch.

Dean focuses once more on the phone, smirking. "Good-looking guy. Bet you had trouble keeping your hands off him."

He hasn't got a clue how accurate that is. If he had, he wouldn't be so blasé about it. Transfixed, I watch him scroll through the pictures, watch him register that every one of them is of Theo and his curiosity change to confusion.

I'm aware the moment he lands on the photo of Theo and me. Part of me hopes it isn't as incriminating as I think. Perhaps our feelings are only obvious to me because I know they're there, and a casual observer wouldn't even notice Theo's hand on my leg or the intensity between us.

But I'm deluding myself; I see it in Dean's reaction, the way his face spasms with shock before draining of expression. For the longest time, he doesn't move. He simply stares at the screen, as though unable to peel his gaze away.

Eventually, he looks up at me. He's grinning, but it's a forced kind of grin. "This is a joke, right? You were just fooling around."

Unable to give him the reassurance he's seeking, I merely shrug, waiting for the truth to sink in.

"Come on." Dean continues to smile in that manic way. "Joke's over, OK? Seriously, you had me going there for a minute."

I close my eyes, shutting out the desperate hope in his expression, and rub my throbbing brow. I always knew this would be difficult, but on top of everything else, I'm not sure I can handle it.

"Wait." Suspicion slinks into Dean's tone. "You're not joking. Are you?"

When I open my eyes, his smile has faded. I shake my head. A rugby ball lodges itself in my throat, preventing me from getting the words out.

Dean nods. With a studied composure, he glances from me to the photo. "So...you're like him now?" He jabs a finger at the screen.

"Theo. His name's Theo." Much as the sound of his name tears me up inside, it hurts less than not saying it at all.

"Whatever, but you're... You and him... That's what you're telling me?"

"Yes. No. Shit, Dean, I dunno."

Dean snorts. "You don't know? Come on, Luke, it isn't that hard. Either you're a homo or you're not."

I scrub my hands over my face, trying to find the words to make Dean understand. "I do like girls. Fancy them, I mean. I just—"

"Enjoy fucking guys? Great." Dean's calm splinters. In a sudden violent movement, he hurls the phone at me, aiming for my face.

I put up a hand in an automatic gesture to protect myself, and it bounces off my palm onto the carpet. I consider trying to explain that I hadn't planned to fall for Theo—hell, things would be so much simpler if I hadn't—but the contempt curling Dean's mouth stops me.

"So," he spits out the syllable, "when exactly were you planning on telling me? Or weren't you? Maybe you didn't think I had a right to know my so-called best mate's a cocksucker."

"It isn't like that. How was I supposed to tell you something I didn't even know myself?"

"Sure. You just woke up one day and thought, 'I know, I'm bored of girls. Why don't I try sticking it up some guy instead?' You've honestly gone all these years and never suspected? You expect me to believe that?"

I shake my head, staring at a crack in the ceiling. No, I don't expect him to believe me. How can I when it isn't true. Not entirely. Still, telling him about Max probably isn't the best idea right now.

"Oh my God." Dean's voice rises. "All those times you slept over, were you secretly eyeing me up behind my back?"

"Don't be an idiot." I glance at him, more weary than irritated. "We're mates, brothers."

"Yeah." Dean regards me and his expression reveals nothing but betrayal and disgust. He turns away. "At least, I thought we were."

The accusation kicks me in the gut. I bolt upright, panic filtering through my numbness. "This is me you're talking to. I haven't changed. I'm still the same person. Still me."

Dean pauses in the doorway but doesn't look back. "No," he says, "you're not." Then he's gone, slamming the front door with a force that reverberates through the empty flat.

Chapter Eighteen

The soft closing of the front door jerks me from a doze. A moment later, the hall light flicks on, shining through the open door to my room. Since when had it got so dark?

Mum's silhouette appears in the doorway. "Luke, what're you doing here?"

"Huh?" My throat cracks like soil after a decade of drought. The question makes no sense. Am I not meant to be here? Is there somewhere else I'm supposed to be?

"I thought you'd be at Dean's," Mum says. "His family were having a barbecue. He was going to ask if you wanted to stay over."

He was? Clearly we hadn't got to that particular part of the conversation before he decided I wasn't someone worth knowing anymore. The memory of his expression, twisted with disgust and disillusionment, springs up to knee me in the stomach.

"Luke?" Mum's voice radiates concern.

I realise my fists are clenched on my thighs, nails eating into the palms. With an effort, I uncurl my fingers. "He…must have changed his mind." Despite my attempt to sound casual, hurt pulses through every word. Even to someone who didn't know me inside-out, it would have been obvious.

Mum doesn't speak right away. She crosses to draw the curtains against the blackness, always tinged a dirty orange from the streetlamps below. It's a far cry from Cornwall, from those nights lit only by stars and the silvery sheen of the moon. I thrust the memories down, burying them in the depths of my soul.

After switching on the bedside lamp, Mum sits on the edge of my bed, the way she used to when I was sick or woke from a nightmare. "I wish you'd talk to me."

I avert my face, staring at the wall. I can't tell her, can't handle having another person I love look at me with incomprehension, as though I've become a stranger overnight.

Mum lays a warm hand on my thigh. "You can tell me, whatever it is. I just can't stand to see you so unhappy." She pauses, before asking, "Did something happen with Zara?"

The lamplight throws wavering shadows over the faded wallpaper. I keep my gaze on them and nod once. It's all I can manage.

"Oh, Luke." Mum rubs my leg, her tone gentle. "I'm sorry. I know how much you liked her."

It would be so easy to go along with it, to wallow in her sympathy and let her assure me there will be other girls. But I can't do it. I turn to look at her, see the genuine tenderness and compassion in her eyes, and I can't keep up the pretence.

Grimacing at the stiffness in my muscles, I struggle into a sitting position and bend to retrieve my phone from the floor. Aware of Mum's anxious gaze, I scroll through the photos, skipping past the one Zara shot by the pool—it's just too intimate—and find the picture of Theo on the cliff.

I intend to hand the phone straight to Mum, but Theo's eyes snare mine and hold them. His words to me during that last incredible night come back to me. "Whatever you want to do, tell people or not, is fine with me." and my reply, "I don't want this to be a secret. I'm sick of sneaking about behind people's backs." Somehow, it's still true. I may have screwed things up with Theo, but I can't behave as though none of it ever happened.

Mum leans into me, peering at the screen. "Who's that?"

"Theo." I pass her the phone. "Zara's cousin."

The queer one. Dean's throwaway remark echoes in my head.

Mum studies the photo. "He looks nice."

"He is." My voice catches, and I glare at a fading bruise above my left knee. *Don't let me break down.*

Mum's quiet for a while. She glances from my face to the photo and back again, trying to understand what I'm telling her. At last, she sets my phone on the bedside cabinet and takes my hand. "Look at me, Luke. Please."

I can't move. Anxiety weighs like a barbell on the nape of my neck, making it impossible for me to raise my head.

"Luke?" Mum cups my chin, her fingers soft but insistent.

I put up no resistance as she tilts my face to meet her eyes, don't have the strength to try and hide my unhappiness.

"Oh, sweetheart." She pulls me into a hug, wrapping me in her arms.

I collapse onto her shoulder and sob. Mum doesn't speak. She simply holds me, rubbing soothing circles on my back, and lets me cry.

And, once I've calmed down, she listens. She listens while the words I've held hostage for days tumble out of me. I tell her about Theo, the dizzying realisation that I was falling for him and that he might feel the same; about the strain of hiding how we felt from Zara, all the frustration and misguided jealousy, and the horror of that last morning when she caught us together. Finally, I tell her about Dean, the spiteful things he'd said and how he looked at me, as though I'd betrayed his trust in the worst way imaginable.

When I'm done, my entire body sags. Exhaustion and relief have turned my bones to sludge. Talking felt good, therapeutic. Hard as it was to begin, once I did, I couldn't stop. However painful the process, I needed to get it out, like extracting poison from a wound before it turns gangrenous. But now, as the initial rush fades, the doubts set in. Mum still has her hand on my back, but she isn't saying anything.

"Are you disappointed in me?" I keep my face buried against her shoulder.

"What? No." Mum tilts my chin, her gaze fierce on mine. "You must never, ever think that. There's nothing you could do that would make me love you less. I just…I hate the fact that you were going through all this and I didn't know."

"That's silly. You couldn't have known."

"Well, I should have. You should've told me."

I imagine it, trying to explain the whole impossible mess over the phone. My mouth twitches in a wry smile. Mum smiles too, conceding the point. She puts her arm around me, and I lean into her. Grown up as I am, it's comforting.

"What am I going to do about Dean?"

Mum ruffles my hair. "Try not to worry. He'll come round."

"You didn't see him." I cringe again, remembering. "The way he looked at me, it was like he didn't even know who I was."

Another thought occurs to me. Has he told his parents? Did they spend the barbecue I was meant to be a part of lamenting how I've deceived them, how I'm not who they believed I was? Nausea rises in my throat. And what about the bookshop? Will my job still be there for me in September?

"Sweetheart," Mum's voice, firm and reassuring, trickles through to me, "Dean's bound to be shocked. That was a big thing you sprung on him, and young men—well, men of any age really—aren't always good at dealing with these situations. You should know that better than anyone."

Mum's right, of course she is. The sort of piss-taking that goes on in the school changing rooms should have prepared me for Dean's reaction. Honestly, I'm not sure what else I expected. Somehow, though, I managed to fool myself into hoping it would play out differently.

"He just needs time," Mum says. "You'll see."

I wish I had her confidence. It's only now dawning on me how lucky Theo is to have Giles. By all accounts, when Theo came out to him at fourteen, Giles took it in his stride. Whatever his faults, and I could amuse myself for many happy hours listing them, there can be no doubt Giles has been a true friend to Theo.

"And the same goes for your young man," Mum adds. "Just give him time."

I shake my head. "After I helped wreck things between him and Zara, I'm pretty sure Theo wants nothing more to do with me, and even if he does," my stomach twists at the thought, "he has no way of getting in touch."

"Trust me," Mum squeezes my hand, "if he really wants to find you, he will."

"And if he doesn't?"

"Then you're better off without him."

My eyes stray to my phone, to the image of Theo still displayed on the screen. Maybe I would be better off. My life was certainly a lot simpler before it collided with Theo's, spinning it off-kilter. Still, I can't quite talk my heart into believing it.

***

The summer passes in a haze of sweltering heat and thunderstorms that hurl spears of lightning from the sky. I spend much of it sprawled on my bed, the windows thrown wide to let in what little breeze there is, eating when Mum reminds me, showering when the stink of my own sweat becomes too much even for me to stand.

Before Cornwall, I would have drowned my emotions in the surf. I would've taken my board down to the coast every day at dawn and hurled myself into the waves until nothing else existed. But not now. Now, I can't think about the sea without being reminded of Theo, and the prospect of surfing without my beloved Spitfire gouges a strip from my heart.

So I read. Finally, after so many false starts, I get stuck into *A Game of Thrones*, quickly becoming absorbed in George R. R. Martin's world of ruthlessness and power, battles and political intrigue. Within days, I'm forced from the safe haven of the flat to raid our local library for the rest of the series.

When I stagger to the front desk under a stack of heavy volumes, the grandmotherly librarian glances up at me, eyes twinkling behind gold-framed spectacles. "You'll never read all those in two weeks."

But I do, and a fortnight later I'm back in search of something new to lose myself in. The same librarian spies me browsing the shelves in the fantasy section and bustles over to help, soon despatching me with novels by David Gemel and Terry Goodkind. I've always read, but never so obsessively. Then again, I've never been this intent on escaping my own existence. Among the pages of a book, I can inhabit another world. My problems shrink into the background, and I get caught up in someone else's struggle until I practically forget who I am.

Only at night, when my eyes are so gritty with tiredness that the words blur into gibberish on the page, and my body trembles from exhaustion but won't let me sleep, do the thoughts succeed in sneaking past my weakened defences. I lie awake, replaying everything that happened in Cornwall, regretting all the things I should have done and didn't.

It seems so obvious to me now. We should never have gone behind Zara's back. That night on the cliff, the night Theo persuaded me to stay, we should have told her then. OK, there was no guarantee the relationship would've worked out, but at least we could have explored our feelings without the strain of all that secrecy. Zara would still have been upset, there was no getting around it, but we could have spared her the pain of our betrayal.

The worst thing, the thing that really eats at my gut, isn't Dean's rejection or the separation from Theo. I behaved badly, plain and simple, and now I'm paying the price. Hard as it is to swallow, there's a poetic justice in that. The punishment feels almost purifying, like serving time for a crime you deeply regret committing. I'll suffer through it because it's what I deserve.

No, what has me tossing and turning into the early hours is the conviction that I'm mostly to blame. Not that Theo doesn't bear a portion of the responsibility, but his position was always more precarious than mine. He had so much more to lose, and in his effort to keep everyone happy, he ended up making no one happy at all. I should have been strong enough for the both of us, ensured we did the right thing.

And now I've abandoned Theo to pick up the pieces. Spending the summer holed up in my kiln of a room might be miserable, but it's nothing to what Theo must be going through—Zara despising him, his best friends' relationship in tatters, unable even to visit his sister because his dad's the biggest arsehole on the planet, and all this after the shit that went down with Francis.

If only there was something I could do to make it up to him. I stare into the darkness, tinged pink with the approaching dawn, and scour my brain for the answer. It isn't like I can do anything about Zara; I've done more than enough damage there as it is. I'd promised to help Theo hunt down his painting, but on my own with zero knowledge of the art world, I wouldn't have a clue where to start. Which leaves...what?

My heart ricochets in my chest. It couldn't possibly do any good. I'm crazy for even contemplating it. Yet, once the idea plants itself in my mind, it refuses to be dislodged. The question is, do I have the nerve to go through with it?

***

At my first sight of the house where Theo grew up, I almost bottle out. It presides over the valley below, basking in the early afternoon sun, a sprawl of pillars and honey-coloured stone, gables and elegant chimneys. But for the silver Jaguar parked outside, I feel as if I've stepped into one of those period dramas that have Mum glued to the telly on Sunday nights, the ones where someone's daughter running off with the wrong sort of man is about as exciting as it gets.

I shade my eyes and scan the grounds. To my left, sunlight glints off a distant stretch of water. A wooden jetty just into the lake, attached to…is that a boathouse? To my right, sloping lawns meld into swathes of yellow corn fields, which in turn give way to olive-green woods. This must be where Theo played as a child. It beats a potted plant and a couple of window boxes, that's for sure.

I approach the house, my feet dragging. All the talk of racehorses and old masters should have prepared me, but it's impossible to be unimpressed by so much grandeur. My fists clench in the pockets of my jeans. I won't be intimidated.

Rowanleigh hadn't been hard to track down. An internet search on one of the library's computers followed by a ninety-minute train ride brought me to the pretty village of Hathercombe. From there, it was a short hike uphill to the gated entrance marking the Scott-Palmer estate. What I hadn't anticipated was that the driveway itself would be a hundred miles long. With the heat searing the nape of my neck and sweat streaming down my back, the walk seemed to take forever.

In my effort to make a decent impression, I'd dug out one of the few tops I own without a slogan or band logo plastered across the front. This happens to be a navy-blue polo shirt, two sizes too small, and which currently has my biceps in a stranglehold. Its one saving grace is that the dark colour hides the damp patches pooling under my arms.

The front steps are a lot more daunting up close. I take a fortifying breath, heart bouncing around like a grasshopper, and force my legs to carry me up. At the top, an oak-panelled door bars my entrance. Beyond it, somewhere in the bowels of this elegant house, is the man I've come to see. I swallow hard, square my shoulders, and ring the bell.

Immediately, the door flies open. Anyone would think they're expecting me. Not that the man shielding the threshold, as though to protect the house's secrets from unworthy mortals, is exactly welcoming. He looks nothing like Theo, has none of Theo's softness. He's all angles and sharp features, with a prominent jaw and dark hair swept away from a proud forehead.

Eyes, green and cool as sea glass, flicker over me with disinterest. "If you're here about the job, it's already gone," he informs me and starts to shut the door in my face.

"No." Without pausing to think, I stick out my foot. His gaze narrows in a way that screams danger. "I mean, I'm not here about the job."

For a moment, I'm convinced Theo's dad will slam the door anyway, crushing my foot to splinters and bringing my surfing days to an excruciating end. Instead, he takes me in, lip curled, cataloguing my shaggy hair and the scuffed toes of my trainers.

"Well, what do you want?" He has a clipped drawl to rival Giles's. "Much as I'd love to stand on the doorstep and chat all afternoon, I'm rather busy."

What a prick. Theo certainly didn't inherit his sweetness from his dad. Is this the sort of reception Francis got when he came looking for Theo? Probably. Well. I'd slit my own throat before emulating him, but a little of his self-assurance would've come in handy.

On the train I rehearsed what I was going to say, had my speech all figured out. Now, face-to-face with Theo's dad, his disdain reducing me to the size and desirability of a flea, my mind goes blank. Still, I have to say something. If I don't, he'll order me off the property and I'll lose my chance.

I inhale and pull my shoulders back. We're around the same height, but I'm broader. The knowledge bolsters me, and I'm able to sound more confident than I feel. "It's about Theo. I—"

"No." His arm shoots out as though to fend off an attacker. "Stop right there."

"But—"

"Contrary to what my son may have told you, I'm not running an escort agency for fucking poofters. If you're not gone by the time I get home, or if you dare come knocking on my door again, I'm calling the police."

Theo's dad brushes past me, almost knocking me down the steps, and leaps into his car. A second later, it roars along the driveway like an enraged dragon. I stare after the Jag until it disappears from view around a bend. He could at least have offered me a lift.

I sigh and descend the steps. Could that have gone any worse? Of the numerous scenarios I'd prepared myself for—scorching rage, insults, even being escorted from the premises in handcuffs—not getting the opportunity to say my piece wasn't one of them. I'd come all this way, screwed up my courage to confront Theo's dad, and it had been for nothing.

I trudge back along the endless driveway. Sweat trickles down my spine and my mouth feels dryer than The Atacama. I'd passed a small pub in the village. Maybe I'll stop there before heading home, buy myself a Coke and sit in the shade.

"Whoa there!"

I pause, turning. A girl, about my age, marches towards me in wellies and mud-spattered jodhpurs, a men's shirt rolled up to the elbows. Her hair, golden brown like Theo's, is pulled into a messy bun, but she has the same green eyes and strong jaw as the man who'd just left.

"You're Clemmy," I realise.

She bats my words aside. "I know who I am. The question is...who're you? No, actually, don't tell me. You're one of Theo's hangers-on, aren't you? Like that other creep who came sniffing around a few weeks back."

I blink. Did Theo's sister just call me a creep?

"Mind you," Clemmy regards me as though I'm on display at a cattle market, "you don't look much like the last one. More of a carthorse than a thoroughbred."

Without a word, I pivot and continue my trek along the drive. I'm hot and thirsty, the sour taste of failure strong in my mouth. No way I'm standing around in the blistering heat to be made fun of. *God, Theo, where did you come from?* Longing for him blindsides me, wrenching at my stomach.

"Hey, hold your horses." Clemmy calls after me. "Where're you going?"

"Home."

"Oh, for heaven's sake. Wait a minute, will you?"

Curiosity wrestles with my desire to make a quick getaway. Curiosity wins, and I stop so Clemmy can draw level.

"This is why I hate people." She brushes a loose strand of hair off her face with an impatient hand, leaving a smudge of dirt on her cheek. "You insist on misunderstanding everything I say. It's like you're determined to be offended."

I raise an eyebrow. "You called me a carthorse."

"So? I love horses. They're my life. I'm hardly going to use one as an insult, am I? But, of course, you had to jump to conclusions."

I shake my head, suspended somewhere between amusement and irritation. Theo told me his sister was horse mad, but he omitted to mention just how…eccentric she was.

Clemmy assesses me in a single glance. "You need watering. Come inside, and I'll get you a drink."

"I dunno." I peer down the driveway, expecting the Jaguar to reappear at any minute. "Your dad threatened to call the police on me."

She waves away my concerns. "You mustn't mind him. His tongue's sharper than his teeth. Anyway, he's gone to look at a horse, won't be back for hours. Come on."

Clemmy clicks her tongue as though cajoling a nervous colt. I shelve my misgivings and follow her towards the house. Instead of climbing the front steps, she veers along a path that skirts the edge of the building.

"What?" I ask. "I'm not respectable enough to use the front door?"

"Not you, idiot, me." She gestures at her boots. "Mrs. Jenkins will have foals if I tread mud all over her clean floors."

Clemmy leads me through a side door and into a sort of lobby area. She kicks off her wellies, tossing them into the jumble of riding crops, golf clubs and bridles. Anxious not to incite the wrath of Mrs. Jenkins, who I'm guessing must be the housekeeper, I take off my trainers and follow her down a passage panelled in dark wood.

The kitchen is clean—courtesy of Mrs. Jenkins, I assume—but cluttered. Junk mail and unopened bills threaten to spill from the dresser onto the flagstones, and copies of *Horse and Hound* and *The Racing Post* litter the farmhouse table. The moment we enter, an old chocolate Labrador waddles over to greet us, tail wagging.

"Hey, girl." Clemmy bends to pat her head. "I've brought a friend to see you. Cocoa, this is…" She glances at me. "Sorry, I don't know your name. Should've asked you that before, I suppose. I'm hopeless at this social interaction lark."

"It's Luke." I get down on my haunches. "Hi, Cocoa."

The dog approaches, sniffing my hand before licking it with a warm, wet tongue. She sits next to me and thumps her tail.

"I think she likes me." I scratch her behind the ears. "At least I haven't completely lost my touch with the girls."

"I wouldn't let it go to your head. Cocoa adores everyone."

While Clemmy rummages in the fridge, I pet Cocoa and examine my surroundings. I can't help picturing Theo in this room, sprawled in the armchair by the Aga, his nose in a book and Cocoa at his feet.

The smack of glass on wood shatters the illusion. Clemmy waves me over. "You want this or what?"

I give Cocoa a final stroke and join Clemmy at the table, accepting the glass she shoves towards me. Cocoa retreats to her basket in the corner, where she curls up and watches us through half-closed eyes.

I sink into the nearest chair, swallowing half my drink in a single gulp. It bubbles down my throat, sweet and lemony and ice cold.

"So," Clemmy leans against the worktop and surveys me over her glass, "what's so important that you came to see Theo without checking he was even here?"

"I didn't. I mean, I came to see your dad." I rest my chin on my folded arms. My plan seems so futile now. What had I really expected to achieve?

Clemmy's eyebrows shoot up. "Dad? What on Earth for? I'm guessing you weren't trying to sell him a horse."

"Hardly. It's just, well, Theo's been through a rough time, and your dad...he's completely turned his back on him. I thought, if I talked to him...I dunno. It was stupid."

"Pretty stupid, I'd say, but brave, too. You must care about my brother a lot."

My throat tightens. I reach for my glass, downing the remainder of the lemonade. I'm aware of Clemmy regarding me, expression pensive, and brace myself for the inevitable interrogation.

She hops off the counter and heads for the door, beckoning me to follow. "This way."

Baffled, I hurry to catch up with her. Clemmy shows me from the kitchen and up a back staircase to a small landing. We twist along a series of passages, and I glance around, wondering which of the many bedrooms we pass belongs to Theo. Is it comfortably messy like his room at the cottage, or utterly barren as though no one has ever slept there?

At the top of a second staircase, narrower than the first, Clemmy pauses outside a closed door to look me in the eye. "What you said about Dad turning his back on Theo, it isn't true."

I open my mouth to argue, but she raises her palms in a silencing gesture. "No, don't say anything. I knew you wouldn't believe me. That's why I've brought you up here. You need to see this."

She pushes the door, which swings inward with a creak, and indicates for me to go in. With no idea what I might find, I step over the threshold. The attic space stretches ahead of me, dusty sunlight filtering through tall windows at the far end. Cardboard boxes line the right-hand side in teetering stacks, while on the left-hand wall...

My heart jumps. Displayed against the bare plaster, like exhibits in a long-forgotten gallery, are paintings.

Slowly, without really knowing what I'm searching for, I move from one canvas to the next. I pause by each one, not so much to study the artwork, but to read the signatures. Hockney, Reynolds, Constable—the remembered names leap out at me, interspersed with others I don't recognise. When I reach the final painting, I stare at it for an eternity. Excitement tingles in the pit of my belly.

At last, I rip my gaze away to face Clemmy, who's studying me from the doorway. "I don't understand. Theo told me your dad got rid of them."

"He did."

"So, how...?"

Clemmy sighs. Crossing to stand beside me, she examines the painting that snagged my attention. "Dad's never been good with words. We're alike in that sense. When Theo came out to him last summer, he reacted the only way he knew how. He shut down, refused to acknowledge it. Dad hasn't mentioned it to me, not once, but I know him well enough to see how cut up he is."

"And you think Theo isn't?"

"Just shut up and listen. I'm not defending Dad, but I'm the one who's had to live with him this past year. Fact is, although he'd rather eat manure than admit as much, he misses Theo. Most of all, he feels bad about everything that happened after Mum died."

"Yeah, really seems like it." I can't keep the derision from my voice.

Clemmy's eyes flash. She jabs a finger towards the paintings. "Do I have to spell it out? Dad has zero interest in art. He's never seen the point in it. Theo, though, he was more upset about the loss of Mum's collection than the rest of her things put together. Why else would Dad go to such lengths to recover a load of paintings he couldn't care less about unless he was trying to make amends?"

I let the revelation sink in. There's no denying Clemmy's logic, and yet I struggle to match these actions with a father who's capable of ignoring his own son for an entire year. "Have you told Theo?"

"Not in so many words. Don't look at me like that. Of course I've spoken to him, tried to get him to come home, but he's seemed distracted lately. Trouble is, I'm not even supposed to know about all this. It was an accident. I came up here the other day to hunt down my old riding boots for one of our work-experience girls. It's weird." Clemmy frowns, scrutinising the painting. "I could've sworn this was the one Mum gave Theo before she died. He always loved it because the mare looks so like Epona. She was his first pony, you know. Still, I must have got that wrong."

The tingle flares to life in my gut. The moment I'd seen the painting—a lush meadow under a summer sky, the horse dipping her head to drink from the bubbling stream—I knew what I was looking at. I didn't even need to read the signature. All the same, it takes Clemmy's confirmation for me to truly believe it.

I grasp her by the arm. "Theo has to know about this. You have to tell him. It's important."

Clemmy rakes my face with that shrewd gaze of hers, apparently unfazed. "What about you? Does Theo need to know you came?"

I think back over my grand plan, the determination that gave me the nerve to go through with it. Then I recall the run-in with Theo's dad, his slur about an escort agency for poofters, the way he'd stormed off in his car. In my effort to help, I'd somehow succeeded in making things worse.

"No," I say at length, "he doesn't need to know about that."

Chapter Nineteen

My visit to Rowanleigh convinces me of one thing: I infinitely prefer fictional worlds to my own. I sink back into my solitary routine, finding comfort in Terry Goodkind's *Sword of Truth* series. At least I'm sleeping better. My encounter with Theo's dad might have been an epic failure, but knowing I've done what I can gives me some peace of mind. Each night, before I drift off, I wonder where Theo is now, whether Clemmy's told him about the paintings.

***

On the final day of the holidays, I drag myself from the flat and head for the high street in an attempt to get my shit together. If I turn up at school looking like some poor imitation of a hippie, all unkempt hair and straggling beard, everyone will know something's up, which, frankly, is the last thing I need. With Cornwall behind me, I want nothing more than to return to normality and forget this disastrous summer ever happened.

Always assuming I'm allowed to.

As I negotiate the swarm of back-to-school shoppers, the possibility I've mostly avoided thinking about hovers at the fringe of my consciousness, the possibility that Dean might have talked. By now, the gossip has had plenty of time to gather momentum. Far from the inconspicuous start to the year I'm after, I could end up being the recipient of incredulous stares and whispered conversations. And my teammates… Whenever I imagine the ribbing that would await me in the changing room, my stomach curls itself into a ball.

With my hair tidied up, and bearing a new Metallica T-shirt I unearthed at the market, I walk home in the late morning sunshine to pack my schoolbag. I can only hope my instincts are correct and Dean isn't a complete arsehole. Twelve years of friendship must count for something, right?

I unlock the front door and inhale the fresh scent of lemons. Mum, using one of her rare days off to clean the flat, looks up from where she's scrubbing the bath. She awards my improved appearance with a warm smile, but otherwise doesn't comment.

Later, she cooks lasagne—my favourite—for dinner. It's good to have my appetite back. I was starting to worry it had gone on a permanent hiatus and I'd wind up looking like Christian Bale in *The Machinist*.

I'm polishing off a second plateful when my mobile rings. I grab for it and glance at the caller ID. I've long since given up any hope of hearing from Theo, or anyone else for that matter. I'm not sure why I insist on carrying my phone around with me. Habit, probably. The name flashes at me from the display. My heart skydives, then rockets into my throat.

"Dean," I say in response to Mum's silent question.

She smiles at me in this knowing way, patting my back as I squeeze past her into the hall. Can't say I share her optimism. Between the two possibilities: that he's calling to apologise or merely wants to warn me off talking to him at school tomorrow, my money's on the latter.

I step into my room and put the phone to my ear, aiming for casual, despite the weight in my chest. "Hey."

"Hey." Dean's voice cracks. He sounds as nervous as I feel.

In the uncomfortable pause, I nudge the door shut behind me and cross to sit on my bed. I let the silence stretch between us. Dean was the one who walked out. I have no reason to make this easy for him.

Finally, he clears his throat. "So, um, about tomorrow…"

My knuckles whiten on the phone. I shouldn't be surprised; it's what I was expecting. Still, the rejection knocks the wind out of me.

"Yeah." Dean gulps. "I'll, uh, pick you up on my way to school in the morning as usual, OK?"

It takes a few seconds for my brain to catch up, to process his actual words as opposed to the ones I'd been anticipating.

"You are OK with that, right?" he asks. "I mean, if you'd rather I didn't—"

"No," I cut him off, "that's fine."

"Great." Air gusts across the microphone, a breath he must have been holding.

There's another tense pause. It's weird. All the hours we've spent talking over the years and without a single moment of awkwardness. I wonder whether we'll ever get that back.

"Well," Dean says at last, "see you tomorrow then."

"Yeah, see you."

After we hang up, I sit for a while and stare at my phone. The steel-capped boot that has been crushing my windpipe for weeks, eases off. Dean hasn't told. If he wants us to show up together like we always do, he's as anxious to avoid questions as I am. Regardless of where our friendship stands, I'm grateful to him for that.

***

Dean pulls up to my building ten minutes early next morning. He doesn't say anything when I climb into the passenger seat, doesn't even glance my way, but neither does he make a move to start the engine.

I dump my schoolbag on the floor at my feet and wait for him to speak. Beyond my window, the residents of the Brickwell Estate emerge from the high-rise blocks—tired-looking men and women collapsing into beaten-up cars, gangs of youths sharing a joint before school. At times like this, I could murder a cigarette, to have something to occupy my hands. I settle for fiddling with my seat belt.

"Look," Dean drums his fingers on the steering wheel, a sure sign he's nervous, "I'm sorry, all right?"

I glance at him. "Are you?"

"Think I'd be here otherwise? I reacted badly the other week, I see that, but it was a shock, you know?"

"This hasn't exactly been a walkover for me either."

"No." He stares down at his lap. "No, I get that."

We relapse into silence. Dean continues tapping out a rhythm on the steering wheel. It would be irritating if it weren't so familiar.

"I told Yasmin. Hope you don't mind."

I shrug. I wish he hadn't, but Yasmin isn't the sort of girl to spread gossip. "What did she say?"

"Um…" Dean fidgets in his seat. "She had a real go at me, actually. Said I was a terrible mate and that you must have been going through enough without me walking out on you."

"Smart girl, your Yasmin." I imagine Dean's normally easygoing girlfriend laying into him and I half smile.

"Yeah." For the first time since I got in the car, Dean catches my eye. His smile mirrors mine. Tension still vibrates between us, probably will for a while, but it ebbs a little.

Dean starts the engine and pulls into the rush-hour traffic. "I'm guessing, since you came home when you did, that it's over between you and this...Theo."

"Yeah." I don't elaborate. No doubt, over the next few days, I'll end up telling him the whole miserable story, but not yet.

Dean nods. "OK, so I've been thinking. You do fancy girls, right? That's what you told me."

"Yes." Caution stretches my response into several syllables. I have a sneaking suspicion where this is headed.

"So, technically, if you wanted to, you could just stick to going out with girls and forget the...other thing."

I wince. The idea that I'll ever feel about anyone, guy or girl, the way I do about Theo, is unimaginable. Somehow, though, I don't think this is what Dean needs to hear. "Listen, I appreciate what you're doing, but—"

"No." Dean shakes his head. He has the decency to look sheepish. "Sorry. Forget I said anything."

We drive the rest of the way in silence. I don't let it bother me. For the time being, it's enough that he's here, despite his discomfort, trying to put things right.

"So," Dean finds a space in the school car park and kills the engine, "what're you telling people? I mean, are you gonna...?"

"Come out?"

"Yeah."

I focus on retrieving my bag. "Dunno. When I was with Theo, I thought I would, but now... I'm not sure there's much point."

"OK." He swallows. His hands clench on the steering wheel. "But just so you know, whatever you decide is fine with me. I'll have your back one hundred percent."

Dean sets his jaw and I can tell he's sincere, although he can't entirely mask his terror at the prospect of his best mate going public. It's my turn to swallow. Unable to cobble together the words to express just how much his support means to me, I punch him lightly on the arm. Dean bumps my fist with his, flashing me a passable replica of his old grin, and I know he understands.

***

I'm glad to be back at school. Who would've thought it? But the routine of lessons and homework and hanging out with the lads restores some equilibrium to my life, gives me something to focus on. Rugby helps most of all. Mr. Edwards launches straight into training us for the opening match of the season, which will pit us against Brookminster Grammar, our biggest rivals. In the changing room, surrounded by the familiar banter and coarse jokes, the memory of those crazy weeks in Cornwall fades into the shadows. Out on the field, caught up in the breathless chaos of the scrum, I forget everything but the game.

At other times, the hurt resurfaces every bit as hard as it did during those first awful days. When I'm least prepared for it, something will remind me of Theo—a glimpse of golden-brown hair or the way someone holds their pencil—and the feelings cannon into me in all their painful intensity.

In spite of my efforts to act normal, it's obvious to my friends and teammates something's up. Every now and then one of them will pat me on the back or cast me a sympathetic look, putting my distractedness down to the breakup with Zara. I don't correct them. It's easier this way, at least until I'm clearer about what I want to do, and who, if anyone, I want to tell.

"You know," Dean says one evening while driving me home after a particularly brutal training session, "when I said one day you'd fall for someone so hard you wouldn't know what hit you, this isn't quite what I meant."

"Which bit? Me falling for a guy, or the fact that I'm a total head case?"

"Oh, you were always a total head case."

I cuff him on the shoulder, and am rewarded when he cracks up. Dean's having trouble dealing with my sexuality. Weirdly, I think he would've found it easier if I were gay. He just can't comprehend how I can be equally attracted to guys as I am to girls, and he squirms whenever we stray onto the topic. He's stuck by me, though, and that's what matters.

Yasmin's been great too. When we bumped into each other outside the cafeteria on our second day back, she pulled me into a hug and told me I'd be all right. The funny thing is, I almost believed her. I'm not all right yet, nowhere near, but in time, when the bruises on my heart have faded, I think I will be.

***

On the second Friday of term, Dean invites me to hang out at his place after school, just as he has every day for the past two weeks. I suspect this is his way of making up for being such a poor excuse for a friend over the summer.

Much as I appreciate the effort, I shake my head. "You need to spend some time with Yasmin, or she'll decide you're a useless boyfriend as well as a shitty mate."

When the final bell rings, I join the tide of students pouring through the front gates, but don't turn towards home. A sultry stillness drags at the air, summer clinging on with grim determination. The prospect of returning to the stuffy flat doesn't appeal, so I cross the road to the park and settle on a bench to do my homework.

I open my Sociology textbook and leaf through to the chapter I'm supposed to read before my next lesson. Shouts and laughter drift towards me from the kids' play area. The sun warms my back, and I inhale the scent of freshly mown grass mingled with smoke from a bonfire.

I'm working tomorrow, but on Sunday, perhaps I'll hop on a train to the coast, hire a board and catch some waves. My pulse surges in agreement. I'm ready. It's time I got on with my life.

"Luke?"

I'd know his voice anywhere. All the same, I have to look up, have to see for myself to believe it. And there he is, hands dug in the pockets of his jeans, hair flopping over his forehead. The sight of him slams me into the bench. I can't breathe, can't speak.

Theo scuffs the grass with the toe of his trainer. "All right if I sit down?"

I nod, and he lowers himself onto the bench beside me. Starved of him for weeks, I want to drink him in, reacquaint my memory with every detail, but I don't. It will only make things harder in the long run. With an effort, I tear my gaze from him to stare down at my book. I don't ask why he's here, partly because I already have a pretty good idea, but mostly so I can hold onto the tiny grain of hope a little longer.

"So," Theo says after a while, "how've you been?"

I flip a page back and forth. "Oh, you know. All right. You?"

Theo shrugs. He's quiet for a moment before he speaks, confirming my suspicions. "Luke, I wanted to say thank you. That must've taken some guts, going to see my dad."

"Yeah." I cringe at the recollection. "Fat lot of good it did. How'd you find out, anyway? Did Clemmy tell you?"

"She filled me in after the irate phone call from Dad. He said if I continued treating his house like a brothel for delinquent queers, he'd disinherit me, and I read between the lines."

"Shit." I massage the bridge of my nose. "Sorry. Didn't mean to make things worse for you."

"You didn't. Seriously. Clemmy told me about the paintings. I couldn't believe... Finding out he's been collecting them all this time... I didn't know what to think."

"Have you been to see him, your dad?"

"Yeah." Theo toys with a hole in the knee of his jeans. "He didn't seem especially pleased to see me, but he didn't kick me out either."

"Progress." I dart him an encouraging smile.

He smiles back at me. "I reckon so."

I can't help it. My gaze lands on his mouth. I'm bombarded with remembered sensations—the hunger of his kisses, his skin hot and smooth under my hands, the lean firmness of him pressing me into the sand. Now that he's done what he came for, panic squeezes my throat. I'm not ready for him to leave, not yet. Maybe not ever.

"How's Zara?" I ask to forestall him.

"Haven't seen her since she went home. We spoke on the phone the other day, though, and she sounded OK. She was full of some party she and her friends are going to this weekend."

A weight I'd scarcely realised I was carrying slips from my shoulders. I'm glad Zara's been able to pick herself up. Of all the regrets I lugged home with me from Cornwall, hurting her was the heaviest.

"And," I hesitate over my next question, "what about you and her?"

Theo frowns at his palms, as though he might find the answer there. I have the crazy urge to reach out, to take his hands in mine and never let go. I look away, focusing on the kids swarming over the climbing frame.

Theo sighs. "It's been…difficult. After you left, Zara didn't speak to me for days. I wondered why she stayed at all. Looking back, I think she did it to punish me. I couldn't blame her, but I'm not sure how we would've got through it without Giles."

"He stayed on too then?"

"Don't think he could face flying out to Tuscany without Meredith. The breakup really shook him. I've never seen him like that over a girl before."

Giles hadn't been so concerned about Meredith while he was kissing Zara. The jibe leaps to my tongue. Once, I would have said as much, but not anymore. I'm hardly in a position to judge.

"He was a rock," Theo says. "He didn't take sides, didn't chew me out for behaving so badly. He was just there, for both of us. He took Zara out a lot. What with the atmosphere between us, I think it was the only way he could cope. They spent a lot of time together that first week. Actually, they had a sort of...fling." Awkwardness creeps into Theo's tone.

I glance sideways at him. He's studying me, watching for my reaction. I dismiss the revelation with a lift of my shoulders. The idea of Zara and Giles together really doesn't bother me. If I'm honest, I half expected it. "How did that turn out?"

A grin teases the corner of his mouth. "Total disaster about sums it up."

"Seriously?" I choke on a laugh. "That bad?"

"Worse. Well, it was never going to work out. It was a comfort thing, I suppose. For about a week, I had to endure them being all lovey-dovey. Then the fighting started. It ended with Zara tipping an entire bottle of wine over Giles's head and him storming off in his car."

This time I laugh properly. "Wish I'd seen that."

"No, you wish you'd been the one holding the bottle."

"You got me."

We exchange a look full of complicit amusement. For an instant, it's as if we've been transported backwards in time, to the days before it all got so complicated, when everything between us was new and exciting.

I avert my gaze. "Where's Giles now?"

"Our flat in Oxford. I joined him there a couple of weeks ago. Since then, I've been forced to listen to him calling Meredith several times a day to declare his undying love and beg her to give him another chance."

"And will she?"

"I don't know. Maybe...eventually. She's going to make him work for it, though."

"Good for her." I experience a rush of pride.

"Yeah." Theo pulls a wry face. "In the meantime, guess who gets to play the role of go-between."

"Awkward."

"You can say that again. Meredith was going to move in with us—made sense, since she spent so much time at the flat—but that won't be happening now." Theo rakes a hand through his hair, a gesture so reminiscent of him that it wrenches at my heart. "Still, one good thing came out of Giles and Zara's brief romance. She was so mad at him after he walked out that she actually spoke to me."

Without consciously deciding to do it, I shift position so I'm angled towards him. "How'd that go?"

"Tough." Theo examines his laces. "Still is, to be honest. We're a long way from where we were. Maybe we'll never get back what we had. I don't know." He looks up at me with a determined smile. "At least everything's out in the open now and we're on speaking terms. It was Zara who told me which school you go to."

I blink. It's a concession on Zara's part I hadn't expected.

"I would've called," Theo adds, "but Zara deleted your number, and she couldn't remember which building was yours. The school was the only place I had a hope of finding you."

"So you could thank me?" It's so like Theo to want to do it in person, but I can't quite believe he's gone to so much trouble.

He regards me with an odd expression. "To see you, idiot. I've waited outside the front gate every afternoon since Monday looking out for you."

"I don't normally come out that way." I try to wrap my head around his words, am barely aware of what I'm saying. Theo wanted to see me. He's staked out my school every day this week, waiting. For me. "I usually go in Dean's car. He parks around the back."

Theo's brow clears. "That would explain it. I was worried, thought you might be off sick."

My eyes latch onto his and don't let go. We scour one another's faces, searching for something, anything, to hold onto. Between us, the air ripples with the implications of what's been said. And what hasn't.

"Theo," my voice fractures, but I need to know, "why are you here?"

His forehead creases. "You knew I'd come, once I'd sorted things out with Zara…didn't you?"

"How could I? That night, before I left, you wouldn't even look at me."

"I thought you understood. You said you did. I had to salvage things with Zara, had to at least try. If I looked at you, I was terrified I wouldn't be able to let you go. I thought you knew."

I stare down at the ground. "I thought you hated me. I thought you blamed me for messing things up with Zara."

Theo swears under his breath.

I dig the toe of my shoe into the dirt. The past weeks have been the hardest of my life, and now I find out it was all for nothing. I brace myself for the anger, but it isn't there. Perhaps that will come later. For the moment, it's enough merely to have Theo here, sitting beside me.

"Luke, look at me."

When I do, Theo's gaze locks with mine. Reaching out, he rests a hand on my leg. "Can we start again? Properly this time. No hiding. No pretence. Can we?"

My breath hitches. His touch burns through the fabric of my school uniform; a pulsing warmth spreads along the inside of my thigh, and I'm grateful for the book lying open in my lap.

"I mean," he withdraws his hand, "if I'm too late, if you're not interested, I'll understand."

Uncertainty clouds his expression. For one insane moment, I couldn't give a damn that we're surrounded by potential witnesses. I want to cradle his face and kiss his doubts into oblivion. But I don't. I recognise one of the older kids loitering near the swings as Max's younger brother, and being spied getting off with a guy on a park bench isn't exactly how I'd choose to come out.

"I wish you wouldn't look at me like that." Theo's eyes darken, his face relaxing into a faint smile.

I stand up, shoving my book into my bag, and flash him my best come-and-get-it grin. "Ready to see how the other half lives?"

Theo raises an eyebrow, and I laugh, seizing his hand to pull him to his feet. "Come on, rich boy, I'm taking you home."

THE END

About the Author

Jamie lives in a tranquil spot close to the River Thames in Berkshire, England, and has always been just a little out of place—the only redhead in a family of brunettes; an introvert far more at ease with dogs than with people; a connoisseur of simple pleasures in a society intent on the quest for wealth and fame. Despite an outward cynicism, Jamie is a romantic at heart, and, when not immersed in a book, can mostly be found writing emotional stories where young men from all walks of life are thrust headlong into the breathless, euphoric, often painful whirlwind called love.

Connect with Jamie

Website: www.jamiedeacon.com
Facebook: www.facebook.com/jamiedeaconauthor
Twitter: www.twitter.com/jamiedeacon82
Boys on the Brink Reviews: www.boysonthebrink.com

CPSIA information can be obtained
at www.ICGtesting.com
Printed in the USA
LVOW08s0014200317
527767LV00001B/26/P